MAXIMUM CAPACITY

MAXIMUM CAPACITY

A NOVEL

TROY SUESSE

NEW YORK
LONDON • NASHVILLE • MELBOURNE • VANCOUVER

MAXIMUM CAPACITY

A Novel

Published in New York, New York, by Morgan James Publishing. Morgan James is a trademark of Morgan James, LLC. www.MorganJamesPublishing.com

Publisher's Note: This novel is a work of fiction. Names, characters, places, and incidents are either products of the author's imagination or used fictitiously. All characters are fictional, and any similarity to people living or dead is purely coincidental.

Proudly distributed by Ingram Publisher Services.

ISBN 9781631956423 paperback
ISBN 9781631956430 ebook
Library of Congress Control Number: 2021938723

Cover and Interior Design by:
Chris Treccani
www.3dogcreative.net

To James W. Suesse Jr.,
who committed his life to giving and loving
and was a divinely positive influence
on everyone he touched.

TABLE OF CONTENTS

ACKNOWLEDGMENTS

Creating and shaping a novel through to publication is a life event that requires contributions from not just the author but everyone who surrounds them. Success does not happen without the collective influence of a faithful backing of family, friends, and colleagues. It is with deep sincerity that I offer my recognition and gratitude:

To my mother, Anna, who wholly and selflessly dedicated her life to my happiness, wellbeing, and success.

To my wife, Stephanie, for being the central pillar in my life and for allowing me to devote the time and energy necessary to carry this novel through to publishing. You are a profound inspiration to me.

To my children, Zachary, Holly, and Heather, and my brother, Brian, and his wife and children, and my entire family for becoming my closest advocates. I am incredibly blessed to have all of you in my life.

To editor, Amy French, whose literary mastery and ingenuity set the course for this novel.

To editor, Cortney Donelson, for her faith and confidence in me and this story.

To my friends and colleagues for making a unique and lasting impact on the fabric of my being, which I cherish greatly.

To my readership, without whom sharing this fascinating dystopian adventure would not be possible.

To the entire author support and leadership team at Morgan James Publishing for accepting me as a member of their professional family and for providing me the opportunity to captivate the imaginations of science fiction and dystopian enthusiasts around the world.

A very heartfelt thank you—from me to each and every one of you.

CHAPTER 1

Do What You Must

The bustle and babel of spectators settling into their seats in the colosseum hushed immediately as a woman's luminous face appeared on the giant screens above the crowd.

"Welcome, *good* citizens of the Delmarva Peninsula, the Chesapeake Municipality, and of our beautiful planet Earth."

Her voice was calm and steady, almost hypnotic; her expression serene. She was stunning with her long, wavy, dark orange hair and bright green eyes. Audience members trained their sights on her as the stage crew performed a final pre-event inspection of the huge death cage below.

"I am Kamalei Ricinulei, Master of Expulsions. And on behalf of the Venom Society, I commend you for attending this afternoon's celebration of survival. You are here because you recognize your duty to express your will to live through your will . . . to kill."

At the mention of the Venom Society, the screens displayed a group of blank-faced individuals in a VIP seating area. Their alabaster complexions matched Kamalei's. But unlike her, they all wore top hats and dark glasses, despite the dim lighting in the colosseum. In unison, they stood, bowed slightly at the waist, and then sat back down.

Next, fourteen men, seven women, and three children made their way to a staging area quietly in a line, their ankles shackled and chained together. One by one, their faces were shown on the screens, along with the charges levied against them.

First came the tearful face of a frightened social worker. Her charges, written on the screen, read: "Selfishly stole food from her elderly neighbors in service of her own gluttony."

Kamalei's voice continued over the images of the accused. "*You* are called upon today to cast punishment upon the wrongdoers among us."

The screens showed a teenage boy with a spiked crop of hair running from his forehead to the base of the back of his head. His charges read: "Habitual bully of his block with an extensive history of looting. Charged with mischievous destruction of property, arson, and theft of clothing and infirmary supplies." These were relatively minor offenses, compared with those of some of the other detainees, but numerous enough to land him in the Expulsion.

The next participant to fill the screens was a trim, muscular young woman. As she entered the cage, Kamalei emphasized the charges against her by reading them aloud. "Armed robbery and assault with a deadly weapon." Audience members turned to one another and traded looks of disdain.

Then Kamalei's face returned to the screens, larger than life.

"We are starving," she said. Her tone remained steady, but her intensity grew as she enunciated her words with increased precision. "We are sick. We are *dying*. We must join together as one and respect the needs of all *good* people on Earth. And yet, there are *those* who decide to commit crimes against their neighbors." She waved her left arm toward the lineup to remind the audience exactly to whom she was referring.

An ominous roar of applause rose from the crowd as a heavy black curtain lifted to reveal the huge cage in which the day's challenges would unfold. Three distinct killing features, all side by side within the cage, included converging walls of spikes, flaming harpoons, and a tank of molten steel. Most of the competitors, but not all, would perish as they fought one another in attempts to successfully navigate these obstacles. The audience was seated upon raised platforms surrounding the entire cage, and all onlookers had a clear, downward view of everything that took place.

"Today, ladies and gentlemen, we sacrifice individuals whose behavior we can no longer tolerate," Kamalei said. "Their violation counts demonstrate that they do *not* respect the doctrine of our land. Their fate lies in *your* hands." The camera angle shifted, and Kamalei came into full view—a tall, imposing figure in a tight-fitting bodysuit and high heels. She raised both arms high, palms up, to acknowledge the crowd. "DO WHAT YOU MUST!"

Those words were a signal to the ground crew to activate a display of laser lights and pyrotechnics. The first participant was extracted from the staging area by a huge mechanical arm with steel claws, her legs kicking and dangling, and introduced into the death cage. Each remaining participant would follow, one by one. By the end of the Expulsion, most of the competitors would end up dead.

Once inside the cage, competitors knew, there was only one way out alive. Amid their deadly trials, they would have to find one of three specially designed protective capsules and lock themselves in it. Each capsule could hold only one individual. The competitors' only instructions: Kill or be killed.

A large man near the back of the colosseum held up a sign that read, "Death to Miscreants!" He shouted the words, spawning a chant that spread throughout the venue.

Just a few seats away, a shy, unkempt fifteen-year-old girl sat silent and small. Her name was Zinnia Blue, and despite the warmth of the day, especially inside the colosseum, she wore an oversized jacket.

Through the afternoon and into the night the competitors tried to outsmart, outrun, and outlast one another. Some became victims of the killing devices that were emplaced in the cage. Some died directly at the hands of other competitors. Two individuals found safe havens inside capsules. Only one capsule remained, with three competitors desperate to find it.

Zinnia sat in a daze for a few moments until a shriek abruptly pulled her attention back to the event. A man's bloodied arm protruded through the steel bars of the cage, then fell limp, his body impaled and trapped between two walls of spikes. Another competitor had been successfully terminated. The crowd around her let out a clamor of approval, but Zinnia bent over in a fetal position with her arms covering her head—a futile attempt to diminish her awareness of what was going on around her.

Expulsions had been regular occurrences throughout her life, but this was the first one she attended. She understood the prevailing view that the deaths of wrongdoers inside the cage helped to ensure the good people of society could live longer. She saw and heard the approval of the crowd around her and felt it in the vibrations of their applause. But she didn't share their enthusiasm. She didn't really want to see any more. Still, after a moment or two, she lifted her head and forced herself to watch the Expulsion play out.

Attentions turned to the two remaining participants. They found themselves in an unenviable standoff. Each had been told that if they survived the competition, they would get another chance at a law-abiding life. The alternative was death. Each considered the one remaining capsule to be their only chance at salvation.

The closing challenge in this Expulsion found the two finalists clinging with their hands and toes to knobs on the inside walls of a large, cylindrical vat. The vat was partially filled with a molten ferrous material that fed an assembly line of a nearby steel production mill. One competitor was a middle-aged man with a graying, bushy beard and mustache. The other was the physically fit female, many years younger than he, who had been last to enter the cage. Both were short of breath.

Just prior to the Expulsion, while in the holding chamber, the duo had made a pact to team together to ensure their mutual survival for as long as possible. Neither wanted the other to suffer a terrifying fall into the melting pot. But at the same time, neither wanted to take this death plunge of their own volition.

Dangling from the ceiling of the cage, at the center of the vat, was a rope ladder, an obvious escape mechanism. The competitors adopted cold stares at one another as they contemplated their next moves.

Both were shaking from the slow onset of muscle failure, but neither was willing to let go of the knobs. A loud pressure release valve began spraying a yellow fog into the barrel—a noxious gas designed to displace the competitors from the side walls and induce movement. The crowd let out another loud cheer. Audience members had been instrumental in triggering the gas flow. Prior to the event, they were given the ability to influence the killing devices using individual joystick transmitters.

Almost simultaneously, the two competitors leaped from the wall and grabbed at the ladder. The young woman got the better position and ended up just above the older competitor's head. They began carefully placing their hands and feet up consecutive rungs. Clearly, the younger competitor had superior coordination, as she began to increase the distance between them.

The man knew he had no chance of catching up, so with one last surge of energy, he reached up and grabbed the woman's ankle. He aimed to use his body weight to dislodge her from the rope ladder. But the effort was quickly quashed when her calloused, bruised foot met with his forehead. A heavy downward thrust was enough to stun the man. He released his grip on the ladder and fell backward with arms flung overhead. He splashed down into the pit of molten steel and sank quickly out of view.

The woman made her way up the ladder and over to a waiting escape capsule—the final survivor.

The event ended with the ceremonial sounding of a foghorn, and Kamalei dismissed the onlookers. "That concludes our Expulsion this fifteenth day of February, 3022. Farewell, *good* citizens," she called out as her image once again filled the big screens.

It would take time for the large crowd to egress from the colosseum. Zinnia, short-stepping in concert with the thick herd, wondered when she would awaken from this nightmare of a life.

CHAPTER 2

The Venom Society

The colosseum began to settle, and the cage lights to dim. Members of the Venom Society's Delmarva Leadership Council made their way down from their VIP seats to greet Kamalei. Upon his approach, Regional Grandmaster Marcus Webb indicated his pleasure with her work in organizing and conducting the event by raising just one eyebrow of his otherwise stone-cold face. Kamalei felt the beginnings of a grin in response, but she caught herself in time to obscure any emotion.

Without saying a word, simply twitching his head to the right, the grandmaster next indicated he was ready for the group of four to move to a secluded holding area for a debriefing on the Expulsion they had just witnessed. It was customary to discuss the mental and physical characteristics of the winners and, most importantly, what would become of them.

The council members formed a perfect single-file line and proceeded to a chamber where the three escape capsules from the Expulsion were lined up, side by side. Each held one survivor. The first was a twelve-year-old boy, who had secured his capsule because he was an exceptionally fast runner. The next was a forty-two-year-old man who had shown remarkable athleticism but who had fractured his ankle—an injury that would require long-term medical attention. And the third was the woman who had managed to escape the pit of molten steel by outclimbing her elder competitor.

As the Venom Society leaders stood in half-circle formation around the capsules, the grandmaster addressed Kamalei, "Well done, Councilor Ricinulei. I do hope you'll remain at the head post for Expulsions in this municipality."

"Of course," Kamalei responded, again staving off a smile.

The grandmaster was a notorious perfectionist. It was rare for him to express approval at all and even more unusual for him to do so without also sternly noting flaws to be addressed. But after only three months in a position coveted for its high visibility, Kamalei had just received praise twice in front of her colleagues.

The grandmaster continued, shifting his attention to his next in command, Deputy Trent Chulah. He was perhaps the most loyal to the grandmaster and demonstrated that by taking on a role of taskmaster, employing a naturally terse, militaristic cadence in his interactions with others. He was willing to do whatever his superiors asked, without question. Grandmaster Webb found him particularly amenable when called upon to punish individuals considered a threat to the society or its objectives. The harsher the punishment to be inflicted, the more Chulah relished the assignment. His enthusiasm for dominance was visible through a glint in his eyes and evident in every instance in which he employed measures more extreme and innovative than ordered.

"To what use shall we put the miscreants?" Webb asked his deputy.

Chulah had prepared an answer that he expected to win his superior's approval. "Well, sir, as I see it, our greatest current need is for skypod construction workers. A combination of overcrowding and homelessness has made Sector 5 a trouble spot ever since the partial collapse of skypod 43Z, displacing its residents. Sector leaders are desperate for *expendable* labor to rebuild the structure." Here, Chulah's voice became a bit breathy with enthusiasm." As you know, those high-altitude jobs are, ahem, quite high-risk."

Webb sank lightly into thought as he considered the proposal.

Overcrowding. Overpopulation. With more than twenty billion people, the Earth simply had too many mouths to feed, house, clothe, transport, and care for. The problem, recognized centuries ago, was the core impetus for the Venom Society's rise to power. The first mentions of the group in historical archives told of a few dozen tall, pale participants who attended a global summit on overpopulation. Those individuals reportedly had captivated other attendees by introducing unheard-of innovations in food production, medicine, space travel, and construction.

Perhaps the most breathtaking innovation the Venom Society had engineered in the realm of construction was the invention of skypods. These were towers that required little or no space on the Earth's surface but enabled thousands of people to live and work high above. The skypods were designed to allow sunlight to pass through to ground-level communities. They were connected with lateral support beams that enhanced stability but allowed for some sway in heavy winds. Some skypods reached altitudes so high that jet planes had to adjust normal flight vectors as an anti-collision measure.

Transport across towers and between upper and lower levels was managed in various ways. Magnetic elevators proved to be a popular low-maintenance transport method, used within structures, by virtue of their magnetic levitation capabilities, while hovercrafts were a common means to move humans from one skypod to another. In great numbers, the structures formed a whole new layer of steel abodes surrounding much of the Earth's perimeter.

The grandmaster stood still and erect over a report detailing the attributes of the Expulsion survivors. He appeared especially tall as he did not bend to view the details but glanced down and ran his slender pointer finger along the portion describing their physical condition. He said nothing, and his silence spoke volumes.

Another member of the entourage, Myra Poda, eager to become a noteworthy contributor to the boss's resolution, seized the opportunity to one-up Chulah by cautiously interrupting the grandmaster's thought and offering a more palatable proposal.

"Orrrrr, if I might suggest, sir, while our sensitive experimentation in the underground lab has progressed well, we're quite low on test subjects in this municipality. I motion that all three of today's winners be placed there. It seems quite obvious to me that a twelve-year-old boy, a medium-aged male with a lame leg, and a lightweight female, together, would be of little value to the efforts of the heavy labor associated with pod construction."

Her comments propelled the grandmaster into deeper contemplation. His eyebrows drew constricted and wrinkled. He clenched his fingers into a fist, pressed it firmly against his chin, and turned his back to the others to avoid further interruption.

The lab to which Poda referred was one of several in the tristate area, which were widely regarded as outstanding successes of the Venom Society. Commoners were aware that the labs produced a steady stream of medical advances, but no one knew much about how they operated. And no one had enough gumption to inquire.

Indeed, well before the Venom Society was building skypods, its earliest known members were impressing global leaders with their scientific prowess. Their most striking contribution at the overpopulation summit, and the one that ultimately spawned their name, was a cure for the deadliest disease on Earth at the time, zaraseptosis.

They engineered an effective concoction, which, if administered soon after diagnosis, could sometimes cure the disease. The catch was that the ingredients for this precious potion were scarce. The primary components included an extract from a rare plant, the Venus Giganta, combined with animal and insect venom. A lesser advertised fact was that aside from its beneficial medicinal qualities, a slightly modified version of the potion could be used as a deadly weapon.

The US president at the time was quoted as describing them with admiration, "This . . . this venom society—I don't know what else to call them, or even where they came from—they are providing solutions that have eluded the rest of us for generations. We don't know much about them, but they seem to know everything!"

With the realization that sacrificing these Expulsion winners to the lab was his most efficient option, the grandmaster turned back around with a satisfied look on his face and gave a nod to Poda.

Chulah, disenchanted that his proposal went unappreciated, made a delicate attempt to verify that the grandmaster agreed with Poda. "If *that* is to your liking, sir, I'll see to it that the winners are well taken care of . . . ahem, *until* such time that their services are rendered to society, that is."

The grandmaster shifted his dark sunglasses up higher on the bridge of his nose with a mere cheek flinch and, again, flicked his head to the right. That indicated the competitors would indeed be sent to the underground lab as suggested.

The Expulsion winners could not hear the conversation from the confines of their tiny capsules. Each waited anxiously—and hopefully—for the latches to release, the capsule doors to pop open, and their next destinations to be revealed. They knew they wouldn't be returning to their home municipality, and that made sense. Their reputations had been destroyed in the Chesapeake Municipality. Plus, how could they live among neighbors who had sought to see them killed? They weren't sure where they'd end up at the end of the day, but they thought almost anyplace would seem like a blessing after surviving the Expulsion.

As they sat tight, however, receiving not even a glance from the officials who stood above their capsules, hope of a new life in a new place began to melt into fear and suspicion. The Expulsion winners found themselves wondering if an ominous fate awaited them.

That was perceptive.

With the destination now selected, the capsules were maneuvered onto the rails of a track that led downward into a dark tunnel. Chulah, disappointed that Webb had favored Poda's proposition over his own, quickly attempted to redeem himself. He keyed a set of coordinates into the capsules' control units, which commanded their automated navigation systems to deliver the capsules to the exact location that the grandmaster indicated, and off they went. Watching as the capsules exited the holding area, the congregation showed no emotion.

The grandmaster made a concluding statement, "Very well, then. That is acceptable. We are successfully accomplishing the objectives that our forefathers entrusted to us, bit by bit."

In unison, the rest of the pack nodded in acknowledgment.

With the day's work complete, the Venom Society officers exchanged goodbyes, issuing a symbolic hand gesture. They presented the thumb and forefinger of their right hands in the shape of a *V*, held tightly against their chests. Then, in a single file line, they departed the colosseum.

CHAPTER 3
Zinnia

Zinnia burst through the front door of the orphanage and headed straight for the communal restroom, leaning forward a little more with every step. Her face ashen, she elbowed other residents out of her way. She had suppressed a queasy feeling ever since leaving the colosseum, and she couldn't fight it any longer.

Hovering over the commode, she retched a few times, but very little came up. She hadn't consumed much in the last twenty-four hours. She lay on the floor, pressing her face to the cool porcelain, and waited for the world to stop spinning.

What she had just witnessed played over and over in her mind. The Expulsion. Fresh visions of the event filled her with conflicting emotions. She knew the rationale for the killings. They were meant to punish people who had committed crimes against their neighbors, their communities, and to deter others from doing the same. She saw logic in that, even if it was a brutal logic. But she also felt empathy for the competitors. Her family history and her own life had taught her how hardships can drive a person who wholeheartedly wants to do right to do wrong.

Her eyes got glassy as she fell into a moment of reflection. Seeing the bloodied arm protruding through the Expulsion cage, and then falling limp, had been a very personal and dark moment for Zinnia. She feared it was also a prophetic one.

Zinnia was a thief and had been one for about five years. It all started when she was forced to become the primary caregiver for her younger brother, Xion. He was malnourished, and his meager daily food supply at the orphanage was insufficient to strengthen him. Most of the subsistence there were prepackaged edibles designed by the Venom Society to have a long shelf life. But that came at the price of lacking high nutritional value. Not to mention, much of what was offered to the residents was unappealing to Xion, who lost more of his appetite the sicker he grew.

Zinnia began taking small items from the school cafeteria, neighboring residents, and even the tables at the market, to supplement Xion's diet. She wasn't a particularly good thief and got caught red-handed on numerous occasions. But often, the locals felt sorry for her and turned a blind eye. As a result, most of her misdeeds met with only minor consequences. She was reprimanded and reported to local officials. Some of her villainous activity, however, did negatively impact her standing as a trusted citizen.

Just a day prior, in fact, Zinnia was apprehended for stealing a pack of freeze-dried fish strips wrapped in seaweed. "That's Xion's favorite," she thought to herself. After being admonished by a local police officer, Zinnia made a tearful promise that she would never steal again. The officer reluctantly sent her on her way.

As a result of this incident, however, Zinnia was issued an armband, a non-removable device that made it possible for Venom Society officials to identify her approximate location at any time. It was society's way of identifying criminals as a threat, and anyone who was considered a threat might also be considered for an Expulsion.

Zinnia had resolved a thousand times to stop stealing. But keeping that promise to herself had proven impossible, even though she knew the threat of significant punishment grew each time she broke the law—or thought she knew. Attending the Expulsion, the first she had ever seen, had given her a vision of the future that was all too real. Now, she knew she had to change—not only for her own good but to be able to continue caring for her ailing younger brother.

"Xion!" Zinnia jerked herself upright as she spoke her brother's name. She shook the fog from her thoughts and realized it had been hours since she had checked on him.

She mustered some energy, pulled herself up, and peered into the mirror. The color returned to her face in a rush.

Zinnia didn't look the part of a quick-thinking, highly intelligent, mature fifteen-year-old—partly because she was small for her age and partly because she rarely put much effort into her appearance. The line for the bathroom at the orphanage was long in the mornings, and between school and caring for Xion, Zinnia had little time to wait most days. Her long, dirty-blonde hair was perpetually a mess of knots. She often would disregard her laundry for days and didn't have many changes of clothing to begin with. What she wore, usually a simple dress with her jacket over it, was rumpled and threadbare.

She gave the impression that she didn't care about how she looked. But in truth, as she had grown older, she had begun to care.

Looking in the mirror, she tried to smooth her hair by pushing it behind her ears. She noticed with some satisfaction that this accented her exceptionally big, blue eyes. She had her mother's eyes, she thought. But her musing didn't last long. It seemed silly to dwell on superficial things. After all, survival was what mattered, and that was more than enough to worry about.

As she had done so many times before, Zinnia decided to dig in her heels and face the day's challenges head-on.

Her nausea had subsided, but she was still mildly disoriented. She eased her way out of the bathroom and leaned against the wall to sample the scene inside the common area. She surveyed the large room to see if Xion was there.

The atmosphere was drab, and the air harbored a stale, musty smell. There were no windows to open for fresh air, and the ventilation system was dated. There wasn't much room to play or exercise. Some of the hungry kids tested the doors of the pantry and refrigerator, looking for snacks, but both were locked. Other kids sat patiently stacking blocks or coloring.

Every corner of the space was crowded and cluttered, making it hard for the children to stay out of one another's way. Sometimes that caused scuffles, but mostly, the young residents were of low energy and in dull spirits—at least partly because they weren't getting enough to eat. The food provided daily was sufficient to keep them alive but not abundant enough for them to thrive. Everyone was hoping that the next horn would sound, as it did about once per week, indicating that Venom Society distribution trucks had arrived to deliver their regular ration of food and drink.

Zinnia identified a clear path over to the section of the orphanage where she, Xion, and his best friend, Dalton, all slept. Xion and Dalton were two of the quietest youngsters in the entire place—Dalton because he was shy; Xion because he was weak and shaky.

She found them sitting on the lowest of three bunk beds. That was Xion's sleeping post, but it was also the most convenient bunk with which the two boys could create a small play area. Curtains on sliders were designed to surround each bedding unit, providing some privacy, but the curtains mostly stayed open during the day.

"Having a good camping trip?" Zinnia called out as she approached the boys, who had built a makeshift tent with blankets and pillows.

At the sound of her voice, their heads popped out of their improvised playhouse. Zinnia glanced around to make sure no one was looking her way, then took off her jacket and sat with them on the bed.

There wasn't much light shining inside, but there was enough for Xion to notice Zinnia was wearing an armband.

"What's that?" he asked.

"Oh, it's nothing," Zinnia replied, as she turned her body away from him to obscure his view of it.

But Xion's questions continued. "Can I see? Can I have one, too?"

Zinnia was not prepared to give an honest explanation about what the armband represented. She also knew that she couldn't simply get rid of it. The bands were designed to set off alarms if removed, summoning the Venom Society to come make an arrest.

Quickly thinking of an out, Zinnia pulled a locket from her pocket and handed it to Xion. It contained a picture of their mother, who had given it to Zinnia just before dying. Zinnia was just seven years old at the time, the same age as Xion now. The locket had become a special heirloom and a way to remember their mom. It was also one of Xion's favorite items to play with.

The locket always brought back adoring memories for Zinnia—some were fond and others not. It also triggered Xion to prod her to tell him about their parents, whom he never really knew. Zinnia had to fight back a rush of emotion every time he asked for the story but would always oblige.

Xion took the locket, pressed it to his left cheek, closed his eyes, and began the conversation. "Mommy loved us, right? Tell again about how Mommy loved us, even though she had to go away."

Zinnia answered exactly as she had countless times before. "Mommy had to go away-away, the night that you were born, Xion. They needed her in heaven because she was an angel."

Zinnia never went into uncomfortable detail with her brother about the fact that their mother died shortly after giving birth to Xion as a result of complications. Xion had survived, of course, but was always underdeveloped and unhealthy.

"She spoke to Daddy and to me before she left," Zinnia continued. "She wanted to make sure we knew how important it was to take care of you. You were so tiny and beautiful. And she knew from the start that you were special."

Zinnia silently recalled how her mother held her while uttering her final words, giving her praise and confidence that she and her father could remain strong and take good care of the new baby.

Xion interrupted, as children often do with stories they know well, "But then Daddy had to go, too, right?"

Their father was a good man at heart, but he struggled with a drug addiction for years after his wife died. He became a persistent thief who knew of only one way to feed his kids and his habit. His poor behavior eventually landed him in poor standing with the Venom Society, and he was selected to participate in an Expulsion when Zinnia was just ten years old.

Zinnia recalled her father kneeling before her and telling her that things would be okay as the Venom Society shackled him and removed him from their home. He wanted Zinnia to believe that his absence was just temporary, but deep down, he knew he was never coming back. The locals reported that he had been one of the winning competitors, that he had secured an escape capsule, but he never returned home.

Zinnia answered Xion, "That's right. And he was sad to leave. But he knew we would be okay because we would still have each other."

Losing her parents early in life had forced Zinnia to mature quickly. She and her brother had little in life, in terms of tangible belongings, but they derived incredible inner strength from each other through an extraordinary bond as siblings.

"You'll never leave me, right?" Though his words came out as a question, Xion's tone conveyed absolute certainty of the answer. Zinnia paused before answering him in the affirmative.

Zinnia had always thought stealing for Xion was okay if it ensured his health and comfort. That was what had enabled her not to think much about the people she was stealing from and the pinch of hunger and pain they must have felt. But after sitting in that angry crowd at the Expulsion, she knew not to expect forgiveness.

It was ironic that a big-hearted, loving sister who only wanted the best for her brother had grown into a habitual thief, trespasser, and pick-pocketer just to keep him better fed. It all ended up causing her to be tagged by the Venom Society as a threat to the balance of food and goods in her municipality. At just fifteen years old, she had earned a permanent armband, which allowed the Venom Society to monitor her movements and consider her for selection to an Expulsion.

As she calmed herself down and prepared to visit the canteen for a swig of water, Zinnia helped Xion change from his pajamas into his pants and shirt so that she could take him with her. When Dalton saw the two of them getting ready to leave, hope and excitement filled his face. "I want to go, too," he said to Zinnia. "I'm super THIRSTY!"

CHAPTER 4

Market Day

With their distinctive salutes, eccentric appearance, and aloof mannerisms, Venom Society leaders maintained an aura of mystery and separation from the commoners they governed. Few seemed to wonder how the strange group had risen to power. It was simpler, and perhaps safer, just to accept that their leadership was critical to the greater good of society. After all, the Venom Society had engineered medical remedies and had built habitable spaces that lowered the numbers of homeless and reduced overcrowding. And, of course, the Venom Society had implemented creative means to dissuade anyone from committing crimes.

Deterrents, notably the Expulsion ceremonies, which were held in municipalities worldwide, had been criticized as extreme in the earliest days of Venom Society rule. But objections to any aspect of the Venom Society faded over time and had mostly been forgotten and replaced by demonstrated enthusiasm. For example, people wore clothing with the initials "VS" to advertise their allegiance. And the phrase, "Thanks be to the Venom Society," was often spoken aloud as a token of praise to them for their acts of benevolence.

One event that everyone in Chesapeake Municipality regarded as especially good was Market Day. It didn't occur often—about once every three months. But when it did, the excitement it generated was electric.

Market Day meant free food, and not just the usual rations for which all city residents were eligible. Those regular rations comprised mostly of items designed for long-distance distribution and long shelf life. They were designed to satisfy the most basic nutritional needs, not so much to whet or satisfy an appetite.

Staples included things like nutritional tablets to be swallowed whole and cubes of gum that were engineered to taste like different fruits. The gum could be chewed for an exceptionally long time and contained chemicals that helped appease a growling stomach.

There were also thick, crunchy wafers that culinary scientists tried—without great success—to infuse with beneficial vitamins and minerals. For example, beef-flavored crackers were routinely available and were rich in protein, and green pita chips, categorized as vegetable-flavored, were high in vitamin C. A popular item among children was the block of dried seaweed, which melted away in their mouths when wet with saliva.

Market Day was different, however. At this event, the Venom Society set aside truckloads of fresh foods that ordinarily got routed to the processing plants for dehydration and compression into rations. Instead, the fare was sent to communal gathering places to be given away in its purest form.

The days of self-employed farmers cultivating acres of flatlands and of ranchers herding cattle across wide expanses and of commercial waterman harvesting a plethora of wild fish were long past. As the human population grew, agricultural real estate diminished.

To mitigate that problem, the Venom Society orchestrated food production methods that were faster and required less space. Now, hybrid vegetables grew under artificial light in multi-story hydroponic labs. And seafood, largely bred and raised in self-contained hatcheries, bore little resemblance to their forebears. Still, compared with tablets, gum, and crackers, the prospect of fresh food made mouths water and hearts grateful.

The colosseum stage, where twenty-one people had died in the Expulsion just two days ago, was in the process of being converted temporarily into an open-air shopping venue. It was still dark outside as volunteers prepped their kiosks, but in a half hour or so, the roof would retract and fill the building with the light of the rising sun. Throngs of hungry townspeople were already waiting in the street. All huddled together, edging closer to the front gate, hoping to get first dibs at the day's selection.

Inside, Zander Hightower, a regular volunteer staffer for Market Days at the Chesapeake colosseum, poured a bucket of lightly glowing, lime green fish onto a cutting counter. Zander had no family at home and found solace in offering his time to assist the community. He was gregarious, chatty, and quick to crack a joke. He liked giving other people reasons to laugh. And at the age of sixty-two, he was considering retirement to pursue his passions for traveling and camping.

Zander was delivering the day's lot of fish to Ryker Meadows, his longtime friend and fellow volunteer, for inspection and processing. Most of the fish were about the length and width of Zander's muscular forearm, but one odd specimen was more than twice that wide—and inexplicably puffed up like a balloon.

"Weren't expecting Moby Dick there, were you!" Zander laughed as he tried to get a rise out of his buddy.

Ryker paid no mind to Zander's comedic attempts, as was typical in their interactions. In contrast to Zander, Ryker was a serious and analytical type. He would sometimes get frustrated at Zander's loose humor. He had a slight hunch in his posture and an awkward gait when he walked, but he was an expert at filleting fish. He had quite an opposite personality than that of Zander, leading many who knew the two of them to question how they got along so well.

Half in reply to Zander and half speaking to himself, Ryker pushed his thick glasses, which some regarded as nerdy, high up on the bridge of his nose, examined the bulging fish more closely, and said softly, "What on earth would cause that bloating? A mutation? Was that fish sick? Is it safe to consume?"

Zander listened and paused, and concern overcame his face as he leaned over to take a good look at the swollen fish. "How about we just slide this monstrosity into the trash can with the guts and bones." Then Zander was off to fill his bucket again. Ryker remained to gut and chop the first batch.

The two men had met twenty-five years ago on a project as independent contractors for the Venom Society. Both had backgrounds in engineering and construction and were hired to assist with repairs and upgrades to a local skypod.

On that project, their differing strengths and weaknesses had clicked together like puzzle pieces. Ryker was a master troubleshooter. He had a knack for spotting mistakes in blueprints and consistently modified plans in ways that saved time, expense, and human lives. But his quiet nature often made him seem standoffish, and when he did speak, about problems he had discovered, he came off as finger-pointing or rude. By contrast, Zander was a natural motivator and team builder. Their combined effectiveness led the Venom Society to hire them repeatedly as partners to lead skypod work across the Delmarva Peninsula.

Their partnership ended abruptly one day at a job site when a swinging steel beam caught Ryker in the knee, shattering the joint. Zander was tireless in his efforts to keep his friend's spirits up through multiple operations, and eventually, Ryker regained the ability to walk. Zander was also instrumental in influencing the Venom Society to rehire Ryker into a new assignment that didn't require physical prowess. The Venom Society reassigned Ryker and retrained him to maintain the computer network infrastructure at the Museum of Human Evolution in Washington D.C., where he also documented the progress of skypod expansion. Though left with a limp, Ryker felt gratitude to his friend and to the Venom Society with every step he took, initially.

Recently, however, Ryker happened upon historical documents in the museum archives that stirred questions in his mind about how the Venom Society had acquired such global power. This made him wonder about the society's true intentions. He had a strong inclination to investigate further, but the idea of probing the supreme rulers left him uneasy.

Ryker thought of using the final moments before the market gates opened to confide in Zander and get his thoughts on the matter, but he hesitated. However, to Ryker's surprise, Zander also wanted to talk about the supreme leaders.

"Hey, buddy, quick question for ya," Zander said as he dumped a final load of fish on the cutting counter. He lowered his voice to a whisper and asked, "Do you know anything about the Venom Society's underground labs?"

Ryker eyes lit up, thankful that he didn't have to initiate the exchange. Then, in an equally soft voice, Ryker responded, "Well, I did stumble upon some records in the museum archives that seem to suggest that the Venom Society has conducted some unusual biological experimentation down there, and that makes me wonder about them sometimes. I haven't shared that with anyone before now, Zander, but I know you won't say anything. What have you heard?" Ryker tossed the ball back into Zander's court.

"They offered me a job." Zander confided in Ryker.

"*Man*, they really like you, don't they?" Ryker responded, in a little louder tone than Zander found comfortable. "SHHHHHHH," Zander reminded Ryker, quickly holding one perfectly straight finger in front of his lips.

"I don't know whether they love me or hate me," Zander continued, "but they want me to assist the civil engineers with assessing damage and patching faults in the support walls. They said the work would require utmost discretion and that I would not be granted access inside the tunnels. They want to send me to that remote location in the Appalachian Mountains where there has been moderate tremors and volcanic activity as of late. That's what caused the wall fractures. They need my expertise, but, clearly, they want to remain secretive about what lies beneath the ground in those tunnels. What do you think I should do?"

"Hmmmmm," Ryker mumbled as he thought about it for a couple seconds. "I'd say take the job if it pays well. Just don't overstep your bounds and do as they say or else . . . well . . . you know how they can be when they feel betrayed. *Hey, you know what?* I might be able to dig up some more on that. I have system administrator privileges to a database that only privileged users have access to." Then, Ryker shifted his tone to a pure whisper and leaned in closer to Zander. "I'll have a look around the database and see what I can find."

Zander gave his appreciation to Ryker and qualified his final thought on the matter, "Well, thanks, my friend; I appreciate that. Now, don't get yourself in trouble or anything. I'd just like some assurance that they don't have any ulterior motives. I mean, they do continue to provide us with our basic needs. The food could be better engineered, but at least we do get a steady trickle. And they keep trying to build us new living space wherever they can make room. I don't know, maybe it's just me."

Staying busy helped to shield the two men from the stress and anxiety of the inevitable collapse of the world around them. They saw masses of people struggling merely to eat each day but helping to distribute a healthy source of protein maintained a glimmer of hope inside them.

While Zander and Ryker finished preparing the fish table inside the colosseum, an exuberant crowd of commoners gathered outside. This was their day to indulge in the rare plus-up of premium fare.

Zinnia was among them, and she brought Xion and Dalton along with her to give them an opportunity to make their own selections. They had arrived extra early to be at the front of the line. The boys were a bit more animated than usual. It wasn't often that they got to pick out their own edibles.

Zinnia spent a couple of minutes, just prior to opening, giving the boys some instruction and reminding them to be on good behavior while inside the market. "It's going to be crowded and busy in there. I expect you two to pay attention and stay close to me. Look for items that are healthy for us and are not heavy or bulky. Remember, there is a limited amount of room in each of our bags, and they must be weighed before they allow us to leave," Zinnia explained to them.

Kamalei was already standing at the front gate preparing to make an announcement to the crowd. She overheard Zinnia coaching the boys, and it was clear that they were under her care. Kamalei felt compelled to say something to Zinnia. "Hello, young lady. It is very good of you to provide the boys with proper guidance and mentoring. I'm quite impressed with how you handle them, given that you are still quite young yourself. You make an excellent role model."

Zinnia recognized Kamalei from the Expulsion right away and was flabbergasted that the stunningly impressive Venom Society elite would offer her some kind words or acknowledge her at all for that matter. But Kamalei's pleasant demeanor was comforting, and Zinnia kept her composure.

"Oh. Thank you, Ms. Kamalei. I've been watching over them for quite some time, so I guess I'm used to it by now," Zinnia said.

"My apologies, I should have asked your name," Kamalei prompted her.

"I'm Zinnia. And this is my brother, Xion, and his best friend, Dalton. And you . . . you're even more beautiful in person," Zinnia added a touch of flattery.

"Oh," Kamalei chuckled softly. "Thank you. That's very kind of you to say. Are you their primary caregiver, Zinnia?" Kamalei inquired.

"I sure am," Zinnia replied. "And it has been difficult. Xion is sick and requires a lot of attention."

"I see," Kamalei responded, as she took a closer look at him. Then Kamalei seemed struck with a sense of concern about the little boy's condition.

Kamalei bent over a bit and focused her bright green eyes on Zinnia's. "Keep taking care of your little brother," she said. "You're doing a swell job. You're a *good* young lady. It will be okay," knowing full well that the little boy was in very poor health.

At the same time, Dalton was impatiently tugging at Zinnia's arm trying to get her to bend over as he asked her if they could visit the fish table first. Zinnia's jacket accidentally slid off her shoulder just enough to expose her upper arm before she was able to resituate it. Kamalei caught a glimpse of her armband and was taken aback but said nothing to Zinnia about it. Instead, Kamalei motioned to an admissions officer to allow the trio to get a head start in the direction of the fish stock as the gate opened.

"If you'll excuse me," Kamalei remarked. She stepped back from Zinnia and stood tall so that she could be seen and heard by the onlookers that were farther away.

"Greetings, *good* citizens of the Chesapeake," she addressed the crowd. "The Venom Society welcomes you to Market Day!" she announced as she lifted both arms high in the air, palms up. That drew cheers from the anxious commoners. "We *do* hope you are grateful for these gifts and the bounty that you are about to receive."

Then, Kamalei dragged open the heavy steel gate, and the roof began to retract automatically. A herd of people started inching forward in unison, Zinnia, Xion, and Dalton leading the way. Zinnia, grateful to Kamalei for showing them favor, called back to Kamalei, "Goodbye, Ms. Kamalei. THANK YOU!" The trio headed straight to the fish kiosk.

The rest of the crowd soon filled the walkways inside the open-air colosseum. They were a hurried bunch, like an agitated ant colony, working to maximize their time and yield. Attendees had free run of the market. Each person was given exactly one relief bag to shop with. These were burlap bags designed by the Venom Society to ensure uniformity across all commoners. The bags, all standard issue and standard size, contained scannable devices within the linings as well as the trademark "VS" initials.

Shoppers had to choose their take wisely to manage a balance between volume and nutritional value while remaining within a specified weight limit for the day. Anyone carrying a relief bag would have it inspected and weighed before they exited the market. Venom Society guards, posted at the exits, made sure of it.

Zinnia and the two boys were first to visit the fish kiosk. Zinnia grabbed several select cuts of meat since that was Xion's favorite, and she hoped it might entice him to eat hardier, but she didn't want to fill her bag too quickly. For a brief moment, she lapsed in holding to her commitment to a higher standard of conduct. She considered slipping some extra fish under her jacket for her sick brother, and made a slight motion to do so, but looked up and saw Zander peering down at her and quickly shed the urge. Zander, in all his street smarts, knew exactly what she was thinking. He asked her for her name.

"Zinnia," she replied. "And this is my brother, Xion, and his friend Dalton."

"Well, now, Miss Zinnia, I sure hope today's catch lives up to your hearty expectations. Say, you wouldn't be up to no good there, would ya?"

"No, sir," Zinnia responded, giving him two slow, yet deliberate, shakes of her head left to right.

"Uhhhh-huhhhhh, I didn't *think* so. You had better be good, ya hear? You don't want to become one of the ones who gets marked for . . ." Zander stuttered and breathed a deep, raspy sigh. "Well, you know what!"

"Y—y—y—y . . . yes, sir. I know." Zinnia mumbled as she thought back to the first Expulsion she attended. "I'll be good . . . because . . ." she paused and thought for a second and then continued: "Because my mother wanted me to do great things for my brother and for society. I'm going to save the world one day!"

Zinnia grabbed a side of mac and cheese, tossed it in her basket, and asked the boys to prepare to head over to the fruit section of the market. To her surprise, Xion was holding a scorpion in his hands, unconcerned about its deadly potential. One sting to the little boy's weakened body would surely have been the end of him.

Zinnia jostled the scorpion from Xion's hand and admonished him for taking that risk. Oddly, the scorpion didn't show any signs of aggression. Xion seemed to have established a trusted connection with it. "That's bizarre," Zinnia thought to herself, as she watched the scorpion scutter through a crack in the wall. Zinnia looked at Xion inquisitively as he waved goodbye to the little critter. Shaking it off as a fortuitously harmless encounter with a dangerous arachnid, Zinnia nudged Xion to move along.

Dalton, without saying a word, grabbed his cut of fish, shoved it into his bag, and continued to shadow Zinnia and Xion. He pretty much went wherever Xion went but tended to linger in the background.

In an attempt to conclude her exchange with Zander, Zinnia waved and offered him the popular mantra, "Thanks be to the Venom Society!"

Zander and Ryker used that phrase regularly themselves as a show of trust in the Venom Society. But beneath that trust was an unspoken suspicion that the elite rulers did not want anyone to question their origins or rise to power. Expulsions, apart from punishing individuals believed to be deserving, served as a regular reminder that defying the Venom Society could bring dire consequences. Very few individuals were willing to take that risk.

CHAPTER 5
Kamalei's Realization

Kamalei slalomed her way through a gathering of nervous members of the Venom Society's Regional Council and eased herself into one of the conference room chairs. Her colleagues were busily exchanging pleasantries to one another in a chaotic cacophony of isolated small talk.

Kamalei made eye contact with the grandmaster and offered him a nod as a show of respect for his supreme authority. She then turned her attention to her tablet to review a plethora of notes in case the grandmaster called on her for information. She was unsure exactly why he had even ordered the impromptu assembly. With her increasing authority within the Venom Society, though, she did appreciate the honor of being extended an invitation.

The Venom Society started Kamalei out in local law enforcement, a role that required her to spend substantial time among the people she policed and protected. A visible security force was necessary as long as there was a subpopulation of citizens among them who would consistently disregard the laws of society.

Kamalei quickly gained recognition for her versatility and willingness to take on multiple responsibilities, as well as her extraordinary intelligence and creative thinking. She was promoted to constable of the

Chesapeake Municipality and offered a position in the regional officers corps. As a devoted Venom Society principal, she had a knack for carrying out orders swiftly and with precision.

Grandmaster Webb peered around the table at the disorderly gathering and became impatient with the inharmonious chatter of the Venom Society elites. He was ready to call order to the meeting. He cleared his throat with authority and lowered his dark glasses on his nose slightly as if to give each member of the group the impression that he was looking to see who was not paying attention to him. A mish-mosh of sidebar discussions came to an immediate halt.

Webb sat at the head of the table. His chair had a high back that reached above his head and was shaped like a cocoon. The seat opened toward the table, and elegant wings flared outward and slightly forward on the sides. No one was to occupy it but Webb himself.

The chairs in which the other members sat were far less stately. The table was designed to allow everyone a clear view of the grandmaster with a simple glance in his direction.

The meeting room was perched high above city hall in a tall business skypod overlooking Baltimore's Inner Harbor. Accessible by Venom Society leaders only, it was where the most important meetings took place.

Typically, VIPs gathered here to discuss routine matters, such as construction plans, distribution of resources, food manufacturing, and engineering techniques. This day was a bit different though, as the grandmaster had a particular and pressing matter on his mind that he needed to address with his entourage: the ways and means of getting overpopulation under control in this municipality.

With the number of humans running at a constant critical state, the ruling body had to continually adjust the parameters that defined who would be selected for termination.

The grandmaster drove the discussions. His top deputy, Trent Chulah, assisted by providing supporting information when the boss asked for it and acting as his yes man.

"Welcome, colleagues," the grandmaster opened the discussion. "I've called you here today to discuss several matters that are problematic in the Chesapeake Municipality. I'll briefly introduce the agenda items this afternoon, and then we'll address each in detail."

"The most pressing reason we've assembled today is the growing imbalance between births and deaths," he explained. "I want you to consider how we might best reduce the number of humans here. It is critically important that we manage this as efficiently as possible. We'll come back to this momentarily."

Kamalei grew uneasy in her seat when this agenda item was announced.

"I'd also like to address the issue of rampant disease in the tristate area," Webb continued.

The most prolific killing disease on Earth was zaraseptosis, a deadly parasite. It was highly contagious and, on Earth's crowded streets, capable of spreading rapidly. The only cure for this nasty little bug was a mixture of animal or insect venom and acitaneum—a diluted poison found only in the root of the Venus Giganta, a descendant of the Venus flytrap plant. The problem was that Earth was running out of the precious species of plant. Harvesting its poison and converting it into a life-saving medicine was becoming increasingly difficult.

"We are critically low on our antidote," Webb explained. "The problem lies not in processing what we have. We simply do not have enough natural plant material left on Earth to sustain us for much longer. All efforts to fabricate the species in hydroponic labs have failed. We'll likely need to assign more Expulsion winners to the task of discovering and harvesting more acitaneum in the near future, *wherever* that may take them."

Councilmembers, wanting to appease the grandmaster, exchanged warm gestures and pleasant chatter amongst themselves, giving the impression they were genuinely impressed with his suggestion. Then, they turned to Grandmaster Webb and nodded to communicate directly with him that his idea was a good one.

"Additionally," the grandmaster continued, "we're becoming increasingly overburdened with waste. And, as you may have surmised, a population reduction will produce more human corpses for us to have to manage. I'll need this congregation to consider enhanced mitigation efforts immediately. We simply *must* do better."

The table again broke out into a number of sidebar interactions. That allowed Kamalei a few moments to check her notes, reflect on recent developments in reclamation efforts, and consider her own potential for advancement by contributing to the matter. "This might be a good opportunity for me to impress Webb in a way that could boost my standing in the Venom Society," she thought to herself.

The Venom Society did realize modest success in recycling manufactured waste into day-to-day essentials. However, the volume of human waste and routinely discarded garbage was nonetheless at an all-time high, and waste management sites were filled to capacity. This increased the risk of outbreaks of disease and disorder, and scientists were under constant pressure to design clever ways to minimize this massive build-up of waste.

One solution that Kamalei was instrumental in launching was the construction of enormous vacuum tubes that essentially whisked materials into space. And, yes, that included human bodies. The tubes were constructed of sturdy nanocarbon materials in segments as long as a quarter-mile each. Attached end-to-end, they formed incredibly long tunnels. Motorized repeater modules were placed at tunnel joints to keep materials moving. The tunnel openings housed a vacuum device that sucked items into its wide, beveled mouth. Ejection mechanisms at the far end of the tubes blew the materials into large rocket-propelled waste bins which carried them upward and away from Earth. Some were placed into orbit, creating remote compact landfills that encircled the Earth collecting garbage. Others entered into a trajectory, casting material away from the Earth permanently.

The Regional Council managed large groups of working commoners that included people from all walks of life. Oddly, there was very little vertical movement among ranking members. The commoners grew accustomed to the sameness of their rulers. Many among the officer corps held their positions for long periods of time, making it nearly impossible for others to rise through the ranks. Kamalei was proud that she was the exception.

At the age of twenty-eight, she was decades younger than many of her council colleagues and the only member regarded as poised to ascend in rank.

Kamalei was hungry for continued success and greater power and grew a thick skin in an attempt to match the dispassionate demeanor of her superiors. What she could not let them see, and didn't fully admit even to herself, was that sometimes she found herself fighting doubts about the philosophy of the Venom Society. Showing empathy toward the commoners would have been perceived in the council as a sign of weakness and would surely have led to her demotion, or worse. Still, feelings of culpability followed her. Particularly when it came to capital punishment and the fate of troubled children.

Noticing that the grandmaster was antsy in his chair, Kamalei lightly shook off her thoughts and transitioned her mind back into the present.

Webb gave the tabletop three quick but heavy taps with his pen, a sign that he'd heard enough of the chatter among the officers, and they quickly returned their full attention to him.

With that, Webb moved on to the most important topic of the day's agenda. The cold, hard truth was that for humans to remain a viable species on Earth for as long as possible, a balancing act was required. For every infant born, someone else must die.

"Now, my fellow principals, let us consider the most critical discussion point today. We need to increase the rate of participation in our Expulsions, thereby checking back the population in this municipality," he said.

This time the chatter around the table was louder and more intense. Most of the officers were eager to hear what Webb's solution to that problem would be. Kamalei, on the other hand, dipped slightly in her chair, and visions of Zinnia appeared in her mind. She shook them off and resumed listening intently.

Raising the volume of his voice a notch for a moment, the grandmaster redirected everyone's attention back to himself, "IT APPEARS the current . . . *birth* rate . . . slightly exceeds the current *death* rate in this municipality. Isn't that right, Chulah?" The grandmaster addressed the deputy, without even looking in his direction.

"That is correct, sir. But only by a fraction of a percentage point," Chulah responded.

"That's *too* much," insisted the grandmaster. "As I've indicated a thousand times before, any imbalance at all could decimate our food and medical supplies. Disease and starvation would take a much greater toll on us. ALL of us! As you well know, we, in this very room, are particularly vulnerable to new variations of zaraseptosis. We could lose everything our forefathers worked so hard for."

"I won't let that happen, sir," Chulah assured him.

"Excellent . . . Kamalei, do our Expulsion facilities have ample room to increase participation?" Webb asked.

Kamalei responded quickly and confidently, "Well, sir, most Expulsion events are quite crowded and push the limits of the colosseums. But that is due in part to the fact that we've been allowing larger audiences to attend. There are modifications we can make to increase dissenter participation by perhaps five percent."

"Good. But not quite good enough," Webb countered. Then he leaned toward the left side of the room, where two of his project leads were sitting, and issued an order to them: "Go out and canvass the colosseums and increase the event staging areas by an average of ten percent."

At first, the two project leads sat still and gave each other puzzled looks, wondering whether Webb had misspoken about such a dramatic increase. After an awkward silence, and not witnessing any movement from the group, Chulah chimed in: "You heard him. Get moving!"

The subordinates jumped to their feet and exited the room to do as the premier leader had asked. They were charged with engineering a means by which a significant number of humans would die as part of a major population correction. Most around the table showed no emotion at all. They would do exactly as Webb ordered, or they themselves could face consequences for disobeying orders.

Kamalei, however, was taken aback by the fact that this meant more human carnage at these larger events. Unable to purge the image of the band on Zinnia's arm at the market, Kamalei tried to maintain a straight face to cover her inner emotions. "I'm sure the *good* people of the municipality will appreciate your concern for their wellbeing, sir," she said to Webb, to continue to appease him.

Kamalei experienced a trance like moment, pondering whether Zinnia might be pulled into an Expulsion by the grandmaster's new decree. For what seemed like minutes but was mere seconds, she reflected upon how the Expulsions worked and how participants were selected. Her thoughts turned, against her will, to Zinnia.

All humans, including every newborn, were fitted with smart devices that contained digital information about them. The devices, the size of a grain of sand, were permanently installed under the skin in random places where they were not easily detected or removed. Once fitted, the host was tagged for life.

The Venom Society used hand-held devices to scan individuals and monitor the digital information stored on their implants. The devices looked like phaser guns, and one pull of the trigger produced a report about the individual at whom it was aimed.

The most important piece of information kept on implants for each person was known as their "violation count." This was a number that represented the total quantity and severity of an individual's infractions against society. There were also sensors on most buildings and light poles so the Venom Society could identify those with high violation counts at just about any instant in time. If someone's violation count climbed into the "red zone," that person would be automatically considered for entrance into an Expulsion.

The Venom Society could change the red zone parameters at any time, depending on how much population correction was needed. A lower threshold meant more participants in Expulsions.

Kamalei shook off her cloudy thoughts and recaptured Webb's attention, "Eh hummm, exactly how do you propose we select an increased number of participants for future Expulsions here, Grandmaster?"

"That's exactly what I need you to determine," Webb challenged her, aiming the thin, dark lenses of his sunglasses right at her. "We'll have to make a modest adjustment to the qualification threshold. You will assess what that adjustment should be. Report back to me in three days, and I'll make the announcement to the people of the municipality."

Kamalei stood, issued a nod to the grandmaster, dismissed herself from the meeting early, and exited the room. She felt pressured that Grandmaster Webb was leaning on her hard to implement a way to check the population back in the Chesapeake Municipality. She hurried out of the conference room, allowed the door to click shut behind her, and leaned her back against it for a moment to calm her nerves.

Her mind raced frantically. "What about Zinnia? She could be in serious jeopardy for selection," she thought to herself, having spotted Zinnia's armband at the market. With no one in sight, she took the opportunity to query the Chesapeake Municipality's criminal offender database for individuals with the highest violation counts.

She ran an algorithmic simulation on her tablet that lowered the threshold for selection to the upcoming Expulsions as the grandmaster had ordered. She then displayed the names of all individuals among that population whose violation counts ended up in the red zone, making them eligible for selection.

When Zinnia's name flashed on the screen, Kamalei felt the blood drain from the flesh of her face. She experienced a wave of dizziness. In an instant, she realized that Zinnia would be at even greater risk for selection once the threshold was adjusted, and she didn't want Zinnia's blood on her hands.

CHAPTER 6

Hidden Compassion

Agitated by what she'd just learned at the meeting, Kamalei made her way to the hovercraft transporters more deliberately and briskly than she normally would. An empty craft awaited her there. She issued a voice command to take her to ground level.

She needed to find Zinnia and warn her of what was coming. Zinnia stood little chance of surviving an Expulsion because she was not physically imposing or swift-moving. Kamalei's thoughts raced, in search of a way out for Zinnia.

Perhaps she could encourage Zinnia to work to become a reformed contributor to society through the demonstration of good deeds, thereby reducing her violation count and avoiding selection to the Expulsion.

The hovercraft came to a halt over a cushion of air close to the ground, and the vertical exit door popped up. Kamalei ducked under the door frame and sprang out of the craft, immediately heading in the direction of the orphanage.

As she entered the busy metropolis street, Kamalei realized that she would be easily noticed by the commoners as a high-profile member of the Venom Society. That would surely attract their attention to her, something she did not want while she confronted Zinnia. She needed to proceed stealthily.

Kamalei came upon a vagrant in a sleeping bag, resting in an alleyway. It was an elderly female. The woman kept a stock of used clothing in a cart next to her. Kamalei saw this and thought to herself, "That is how I can go unnoticed."

She knelt beside the woman to ask her assistance. The vagrant lifted her head, clearly startled. She wasn't expecting to be interrupted by anyone as she rested, especially not a Venom Society elite.

"Eh-hum, ma'am, would you mind if I borrowed some of the clothes in your cart for a short while? I have something to give to you to show my appreciation," Kamalei said, offering the woman a voucher. The woman looked at it curiously and realized it entitled the carrier to one hospitality bag for use at the next Market Day. She accepted it handily.

The vagrant was befuddled as to why the beautiful Venom Society leader might want second-rate clothing but did not question her. "Take whatever you want," she muttered.

Kamalei selected a jacket and pants from the cart. While not the stylish attire she was used to wearing, Kamalei knew it would allow her to fit in nicely with the crowd.

The woman slouched back into her resting position, and Kamalei hurried to find a nook where she could change clothes.

Donning the loose-fitting, shabby jacket and pants, Kamalei approached the orphanage, unsure of what the atmosphere would be like inside.

She stood for a moment just inside the door, swallowing a lump in her throat as she looked around for Zinnia. There she was, sitting on the floor in the back, playing marbles with her brother and Dalton.

Finding Zinnia was easy. Informing Zinnia that she was in danger of being selected for the next Expulsion was not.

Kamalei dashed to the rear of the orphanage where the children were playing and tapped Zinnia on the shoulder. Zinnia's eyes rose a little, froze for a moment at Kamalei's midsection, then rose some more, all the way up to the face of the tall stranger—and suddenly, she realized who it was.

"Uh-oh," Zinnia exclaimed. She recognized Kamalei from the Expulsion. "Am I in trouble?"

Kamalei, with a straight forefinger pressed to her lips, responded in a calming, quiet tone. "*Shhhhhhhhhh*, no; you're not in trouble . . . well, not with me, anyway. I need to talk to you, though—*now*."

Kamalei grabbed Zinnia's hand and pulled her along, out the back door of the orphanage, and into the alley where they could talk without anyone overhearing.

"Zinnia," Kamalei said, "I just came from a board meeting with my superiors. There will be another Expulsion in this municipality very soon."

"Oh, gosh, Ms. Kamalei, I don't think I'm ready to attend another one of those right now," Zinnia said, recalling how sick she had become after watching the last one.

Kamalei bent her knees and lowered herself to look Zinnia directly in the eyes. She put her hands on the child's shoulders.

"Zinnia," she said, "you might not have a choice."

Kamalei then explained to Zinnia that her violation count was high enough to make her a candidate. An Undesirable. Kamalei watched Zinnia's head fall slightly forward and waited for a response, but Zinnia stayed silent.

Zinnia had a look of panic on her face. She knew that her recent behavior had not put her in a favorable position. Her mind spun, wondering who would take care of Xion if she were no longer in his life.

Tears streamed down Zinnia's cheeks as she looked back up into Kamalei's eyes. "What can I do? Ohhhhh . . . what can I do?" Zinnia asked. "I can't die and leave my brother with no one to care for him. I promise to stop stealing. But, but . . . if I'm already on that list, it may be too late for me. What am I going to do?"

Kamalei responded with a gesture that felt completely foreign to her: she hugged Zinnia tightly, feeling the child's tears wet on her own neck. Then, Kamalei again made eye contact with Zinnia and offered her a source of hope.

"There is something you can try," Kamalei said. "Something that could reduce your violation count and pull you out of the red zone."

Kamalei went on to explain that Zinnia could possibly lower her violation count through good deeds. "If you commit time to assisting the Venom Society delivery crew with food distribution in this municipality, you will have a very visible hand in sustaining the health and wellbeing of your fellow citizens. You should also consider giving more of your time to cleaning up the rubbish in these streets, as well," Kamalei added, waving one of her arms out to her side, in case Zinnia had not taken notice of the filth in which they stood.

"You need to understand the severity of the consequences of your actions. Here is a copy of the Expulsion Charter," Kamalei continued, handing her a small booklet. "It describes in detail the decree from the grandmaster and provides standard operating instructions for carrying out the events. You're old enough now to take responsibility for the path you choose in life and to understand the ramifications for poor choices. I want you to read this."

Zinnia took the booklet and showed her appreciation for Kamalei's concern, "Thank you, Ms. Kamalei. I understand. I will be okay. I promise. But—but my brother . . . I don't know what is going to happen to him."

"How's that?" Kamalei asked Zinnia to explain.

"Well, ma'am, he has been the real reason behind my decisions to steal. I do it for him. He's very sick. You see, he was bitten by a spider a few months ago, and a terrible infection manifested itself. A blue ring appeared at the site of the bite. While that subsided after a couple of weeks, Xion never seemed to be the same after that. And he's gotten worse. I think he's dying."

Kamalei knew right away that Xion was suffering from zaraseptosis. The disease is fatal if left untreated for too long. "I may be able to help him," she told Zinnia.

Zinnia focused her big blue eyes, excitedly, on Kamalei's, "What are you going to do?" she asked.

"You're right," Kamalei agreed, "if we don't get him some medicine quickly, he will surely die. As you are aware, I am an officer of the Venom Society. I have access to the serum that is used to treat the disease that he suffers from. I'll need to retrieve a vile and administer it to him immediately."

Kamalei also felt she needed to divulge the absolute truth of the matter. "I'm afraid I cannot guarantee a cure, but I can likely give him more time. Some patients respond much better than others. I hope your little brother is one of them. Only time will tell."

Zinnia stared back at Kamalei and nodded as if she understood the situation but had hoped for a better prognosis.

"Now, I'll need you to follow my instructions very closely," Kamalei continued. "Meet me at the infirmary, just down the street, in one hour. Bring Xion with you," Then, in a show of trust in the young lady, Kamalei extended her fist to Zinnia, palm up. She opened her long, powerful fingers, and a device appeared in her hand. "Here, take this fob and keep it safely on your person at all times. It will allow you entry into the infirmary."

Kamalei then directed Zinnia that once she arrived at the infirmary, she was to make her way around the west side of the building to a door that was not visible from the busy street. She told Zinnia to hold the fob close to the electronic cipher lock until the LED screen awakened and prompted her to enter a passcode. She gave Zinnia the code: 0-7-2-0-6-9.

"The electronic deadbolt will release for five seconds, and you will be able to enter," Kamalei continued. "Go immediately to your left, find the large supply closet, and wait for me there. That's where I'll administer the medication. And, Zinnia . . ." Kamalei added, as she leaned toward the girl, closing the gap between them, "*don't* let *anyone* see you enter."

Kamalei rose and turned as if she were about to go and make good on her promise but thought for a split second and realized that there was more to that electronic fob than just a user authentication for the cipher lock. She abruptly turned her focus back to Zinnia, and her facial expression became intensely serious.

"One other thing," she said to the girl. "Do *not* press any of the other buttons on the device. I don't have time to explain, but I need you to comply. If you want me to help your brother, I need you to do exactly as I say."

Zinnia watched as Kamalei disappeared into the crowded street. She then fell slightly backward, making contact with a rickety fence, and collapsed into a sitting position on the ground. Her knees were tight to her chest. She decided to take this time alone to begin studying the Expulsion booklet that Kamalei had given her. Not everyone got a chance to review the supreme orders first-hand, and she had a little bit of time to peruse the document before getting Xion over to the infirmary.

"This charter hereby establishes and executes the parameters by which the people of this land will select for termination, individuals who have committed acts against their fellow citizens," the booklet read.

"Those who have incurred the highest violation counts, above the acceptable threshold, shall be selected. They shall be referred to as *undesirables*. Participation for these individuals is mandatory. They have proven their disloyalty to others and have demonstrated that their cost to society outweighs their worth. They shall be marked for termination."

The doctrine went on to describe how citizens of detestable behavior, who were at the highest risk for selection to Expulsions, were fitted with permanent armbands. That allowed the Venom Society to track their movements as death cages were assembled and prepared.

That brought Zinnia's attention to her own armband, which she tried to adjust into a more comfortable position before reading further.

The booklet explained that a citizen's violation count shall rise commensurate to the severity of their infraction against society, as defined by the ruling body. Conversely, good deeds and exceptional contributions toward the prosperity and common good of society may earn a reduction in one's violation count.

Executioners were citizens who were granted the honor of eliminating undesirables during an Expulsion. They were granted first rights to avenge one or more contestants. Executioners were embedded safely inside the death cage and inaccessible to participants. They were able to physically operate robots, maneuver features within the cage, fire weaponry, and deploy killing devices but only at the behest of a majority rule of observers.

As she read on, Zinnia felt a mix of terror and remorse. She reflected on her actions over the last couple of years. Taking from others was just her way of trying to help Xion. But she knew that she could not use that as an excuse anymore.

"Observers shall be given electronic modules—joysticks—that communicate with a master control unit embedded within the killing devices," the doctrine explained. "No one joystick, in-and-of itself, is sufficient influence to allow the Executioner to deploy a killing device. However, if a majority of onlookers unite against a particular contestant, and enough electronic votes are cast in unison, the collective will shall activate the master control unit, which, in turn, will allow an Executioner to make a kill."

Zinnia's memory flashed back to the first Expulsion that she attended, and she recalled the vivid image of the crowd chanting in unison and a young man's bloodied arm reaching through the cage as he took his last breath. It shocked her back into the fear of her own predicament. She clapped the booklet closed and covered her head with her arms. This was her reality. But she knew she needed to stay strong for her little brother.

Gathering her composure, Zinnia rose to her feet and hurried back into the orphanage to get the boys. Time was running short, and she had to hurry to get Xion over to the infirmary to meet Kamalei.

There, they found the side door that Kamalei had described. It was high-tech and a bit spooky looking, almost like something from another planet. Zinnia held the fob close to the cipher lock as Kamalei had instructed, and the electronic display lit up.

Zinnia read the disclaimer on the screen, which stated that the security network she was about to access was restricted to authorized personnel only, but she ignored it. Then, a password prompt appeared. Zinnia keyed in the numbers, just as Kamalei instructed: 0-7-2-0-6-9, and almost before she touched the "9" button to complete the sequence, the door latch released, and it began to crack open, allowing her, Xion, and Dalton to make their way into the infirmary and over to the supply closet.

Medical supplies and cleaning agents filled the shelves around them. There was nothing interesting to Dalton to hold his attention, but he was fascinated by the fob and asked to hold it while they waited for Kamalei. Zinnia didn't want to do anything that would go against Kamalei's wishes, but she thought it harmless to allow Dalton to look at the device more closely if that would keep him occupied for the next ten minutes or so.

Dalton, having witnessed the fob's role in opening the door wondered exactly what else it might be capable of. To him, the fob appeared to be an expensive toy, something he didn't get a chance to play with often. He held the device high overhead, waved it in a figure-eight pattern, and made engine sounds, as he sometimes did with his toy airplane.

Dalton lost his balance slightly and fell against Zinnia, and the fob came to rest tightly against her arm. To their surprise, Zinnia's armband flashed a series of lights and made a beeping noise. A data transfer took place. Zinnia was mortified that the fob and her armband appeared to be communicating in some way.

She grabbed the device from Dalton with some trepidation that she had allowed Dalton to handle the fob against Kamalei's wishes.

Kamalei arrived at the infirmary with a vile of medication in hand. She administered it to Xion, who appeared frail and thin. She told Zinnia to hold on to the fob so that she could gain entrance into the infirmary later for more medicinal supplies. She added that she would stash some food items there for Zinnia each week but warned her not to tell anyone.

Then, Kamalei saw the three children out the door and turned her attention toward tackling the original orders of Grandmaster Webb—to recommend an adjustment to the qualifying threshold for selection to the next Expulsion.

CHAPTER 7

Evolution in an Advanced Society

Zinnia sat sluggish on the floor at her brother's bedside. Xion lay resting in the lower bunk, drowsy from the medication that Kamalei administered. The stress of having been warned by Kamalei of the danger she was in drained Zinnia of much of her energy. But the day was not over for her.

She cradled Dalton in her lap, rocking him back and forth. He was upset and crying as Zinnia tried to console him. One of the children at the orphanage made a comment to him about his round, oversized eyes. The child meant no harm, but it brought an awareness to Dalton that he looked just a little bit different than the other kids there.

Zinnia felt compelled to explain to the boys why some humans look different than others. They were old enough now to understand the physical effects of evolution on the human population.

"Listen to me, both of you. You must understand that not everyone is the same in physical appearance," she began. "Xion and I are traditional humans. We look just like our surface-dwelling ancestors from thousands of years ago. Nothing has changed. However, there are three other populations of humans that look a little bit different than we do."

Dalton lifted his head from Zinnia's shoulder and looked her in the eye so that he could interject. "Am I one of those kinds?" he asked in a boyish tone.

Zinnia wiped the moisture from his cheeks and confirmed his suspicion, "Well, yes Dalton, you are. But that's not a *bad* thing at all! You are from a family of underground dwellers. They are called Marsupans. That is why your eyes are so big and beautiful," she emphasized to him, hoping that would assure him that he was no less normal, or liked, than anyone else.

"Your mommy and daddy had to go away when you were really, really little, due to the collapse of their underground bunker," Zinnia continued. "That's when you were brought to this orphanage to live with us. We're thankful that you are here, and we love you very, very, much."

The boys listened intently as Zinnia went on to describe in detail how overcrowding led to widely variable living conditions among different subpopulations, and that caused humans to evolve with subtle physical differences.

Traditional humans, which came from an ancestry of Earth's surface-dwelling bipeds, still appeared the same as they had for millennia. Their original habitat remained essentially unchanged. However, radically different living conditions among other sectors of the population produced three modern variant species of humans.

The Astronians were one large population of an adapted variant of humans. They had become adept at living in skypod dwellings high above the surface of the earth. They survived within their elevated communities by perfecting specialized farming techniques that did not require planting in soil. For example, they hung fruiting plants on metal grates and misted their roots to sustain them.

With bloated chests to house their oversized lungs—by-products of the thin air they breathed at high altitudes—they were relatively sedentary beings. They appeared to crave more oxygen with every breath they took.

Their skin was thick and had become resistant to the detrimental effects of the driving sunlight, as they took the brunt of the rays aimed at Earth. Their most obvious evolutionary body feature was their exceptionally long and strong arms and hands. While they remained bipedal beings and walked normally, they grew unusually long, curved fingers and stiff, thick thumbs, which gave them the ability to climb and maneuver from skypod to skypod, just as a sloth would navigate the trees of the forest.

They did add an extra threat to the traditional humans at ground level, though. Occasionally, an Astronian would miscalculate their swinging maneuvers high above and fall to their deaths, sometimes taking out a couple of the ground-dwelling humans in the crowds below.

Another subset of humans, the Hydronians, had adapted to living in aquapod dwellings, which were essentially skypods built on ocean barges. This human variant became accustomed to surviving in the harsh conditions of the ocean's unrelenting sway.

Their skin was scaly with a white hue, indicating a high salt content. Advanced techniques for crop development, hydroponics, and fish farming were employed in their watery world. They were comfortable ingesting conch, raw fish, sea turtle, and other sustenance of the waters. But seaweed was a main staple for them. Whether it was dried and crisp or freshly harvested from the sea, it became a cost-effective way for this group of humans to help feed their growing population. They shared their bounty with the other species of humans who also derived vitamins and minerals from seaweed.

The Hydronians developed a tiny finger-like protrusion at the base of the palm of their right hands, laden with natural toxins. These lethal flanges could stun and paralyze fish and other prey, providing them with a key survival component.

They also mastered water exit and entry techniques—very smooth, sleek, and flawless. Many likened their physical motion to the seals and penguins that shared a similarly impressive talent for navigating from water to land and vice versa.

The other evolutionary variant of humans was the Marsupan race. These humans lived underground for over a thousand years and adapted to remaining largely within the tunnels of the Earth's crust. They developed incredibly sensitive, oversized eye sockets and pupils, which allowed them to better navigate their dimly-lit burrows. Males had stocky, hairy frames. Females were smaller but also developed a muscular build.

There was not a lot of food to be had in the pits of the Earth's crust, so they relied on a steady feed from above ground. As a navigational aid, the Marsupans could spray out sound waves from a specialized tongue click and receive and interpret spatial information from the echoes. They had thick, rugged fingernails at the ends of their fingers, developed over time as a result of aggressive digging and tunneling. The Marsupans provided an abundance of raw materials to the populations above ground for building and manufacturing.

All variants of humans, while they had adapted to differing environments, shared frequent interactions and coexisted well together for the most part. Each subpopulation provided a unique service to the others but also required reciprocation from the others for their own survival. These symbiotic relationships were fueled by an inherent interdependency on one another.

For instance, the Astronians, who derived great benefit from bountiful sunlight, cultivated an abundance of fruits and vegetables, which they would share with Marsupans. But they also required a constant feed of raw materials from the Marsupans for new construction.

The Marsupans were dependent upon the Astronians for solar electric power to be able to mine and process iron ore.

Similarly, the Hydronians relied on the Marsupans for natural resources for use in the production of tools. The Hydronians provided the underground dwellers a bounty of seafood in return.

Zinnia continued to educate the boys about the various interrelationships among humans. "The balance of resource exchange among different variants of humans was fragile," she said to them. "If one species fails to deliver their provisions on time to the others, it could result in a catastrophic loss of life. This common bond of survival demands patience and tolerance for one another. I'm telling you all of this so that you don't get upset if you don't look or think or move the same way other children do."

Zinnia finished educating the boys about the development of the different species of humans no sooner than Xion began complaining of discomfort in his abdomen. As tired as she was by this time, Zinnia was forced to visit the medical supply building to try and scavenge some pain medication.

Zinnia coaxed Dalton into his bunk, told the boys to settle in for a nap, and then made her way out of the orphanage and into the busy street.

Commoners were prohibited from entering the medical supply building without credentials. If they were not assigned to stocking, cleaning, or distribution efforts, they likely did not have a valid reason to enter. Zinnia didn't.

That didn't stop her from testing a back window of the place, though, to see if it was open. She struggled with it for a couple seconds, and it didn't budge.

All of the sudden, she felt three firm taps on her shoulder. A burly man wearing a security badge put a quick stop to her antics before she could get herself into any trouble.

"*Hold* it right there, young lady," the man admonished her as he leaned ominously over her, staring her down. Zinnia turned to him with panic in her eyes. The man was a large, imposing figure with broad shoulders. He wore a black, tight-fitting tactical uniform and carried an abundance of gadgets on his person.

Zinnia's silence spoke volumes about what she thought was going to happen to her. But rather than administer stern punishment, the man saw this as an opportunity to offer a bit of advice to a teenager who seemed out of her true element trying to illegally enter a restricted building.

"Now, you're old enough to know that your violation count will rise if you get caught breaking and entering. And I suspect you saw the 'Do Not Enter' sign posted in plain view—right . . . over . . . there," the man continued, pointing over her shoulder to make sure Zinnia acknowledged the sign. "So, tell me, who are you, and what motivates a young lady like yourself to go against the law of the land today?"

"I'm Zinnia, sir" she answered. "And—well, my brother."

"Your *brother* put you up to this!" the man exclaimed. "*Well*, I think we should go have a little chat with him, don't you?" He grabbed her arm with a grip like a vice.

"NO!" Zinnia lashed out at him, pulling away from his grasp. The man looked at her with a scowl on his face as if to take exception to her defiance.

"Well, sir, what I mean is," Zinnia continued, "my brother—his name is Xion, and . . . well, he is very sick. His stomach is causing him severe pain, and I need to get him some medication very soon. A nice woman—a Venom Society officer—gave him some of her special medicine a few days ago to try to help, but he hasn't improved much. His body needs more nourishment. Sir, I just don't know what to do. I think he's dying."

The man's heart sunk in his chest.

"I see . . . I'm sorry that your brother is not well. But you must be very careful not to allow your violation count to rise. I sure would hate to see you become one of the ones who gets selected for—" the man stuttered and breathed a deep, raspy sigh, "well . . . you know what!"

"I know," Zinnia said, as her bright blue eyes acquired a very somber expression to them at the thought of losing her little brother.

The man continued, "Come with me. I've got a little something that might just help him out. *But* you must *promise* me you are not going to continue to disregard the laws of this land. You hear me?"

"Uh hmmmm." Zinnia nodded her head in total respect of his authority, and out of a good bit of fear too. Zinnia followed him around to the side door.

While displaying a rugged, authoritative appearance, the man was an emotional personality and wanted to make as much right in the world as he could. He won high trust from the Venom Society from his past work for them in the field of security. The Venom Society felt so comfortable with him that, at times, they asked him to stand guard outside of some of their most sensitive facilities.

Most recently, he was asked to install security monitoring cameras at an underground collider site, underneath the historical grounds of Annapolis, Maryland. There, engineers from the Venom Society made great strides in the science of quantum manipulation and its application to the electric power grid, material transport, and space travel.

Through his work in security at high-profile facilities, he became lightly privy to the little-known capabilities within the Venom Society atomic energy programs—things such as advanced neutron collision and nuclear fission techniques. Scientists were able to cause separate and distinct subatomic particles to become entangled. That meant that materials could be acted upon and broken down into individual subatomic parts, moved in a direction of choice, and reassembled in a different location, without losing or damaging any physical matter.

Additionally, space tampering techniques were developed, which could warp the space-time fabric. The process created a four-dimensional pathway through the atmosphere through which objects could travel at the speed of electrons.

Together, these capabilities enabled scientists to manipulate the chemical building blocks of matter to allow matter to be transported almost instantly from point to point. Eventually, to include animals and humans.

From what little bit Zinnia told him, the man gathered that Xion was gravely ill. He also saw good in Zinnia in that she was putting her own welfare at risk for that of her brother. He knew he had to do something to try and help them both.

"Stay put while I go and grab a couple things for you," he said to Zinnia. He poked a series of numbers into the cipher lock, and the door to the storage facility sprung open. He disappeared inside for only one minute and then shot back outside, closing the door firmly behind him.

Zinnia hadn't moved an inch. She looked at the man as if to question what he had in mind for her.

He handed her a few pain-reducer tablets and a pack of protein bars to carry her and her brother through the night.

"There you go. That certainly is better than what most folks get for attempting to break into the local medical storage facility," the man suggested to her with a raised eyebrow and friendly smirk on his face. "Now, you are to tell *no one* that I gave you this stash tonight, you got that?" Zinnia agreed with a double nod in the affirmative.

"Thank you, Mr. uhmmm . . ." Zinnia hesitated because she still was unaware of the man's name.

"Jett . . . the name's Jett," he responded. "It was very nice to meet you, Zinnia. Now, don't make me worry about you anymore, ya hear? Get on home and take care of that little brother of yours. It's getting late, and you have to get up early in the morning for school."

"Yes, Mr. Jett." Zinnia's big blue eyes lit up like stars, having been the recipient of another act of human kindness. This resonated with her inner spirit. She thanked the kind man, turned, and ran for home as the sun disappeared deep into the red western sky.

CHAPTER 8

Success Comes at a Price

It was a beautiful day in Staziak, Alaska, located along the western edge of the Juneau Municipality. A grid of skypods grew busy as scads of unassuming commoners gathered to view the launch of a conventional rocket ship. Its mission: to transport a payload of materials from the Earth to the moon to support the construction of human biodomes. Some commoners perched themselves upon the out coves of their aquapods. Some remained inside of their skyscraping abodes. All were intent on viewing the lift-off.

Excursions to the moon had become routine. This was good news for all humans because it instilled hope in them that one day they would be able to permanently relocate there. Living conditions there, however, were far less than ideal. Scientists endeavored to discover a more suitable habitat somewhere in space that mirrored the standard comforts of planet Earth. After all, no one could predict exactly how much longer mankind could draw from the sustenance of the Earth before it completely collapsed.

That is what motivated the events that were taking place on the east side of town. There, five skypods, arranged in a pentagon formation, were roped off so engineers could perform heavy structural repair work.

Well, not really. That was the Venom Society's cover story for what was actually going on.

Restricting access to this circular series of skypods under the guise of construction work provided a great pretense for a secret deep space launch. One that would take place unbeknownst to commoners and simultaneously to the conventional ship expedition to the moon.

Collider spaceships were inherently difficult to detect by eye. Upon lift-off, observers merely saw a ripple or warble effect in the air as matter traveled, much like the nebulous exhaust from a traditional gasoline engine. The Venom Society had achieved some success with deep space excursions in recent years, but the events themselves were far less widely revealed to commoners. Especially when failures occurred.

Experimentation with molecular human body disassembly and reassembly had been successfully demonstrated within the underground collider rings in New Mexico. But that was in a very limited and controlled environment. And previous deep space flight trial-runs to outer space were only lightly tested with human beings on board. At least that's what the Venom Society wanted everyone to believe.

This launch marked the next step in the Venom Society's quest to appraise the validity of their deep space travel ships with live humans on board. They recruited a skeleton crew to minimize the damage should things not go as planned.

Astronauts eager to make a name for themselves were selected to man the ship. These brave travelers were relatively young, easily impressionable, and somewhat gullible. The lure for them was three-pronged: the promise of rising quickly through the ranks, the possibility of staking claim to new habitable territory, and the fame of being the first humans ever to leave the Milky Way and return, alive, to tell their story.

While this all sounded good to the novice crew, the chief of operations of the Deep Space Division of the Venom Society, Rayven Zeller, and his colleagues were only modestly optimistic that the flight would proceed completely without incident. Zeller was a cold personality. He'd grown that way over the years having been in charge of numerous failed missions that sustained significant losses. Yet, somehow, he managed to maintain a harmonious relationship with each new crew he commanded. Grandmaster Webb deployed Zeller to Alaska, a less densely populated municipality, for a temporary assignment to oversee the Venom Society's progress on human deep space collider flight.

The Venom Society was open about the fact that they had made attempts at deep space travel with ships carrying live animals. And that part was true. But it wasn't the whole truth. The animals, upon return, were nothing more than a mosh of biological cellular debris. Basically, piles of clotty blood puddles.

But the Venom Society would always clean up the mess and discard the remains before the press scheduled post-flight interviews. The good news was that the ship itself usually made it back in pristine condition.

Captain Byron Banes headed the crew. He was an up-and-coming star. He lacked physical prowess, but his IQ was off the charts. While he was highly book-intelligent, however, he had very little common sense.

Accompanying him was a cosmic understudy by the name of Chaz Knightly and two technical navigational assistants, Harris Tungsten and Katrina Strange.

Sounds of rocket boosters drowned out the tittle-tattle of the crowd on the west side of the municipality. That was good enough to begin the countdown for the covert deep space travel attempt on the east side.

As the conventional moon ship took to the skies over Juneau, so did the collider ship. The Venom Society had reached the point where they sat ready to observe, real-time, if human astronauts could withstand transportation via collider technology and return safely to Earth and thus, aptly named this collider ship Curiosity.

Any visual mutation to the air space where Curiosity made its lift-off was muddled by the blast and propulsion effects of the louder and more visible decoy ship just a few miles away. In seconds, both were piercing the Earth's lower atmosphere.

Once the space launches were underway and out of sight, the municipality grew quiet again. Zeller attempted to establish contact with Curiosity at an early molecular reassembly point. "Curiosity, this is home base, Staziak, calling. Please go live at your earliest convenience and confirm your status, heading, and distance," he called out over secure communications.

The control room listened for a response and heard nothing but a scratchy resonance on the transmission channel. Zeller pushed out another call: "Repeat, this is Staziak. calling deep spaceship, Curiosity. Please confirm your status. Over." Again, Zeller heard nothing but a loud silence. He immediately wondered if the communications system had failed or if perhaps something unfavorable had happened to the ship or its occupants.

Zeller and his deep space missions team began to get a bit anxious after repeated failed attempts at syncing communications with Curiosity. But they tried not to panic. They continued to work to establish a connection with Curiosity at some reassembly point, knowing full well the crew may or may not be in-tact.

Zeller got that sinking feeling in his gut that he had experienced so many times before. He had hoped to avoid any failures this time. Not so much out of compassion for the crew of Curiosity, but more because he wanted to take credit for achieving a new level of success in the Venom Society's developments in human deep-space collider transport.

While he knew there was a chance that Curiosity was lost, Zeller didn't want to alarm the others at this point. He ordered them to continue monitoring the communications channel with the hope that Captain Banes would issue a return call. Then, he fashionably exited the control center and headed back to his private office to devise an explanation for his boss, to make the deep space expedition program still appear worthy of preservation.

After repeated failed attempts by his team at Staziak to make contact with Curiosity, Zeller reluctantly decided to inform Grandmaster Webb of the situation. He squirmed in his chair for a bit, contemplating exactly how to address the matter, unsure of how Webb would react. But he was eventually able to muster up the gumption to make the call.

"Well, sir, I'm afraid we've lost contact with another ship. As you are already aware, this time there were humans aboard. I needed to let you know that we do not expect to recover the craft, nor the astronauts on board," Zeller said to the grandmaster. He paused, petrified at what he might hear coming back at him through the earpiece.

"Hmmm, what a pity that is," Webb responded in a sarcastic tone. Zeller was unsure if the grandmaster's sarcasm was directed at him or at the fate of the crewmembers. Before Webb could clarify, Zeller thought he'd lessen any disappointment on the part of the grandmaster.

"Eh hum . . . that's the *bad* news, sir," Zeller continued. "The *good* news is that we believe we know exactly why the ship went missing without communication. My team at the Galileo Center for Space Exploration in Washington D.C. has been reengineering the electronic motherboards in the master control units to resolve this very issue. I expect that they can have a new ship prepped and ready for launch in ten days. I also expect this ship to meet with greater success. With your permission, I'd like to proceed with another human crew for a repeat mission, launched from that location. I think we're on the verge of a great success, sir."

"I admire your confidence, Chief," the grandmaster responded, in a more serious tone this time. "You appear to have your priorities in *good* order. Please continue with your plans and *do* prepare to attend the D.C.

launch in person. I will assemble a competent team to man the new ship. We will administer orientation to them at Galileo Headquarters and brief them on the mission. Our progress shall not be delayed by the loss of a few brave, but unfortunate, pioneers. Our forefathers would not approve of that."

"Understood, sir. We will not waver. Thank you for your patience. I will pick up my things and make my way to Washington D.C. right away. Thank you for your assistance and patience, sir. My best to you."

Zeller concluded the conversation and brushed the back of his right wrist across his forehead to remove a puddle of perspiration. He had dodged another bullet and remained in the grandmaster's good graces.

The crew of Curiosity did not fare so well, however. After two days of searching for signs of electronic communications activity, Staziak mission control still had not heard back from them.

CHAPTER 9
Proximity

With a few adjustments in material engineering and some significant electronic improvements to the master control units, the Venom Society was ready to deploy the next model of deep space flight ships. Scientists in the Deep Space Division of the Galileo Center for Space Exploration, located in a Virginia suburb on the outskirts of the Washington D.C. Municipality, were able to complete the assembly of a replacement craft, which they believed would prove much more reliable than previous ships. That was how deep space travel spaceship, Proximity, was born.

Proximity was perfectly spherical in shape. It carried a collider ring on its frame that encircled its entire girth at the centerline.

Engineers incorporated their most advanced collider. It was designed to move objects almost instantly to predetermined locations. Utilizing this technology, Proximity possessed the rare capability to relocate a payload from one location to another and return it intact. Proximate, as the name suggests, to its original starting point.

How it worked—well, many of the engineers themselves weren't even one hundred percent sure. Each scientist was used sparingly and only for specialized tasks, shielding them from gaining too much knowledge of the overall process. But it did work.

The technology was one where, through subatomic particle manipulation, all matter contained within the circumference of a collider ring was essentially disassembled into its atomic components, entangled with particles at great distances, transported through a temporary space-time tunnel, or warp, and collected and reassembled in a new location. They called that a "jump."

The collider ship was controlled via multiple high-compute power processors located in its fuselage. These components, too, were disassembled and then reassembled at a predefined time and distance.

In more simplistic terms, once the collider was activated, the spaceship and all of its contents were systematically pieced down, transferred to distant locations, and reassembled there.

That didn't bode well, however, for experimental live animal passengers early on. Due to a biological anomaly that scientists couldn't seem to resolve, those unfortunate test subjects were most often not reassembled properly. The Venom Society expected little bumps in the road but had to continue to push on with live passenger collider travel trials. Their forefathers vowed that no matter what happened to the live subjects, it was for the good of the future of the planet. Someone, or something, had to make the sacrifice early on.

The jump process repeated itself millions of times per minute. The contents of the payload propagated continuously until the control module initiated the request for final reassembly of all original parts. This was much easier to demonstrate on paper than it was to actually implement.

The safe distance for particle disassembly and reassembly differed with the size and intensity of the collider employed. But the end result of trillions of jumps was the ability to travel to regions of the universe never before thought reachable.

After several deep galactic test runs with only inanimate cargo aboard, it was time to man Proximity with humans for the first time.

The crew was hand-picked by Marcus Webb. He assembled a multitalented crew with a diverse background and skill set.

After thirty years of civilian aircraft flight service, Captain Phineus Pennington was selected to head the crew. He was a highly intelligent middle-aged man who kept physically fit. A consummate professional, Pennington always carried a serious demeanor about him but would exhibit flashes of humor from time to time.

His master ship engineer was Lieutenant Skylar Epson, who went by the nickname "Skip." He was also very serious in nature and sometimes had little patience for the imprudence of others.

Because the primary objective of this mission was material discovery and sampling, the crew also included a chief lab technician and geologist by the name of Dr. Alandia Moss. With her skill in mineral identification, the crew would be able to suitably collect, package, and transport planetary materials of interest.

Kassie Lomaxx also joined the crew. She was a botanist and biologist. The team needed her expertise to categorize any alien plant, insect, or animal species they might stumble upon.

The least experienced crew member was Max Gilligan. He was a young understudy with lots of upside. His job was to do whatever anyone else onboard the ship asked him to do without asking any questions.

The final crew member, and arguably the most critical piece to the team, was very different than the others. That's because she was not human. DAISIE made the flight. DAISIE, the Deep Space Artificially Intelligent System for Intergalactic Exploration, was the most advanced android ever created. So highly intelligent that if you weren't staring right into her metallic, motionless eyes, you wouldn't know you weren't speaking to a human.

She was pyramidal in shape and weighed in at over nine hundred pounds. She was an engineering marvel, consisting of three horizontally-layered titanium sections held together via magnetic forces. Each horizontal layer could operate, rotate, and function independently of the next, but all sections remained positionally in line and true to maintaining DAISIE's pyramidal form. She moved about via magnetic hover capability and was able to do so silently.

DAISIE was never negatively affected by the extremes of deep space travel, and even under exceedingly stressful conditions, she never got frazzled. And the best thing about her? She always returned from the trip in one piece.

CHAPTER 10

Watch Your Step

Venom Society officers kicked open the school doors and moved in quickly to interrogate Ginny to see what she knew. They had to find out if she divulged anything to her family or friends. They had it in the back of their minds going in that they might need to eliminate her at the end of the day. But giving her false hope of returning home to see her family for dinner, they thought, might just be enough to get her to talk before they made any final decisions about whether or not to spare her life.

Ginny was the head janitor at Magothy Manor High School, located along a riverbank tributary of the Chesapeake Bay, in the heart of the Chesapeake Municipality. She was told by the Venom Society, in no uncertain terms, that even though she maintained all areas of the building, which she so spotlessly kept clean, no commoners were allowed to enter the secure gates located behind one particularly precarious bank of lockers.

The Venom Society had grown to appreciate Ginny over the years. She hadn't been a bit of trouble to them, and she really did a wonderful job at keeping the halls leading up to the secure area spotless. But with surveillance video in hand, confirming that Ginny finally disrespected them by breaching the gates, their attitude turned 180 degrees on her.

The interrogation began in the gymnasium with the typical lead-in questions, trying to get her to admit that she disobeyed orders. She owned up to that very quickly. And she agreed that her poor choices represented a security risk that the Venom Society deemed unacceptable.

To get more comfortable for the longer questioning session, Venom Society elites, which included Grandmaster Webb, Chief Chulah, and Councilor Ricinulei, escorted Ginny to the administrator's office, sat her down, and began to lean on her harder for the details.

Grandmaster Webb "invited" Ginny to stay as he grasped the lapel of his white blazer and adjusted it more comfortably forward on his shoulders to prepare for questioning, "Have a seat, Ginny. We have some more things to talk to you about today."

Ginny, in a very weak, shaky voice, responded "O—k—kay."

Webb whispered into Kamalei's ear, "Soften her up a bit, Councilor. Get on her good side, then turn her right over to Chulah."

"Yes, sir," Kamalei softly acknowledged him. Then, she took a seat across the table from Ginny.

Kamalei aimed her bright green eyes directly toward Ginny's and began to interview her, "Hello, Miss Ginny. My name is Kamalei. I'm here to assist the Venom Society in assessing the security posture of the premises. I understand that you've been a life-long employee here?" Ginny gave her a nod in the affirmative. Kamalei continued, "We'd like to discuss with you what happened this morning, regarding the breach of one of our secure gates. I'm sure you understand exactly what it is I'm referring to, don't you?"

Ginny, with a voice a little less weak and shaky as before, spoke up. "Yes . . . I understand."

Kamalei continued, "Good. How are you feeling today? Can I get you anything before we begin?"

"No, thank you. I'm fine," Ginny responded.

"Great. Now, we're going to ask you to relax and simply answer all questions asked of you, completely and truthfully. Is that clear, Miss Ginny?" Kamalei said to her.

To which Ginny responded, "Of course. I know you all have a job to do."

Kamalei, confident that she had brought Ginny into a cooperative state of mind, was ready to let Chulah take over, "Very well, then. Let's go ahead and get started. Chief Chulah will work with you through questioning, and you'll be on your way home in no time," Kamalei assured her, knowing that wasn't the complete truth.

Kamalei whispered into Trent Chulah's ear as she got up and stepped aside: "Find out what she knows while the grandmaster and I decide what to do with her."

Chulah, with a quick nod, turned his attention toward Ginny. "So, Miss Ginny, certainly you knew you were not authorized to investigate any of our activities here, and certainly, you were previously advised not to attempt to enter our secure passageways, right?"

Ginny, trying to think of a way to weasel out of her predicament, emphatically responded, "Well, yes, sir. I know that your operations are highly sensitive and that no one is to meddle in any way. But I have worked here for so long and never once was I ever able to enter or see beyond those gates. I've turned a blind eye to your activities for almost forty years and, finally, I simply thought I'd see if there was some way that I could help clean up back there. I'm very sorry if I've alarmed anyone."

Chulah jotted down a few scribbles on his note pad and continued, "How long were you inside the tunnel, ma'am?"

"Not long at all," Ginny assured him. "I didn't see much of anything in there. It was dark and dirty, and there were spider webs everywhere. I walked a short way down the hall to try and get a sense of where it led.

After all these years of wondering, I guess curiosity just got the best of me. And, well, after just a couple of minutes I heard footsteps coming from another direction, so I turned around and came back out very quickly."

"How far did you enter into the tunnel, ma'am?" Chulah prodded her.

"Well, I only made it to where I saw what appeared to be some sort of transportation capsules. They were quite impressive. What are they, and where do those things lead to anyway, Mr. Chulah?" Ginny responded with an inquisitive tone.

Chulah turned his head to Ginny, leaned heavily toward her, pushed the brim of his top hat higher on his forehead, and lowered his dark glasses on his nose so that Ginny could see the whites of his eyes very clearly. Then, with an unnerving look on his face, he clarified who was in charge of the focus of the conversation, "I'LL ASK the questions, ma'am."

"Oh . . . of . . . of course, Mr. Chulah," Ginny backpedaled.

Chulah slowly receded back into his proper upright seated position, situated his hat and glasses comfortably, and continued, "Why would you let yourself commit these transgressions after such a stellar history of maintaining a low violation count?"

Ginny thought for a moment. "I don't know, sir. But even if I had seen anything that you would consider sensitive, I certainly wouldn't say anything to anyone. I swear."

Chulah continued to press. "And this isn't the first and only time you've defied orders by breaching the security gate, is it, Ms. Ginny?"

"Well, I'm afraid not, sir," Ginny revealed as she focused her stare toward the floor beside the table, in effect avoiding further eye contact with Chulah.

At this point, Chulah knew he had her in a bind. But he had a hunch that she was hesitant to open up and tell him everything. He suspected that she had explored the secret tunnels to a much greater extent than she was letting on.

And Ginny, well, she knew that to save her own life she had to come completely clean. But she also knew that saying too much could mean the Venom Society might decide to do away with her. Humanely, hopefully.

The discussion continued right there at the schoolhouse for the first half-hour or so. Then Webb decided to take Ginny to a more discreet location to finish the interrogation.

Kamalei assisted Ginny up from her chair and escorted her out of the school and over to Venom headquarters. There they could do more in-depth analysis of her facial expressions and physical gestures as they continued to question her. That part of the interrogation would last another hour.

Once the schoolhouse fell quiet, Zinnia, who was there serving detention for hoarding milk and chips from the lunchroom, popped out of the closet next to the administrator's office. She had assured Zander and Ryker that she would shed her mischievous ways when they challenged her at the market the other day. Jett also set her straight after interrupting her foiled plan to raid the non-perishable food storage shed.

Yet, she continued to suffer a rising violation count as a result of her latest bad decision. She tried to exit the cafeteria with a small stash of food to take back home to feed Xion and Dalton. Although her intentions were good, it went against globally accepted societal doctrine.

Ginny didn't know it, but while she was busily stealing the secret combination to the cipher lock that protected the secret gates, Zinnia was taking down some notes of her own about that combination. Zinnia thought she might take a hike into the tunnels herself one day. Maybe there, she'd find more goodies for her brother. She tucked the combo safely in her pocket.

Frightened when the Venom Society had rushed in earlier looking for Ginny, Zinnia had used the closet as a hideaway. She was the only one at the school who heard Ginny's interrogation take place. She witnessed first-hand the bullish behavior of the Venom Society—and Kamalei as well, the woman who saved her little brother's life, at least for now.

"Why would someone of such compassion be involved with the Venom Society's dark side?" Zinnia thought to herself. "Kamalei seemed so genuine and caring in our previous encounters."

After serving her detention and seeing the interrogation, Zinnia was petrified. She ran back home to check on Xion and Dalton, unsure of what would happen to Ginny.

Unconvinced that she had been completely forthcoming with them, the Venom Society's confrontation with Ginny took an ominous turn. Incessant piercing of the skin and electric shock would surely bring her to full confession, they thought. Ginny was made to lie on a bed of nails, and electrodes were attached to her fingers, head, and abdomen. At the same time Chulah ramped up the voltage of the shock device, he also ramped up the questioning.

"*And* I don't suppose I can CON-VINCE you to be ONE HUNDRED PERCENT straight with me by cranking up this little *electric surge dial* here, CAN I, GINNY?"

Unable to tolerate the pain any longer and fearing for her life, Ginny let out a hideous shriek, "I'M SORRY! PLEASE STOP!" as she deteriorated into a pleading cry. "I WILL TELL YOU EVERYTHING. I PROMISE! NO MORE, PLEASE!"

Chulah dialed the voltage back immediately and decided to give her some reprieve. He unhooked Ginny from the device, sat her up, and offered her a drink of water. She thanked him, gathered her composure, and began painting a complete picture of the security breach for him.

Ginny confessed, "I was alone, as I always am at that time of the morning. The halls were empty. I finished the daily inventory early and had already prepared for the day's ingress of teachers and students. I simply needed to fill some unexpected idle time. That's when, well, you know, I . . . I decided to enter the gates myself."

"I see," Chulah replied, seemingly satisfied with the direction the conversation was now taking.

"I struggled to pull the locker bank away from the gate entrance by myself, but I didn't need much room to squeeze behind it," Ginny continued. "I entered the numbers into the cipher lock and the latches popped open right away. I thought it would be okay to go and take a quick look around. I wasn't in there long at all, honest." Ginny looked up at the clock, hoping maybe Chulah was ready to take a break.

"Keep going," Chulah interjected.

Ginny continued, "I was surprised that the hallway immediately led downward into the underground tunnels. I guess I was somewhat fascinated that a little old commoner like myself had a chance to see the inside of the mysterious tunnels. I knew what I was doing was wrong, Mr. Chulah, but I meant no harm to anyone or anything."

Ginny watched as the chief transcribed Ginny's confession into his notebook. She tried taking another stab at soliciting a dismissal from Chulah. "Look, I'm not feeling so well right now. May I go home now, sir?"

"*Tell me* what you saw down there, Ms. Ginny," Chulah replied, ignoring her suggestion to end the discussion and becoming short and direct with her.

"I . . . I came upon a door. It had a window in it. It was some sort of a lab. I tried to open the door, but it was locked, so I looked in to see what was there. And—" Ginny stopped in mid-sentence, broke down sobbing, and found herself trembling and unable to continue.

Chulah allowed her to recover for a moment but soon ordered her to carry on.

"I was so scared, sir," Ginny admitted. "I don't know what they were. They weren't human," shaking her head and continuing to weep.

"*That's* enough. Now, I need to know exactly *how* you acquired the combination to the cipher lock?" Chulah demanded.

"Well, you see, sir," Ginny muttered, as she caught her breath a bit, "I've been a very enthusiastic hobbyist in the area of drone-building and flying for many years. I'm skilled at maneuvering my micro units indoors. They are small and quiet, and they carry tiny cameras on them. And, well, it wasn't very difficult for me to maneuver one high above the entrance to record your movements as you entered the password into the cipher lock. From viewing the pattern of your finger as you typed the numbers into the keypad, I was able to recreate the combination. For that, I am very sorry."

"I see," Chulah replied. "Sit tight for a few moments while I confer with the grandmaster." Chulah stood, handcuffed Ginny to a water pipe, and made his way into the principal's office where Marcus Webb sat awaiting a status report.

Kamalei sat by Webb's side. She was antsy by this time because she had a good idea about what the grandmaster had in mind for Ginny next, and she was fighting back competing emotions about that internally. Kamalei didn't want to see Ginny suffer any severe punishment, but she was careful not to let her colleagues know that.

Chulah explained to them everything that Ginny had confessed to and then waited while the grandmaster considered her testimony.

Sneaking her aircraft around the building and recording random videos as a hobby is one thing. Surveilling one of the most powerful organized secret societies on earth and stealing a forbidden cipher lock combination from them is quite another. The fact was, though, that is what Ginny did. And, sadly, that would be her last poor decision.

By 5:15 p.m., Grandmaster Webb had heard enough. And he was hungry. He didn't want to spend any more of his precious time on Ginny. Kamalei knew it was time to hand Ginny her punishment, and she began to feel ill, so she excused herself to distance herself from what was about to happen.

That left Webb and Chulah to do the dirty work. Without informing Ginny of her fate, Chulah casually walked over to Ginny, stood behind her, and terminated her. It only took one quick stick to the back of her neck with a hand-held, spring-loaded, poisonous prick. It was a somewhat rudimentary device, given the sophisticated technology available, but it was a tradition that the Venom Society had maintained over time.

This was all very sad because Ginny's violation count was quite low. She had led a good life and served the community well. She walked by the suspicious lockers just about every day and was constantly reminded that she was forbidden to investigate the nature of whatever was hidden behind them. And, just six months before her retirement from service as head janitor at the school, Ginny let herself succumb to her own curiosity.

Her body was thrown into a dumpster, the contents of which were conveniently scheduled to be vacuumed up that evening and swept into low orbit with the town's weekly waste. It was all in a day's work for the Venom Society. And if anyone else suggested that they missed Ginny and inquired into her disappearance, they might face a similar fate. It's how the Venom Society prevented their secrets from getting out. And that was no secret.

CHAPTER 11

Playing with Fire

Zinnia returned to the orphanage and scurried through a bunch of listless residents making her way back to Xion and Dalton's beds. In an obvious hurry, and with something preoccupying her focus, she wanted to make sure the boys were fed and comfortable for the night.

She found them safe and sound, sitting cross-legged on the floor playing a game of marbles. While that was comforting to her, Xion showed even greater signs of malnutrition, and he conceded to her that he felt queasy and did not want anything to eat. She offered him some crackers, but he shook them off as if nothing at all was appetizing. That was a clear sign that the disease had begun to take its toll on him, and it became apparent to Zinnia that he wasn't going to live much longer.

Although the initial dose of medication that Kamalei had given him sustained him for a short while, his condition had reached the point of no return. A second dose was never administered.

This realization weakened his big sister to where she could hardly stand and caused her to turn away in anguish. A cold sweat overcame her body. She shed her jacket, slumped, and fell to a seated position on the floor, knees drawn to her chest, her back against the wall.

She knew Kamalei had every intention of helping Xion, but Kamalei was not a medical practitioner. Kamalei had also been roving and serving as master of ceremonies of Expulsions in two neighboring municipalities. Kamalei's had no ill intent to purposefully neglect to administer the second dose of antivenom to Xion, but she knew all along that his body was not capable of making a full recovery and that giving him an extra month to live was about all she could do for him. And at least for that, Zinnia was grateful.

Dalton was too young to realize that his best buddy was dreadfully close to death, but he unquestionably sensed that something was eating at Zinnia. He looked at her and asked, "What's the matter?"

Zinnia placed her hand gently on his shoulder and replied in a comforting tone, "Oh, I'll be okay, buddy. Everything will be okay." She gave Dalton a hug and nestled him into her lap to console him. Xion kept busy with the marbles.

Dalton couldn't help but notice the band on Zinnia's upper arm as she held him there. He got a good close-up look at it. He noticed a small red button on the bottom of it, curiously positioned underneath a transparent flip-up panel. "I wonder what that does," he whispered to himself. And without giving it any more thought that he would fidget with the controls on his virtual reality headgear, he lifted the plastic cover and gave the red button a push. The screen on Zinnia's armband beeped and illuminated immediately.

Zinnia noticed what the little guy had done and hastily released him from her clutches. She wasn't angry with him. More just curious, as he had been about her armband.

A disclaimer appeared on the small screen of her armband, warning against unauthorized use of the network.

"Oh, my goodness!" Zinnia exclaimed. "Dalton!" she continued as she grabbed his shoulders to capture his full attention, peering at him face to face, "Remember when you placed the electronic fob device against my armband at the infirmary?"

Dalton nodded in the affirmative, a bit frightened that he had angered Zinnia for doing such a thing without her approval.

"*Something* happened! I don't know what, but *something* happened when you did that," Zinnia told him.

Dalton teared up because he thought he was in some serious trouble.

Zinnia assured him that she wasn't upset with him, "NO, no, no, it's okay. Nothing hurt me. Nothing is wrong. It's just that *some kind* of data transfer took place that day. The device that Kamalei gave to us contained more than just the entry codes for that gate at the infirmary. She even said it did. There's an obvious compatibility between my armband and those devices. I just don't know what the connection is."

After realizing Dalton was too young to understand the bulk of her rant, she again reassured Dalton she was not mad at him. "Umm, what I mean is that fob did *something* to my armband, Dalton. But it's okay. It doesn't hurt me or anything. It just made the armband smarter, that's all."

Dalton felt better knowing that she wasn't angry with him. But he didn't know what any of this could mean. He withdrew from Zinnia's grasp and worked his way back over to Xion for another game of marbles. That gave Zinnia a chance to examine her armband a little more closely.

Following the disclaimer, a second screen appeared that prompted her for a password. She assumed it was asking for the same six-digit authentication that Kamalei had given her previously. She paused for a moment trying to recall what it was but then remembered. She hesitated before typing in the code because she was unsure of what might actually happen. Zinnia remembered explicitly what happened to Ginny for stealing a cipher lock code at the schoolhouse and breaching the hidden door.

But Zinnia was adventurous, and she was terribly curious about what Kamalei's other responsibilities within the Venom Society entailed.

With her chin pressed snug against her shoulder and barely able to get a comfortable view of the tiny virtual keyboard, she poked in 0-7-2-0-6-9. The screen lit up immediately in a bright red color, flashing a warning signal. A crude sounding buzzer blared, as if the password had triggered the armband to emit an electronic command. But what in the world could that possibly mean? Zinnia's jaw dropped.

CHAPTER 12
Discovery

"Five . . . four . . . three . . . two . . . one," Chief Zeller counted down, anticipating a burst of thrust from the rocket boosters that pushed Proximity up from the depths of a well disguised portal within the Earth's crust at the Galileo Center. The upper crest of the giant golf ball leviathan came into view of the Venom Society onlookers as it began its ascent. Then, the entire body of the spaceship appeared and rose steadily upward. For a ship of its size and capability, it rose from the depths of the launch basin rather stealthily.

As was typically the case with deep space excursions, the Venom Society made it a point to obscure this launch from the commoners. Once the ship turned to collider power, it would dematerialize almost instantly and vanish into thin air in utter silence.

Chief Zeller's mission was to remain in good standing with Grandmaster Webb by executing a successful deep space mission with humans on board. Proximity's mission, on the other hand, was aimed at continuing the search for a human-habitable planet.

The Venom Society had a rough idea of where to find a planet of interest, but getting there, exploring it, testing its environment and chemical makeup, and returning home safely had proven an elusive feat in previous flights. They believed that somewhere in the swirling gases of the Milky Way Galaxy there existed another star that contained orbiting planets, like those in their solar system, which had atmospheric conditions surrounding them that might be suitable for sustaining life.

One of the largest known stars in the Milky Way, Canis Majoris, is about 4,800 light-years away from Earth. The Venom Society suspected that one of its planets might have the potential for becoming a viable, habitable developmental site.

Shortly after take-off, Zeller, who had made the trek back to Galileo from Staziak at the grandmaster's request, made a call to the crew.

"Galileo to Proximity, this is Chief Zeller. Launch of Proximity appears to be successful. How are things on board?"

Captain Pennington immediately answered the call: "Things are looking up, Galileo. Our jump distance has been determined; collider calibration looks good, and all master control units are functioning properly. As we reach our space-time warp entry coordinates, we'll cut all communications temporarily and initiate collider travel to the target planet. Proximity will contact home base if we need further assistance during travel. Thanks be to the Venom Society. Over."

Zeller responded, "Roger, Proximity. Good luck in your endeavor. Planet Earth and its people are depending on your success. Over."

Skip chimed in, speaking to his colleagues on board, "Crew, we're quickly approaching the coordinates for the space time portal, which I believe will lead us into close vicinity of the target. DAISIE, check our current position and confirm a specific vector for Proximity."

DAISIE, with lights flashing feverishly, provided a swift reply. "Ship's heading is all set, Skip. At our current speed, we will enter the peripheral layer of space-time warp portal in approximately sixty seconds."

"Thank you, DAISIE," Skip acknowledged. "Crew, prepare to enter full collider transport mode. In thirty seconds, I will extinguish the combustion engines and initiate the particle accelerator. Secure yourself into your travel chambers immediately and prepare for particle disassembly."

A clacking and clattering of sounds broke a tense silence as the crewmembers secured the latches of their chambers. "This is what we've all been waiting for," Skip called out to them.

"DAISIE, upon approach of the target planet's location, the collider will begin its timed particle reassembly. Then, as we exit the space-time warp portal, we'll generate a new short-distance heading, with the ship under conventional power, leading us into the airspace of the planet."

"Roger that, Skip," DAISIE confirmed with him.

Captain Pennington said what everyone was thinking, "May we be blessed with a successful transport to our destination. Good luck, everyone. We will be okay. I will see you when we are reassembled."

The spaceship created a vortex, which, by eye, from Earth, appeared to be nothing more than a cloud of dust that disappeared quickly. The collider executed its particle breakdown and entanglement perfectly. Communications went silent. All matter on board Proximity, including the ship itself, was transported into deep space.

Within a few minutes, Proximity exited the space-time warp, and the collider completed particle reassembly of the ship, the cargo, and, thankfully, the crewmembers. To everyone's relief, the entire crew was snug, safe, and sound in their travel chambers. If for no other reason, the initial portion of the journey was a great success at least for that. But they were just getting started.

As Proximity entered the vicinity of the planet, the ship began to establish orbit about twenty-five miles above its surface.

The planet was located roughly 3,800 light-years away from Earth. The crew of Proximity prepared to explore it, unaware of its exact chemical makeup and unsure if it would provide any lifesaving resources for the dying Earth they left just a short time ago.

DAISIE had performed some mathematical analysis of the planet's age and location and deduced that it might contain materials deemed useful to planet Earth. It was on her recommendation that the Venom Society organized this exploratory attempt.

Taking the planet into full view, the crew took note of its gray dominant exterior color. Casual observation from Proximity's exterior camera brought into focus a very dull, dusty, and arid surface. Also evident was a roughly textured, pitted outer layer, suggesting the planet had been a popular target for meteors over the billions of years it was believed to have existed.

The crew noted its likeness to Earth's moon. Knowing the moon was currently under development for human expansion, they were hopeful that this celestial body might possess the potential for human habitation.

Proximity made a slow approach into the planet's upper atmosphere. Dr. Moss collected air samples, tested them, and turned the results over to DAISIE for further evaluation. DAISIE reported nothing out of the ordinary. That was encouraging as Proximity continued to make its way through the lower layer of the planet's air space.

Just one mile above the surface of the planet, Proximity entered hover mode. Dr. Moss and DAISIE continued to monitor air samples for any unusually high or low levels of potentially human-harmful gases or radiation. They were confident that the ship had entered safe airspace.

With some clever maneuvering and a steady approach, Captain Pennington was able to land Proximity safely on the surface of the planet.

He would be the one to bravely take the first steps on the surface. His crew was trained to assist him from inside the ship by examining soil samples for density, minerals, elements, metals, PH, and signs of moisture.

Although the temperature was only forty-five degrees Fahrenheit and the surface for all intents and purposes appeared to be dormant, conditions of the air fell mostly within harmless ranges. That was good news.

But to ensure his complete safety while exploring the surface of the planet, Captain Pennington needed to remain pressurized inside a Space Mission Ambulatory Robotic Terrestrial, or SMART, Capsule. The SMART Capsule was capable of maneuvering over land surfaces, taking photographs, collecting samples, and continually monitoring for unsafe conditions.

After the ship was stable and all remoting systems were a go, the captain strapped himself in the tiny craft. With a press of a button, the containment doors swung open, and the SMART capsule was dislodged from the pit of Proximity's underbelly.

The capsule was a tight fit for the husky captain. This, coupled with the fact that he was a mild claustrophobic, caused him some initial discomfort, both physically and emotionally.

The capsule was lowered to the ground via a retractable liftgate. The crew was in suspense, unsure of exactly how the planet's surface would react to the weight of a foreign object. Skip watched with a blank stare of wonder and disbelief.

But all was well, and everyone breathed a sigh of relief when the SMART capsule contacted, wobbled a bit, then stabilized itself on the dusty surface.

All the captain could see out of the front window was unadorned, lackluster land. Nothing stood out as particularly interesting. In the direction behind him, he noticed a run of hills and some natural stone formations. Most of the stones were uniform in their coloration, size, and shape.

Of note, however, was a line of stones which stood tall, oddly on their ends, and contained a slight hue of orange. They appeared to be displayed in a seemingly purposeful arrangement. The captain thought to himself for a moment: "Some planetary magnetic phenomenon could potentially explain how those stones were stood on end. But I have to wonder how they ended up in this configuration."

He brushed it off, though, and continued to scan the immediate area, recording the topology of the land as the SMART capsule slowly crept along. Surface features were sparse in terms of major mountains, valleys, or other significant land textures. There was no vegetation or life present. The entire setting seemed dull and melodramatic.

Then, he stumbled upon a second series of stones, which, again, presented themselves in a unique and unnatural arrangement. It occurred to the captain that these stones had the same odd coloration as the other unusual assortment he noted back closer to the spaceship. He spoke to himself under his breath. "What the heck is going on with these things? *Something* seems uncanny here." Then, he radioed to Proximity.

"Come in, Proximity. Are you there?" The captain queried them.

"We're here, Captain. We still have you in full view, is everything in order out there? Over," Skip answered him.

"Well, I suppose things are in order, Skip," the captain replied, adding a touch of sarcasm, "*if* you consider being half a light-year away from civilization in a pressurized, cramped, metal pickle barrel, in the middle of nowhere . . ." and he let out an audible sigh. "*If* you call that *in order*," he said light-heartedly. "I'm not sure yet if I am elated or terrified . . . DAISIE, are there any unusually high magnetic fields on this planet?"

DAISIE, always attentive to the captain's queries, responded, "No, sir. Magnetic pole readings are in the normal range for a planet of this size and mass, rotating at this speed, on its current axial tilt. Assuming the core is primarily molten ferrous-based materials, which we believe it to be."

Captain Pennington continued, "Listen, I just wanted to report to you a particular arrangement of boulders, which I've wandered into. There must be a couple dozen of them in total. They appeared ordinary as I casually scanned the planet's surface. However, their color and positioning are far different from the other stones in the natural landscape. What's intriguing about these stones is the fact that they are of similar size and shape, standing on end, and form a pattern that seems non-random. All flat faces of the stones are oriented along the same plane, and they are set equidistant from one another. It's almost as if something, or someone, caused them to end up in this unusual pattern."

"Captain, what does the pattern look like?" Skip inquired.

"Well, the more you stare at them, the more you sense areas of symmetry and relationships," the captain explained. "Each stone tends to reach toward the next succeeding stone. If you connect them with imaginary lines, they seem to form a maze or some other defined pattern. It simply does not strike me as completely random by nature. Somehow, I can't help but think they are all working in concert, but for the life of me, I cannot imagine what they would represent."

"Captain, are you sure the stones have a non-random disposition? We're a *long* way from anyone or anything that would have been capable of affecting the stones," Skip reminded him.

The captain coyly responded with an intriguing rhetorical question, "Ahhh, but *are* we, Skip?"

Silence suddenly overcame the ship, and the crew looked around at each other, at a loss for how to respond to that.

Captain Pennington chimed in again. "Well, these things didn't just fall from space like this, and I see no signs of volcanic or seismic activity nearby. I'll radio again in a few minutes."

The captain continued to peruse the surface while the crew logged the events. DAISIE began to relay data about the unusual stones back to the supercomputing division of Galileo's home base.

There, REX, another high-performing android, received the crew's voice transmissions and images of the boulders. REX was highly intelligent, just like DAISIE. Although he was created in the image of humans, he still looked very much robotic. He contained oversized legs and arms, attached to a massive titanium torso.

REX was maintained and operated as part of the Biology Division at Galileo. The android immediately tried to identify the significance of the layout of the stones. He executed highly specialized mathematical calculations against the positional and directional data using state-of-the-art plasma-cooled processing hardware. He was also fitted with sensing and testing equipment, which allowed him to analyze and identify unknown substances.

REX roamed the supercomputer lab at Galileo Headquarters, which he rarely left. He interacted with DAISIE regularly, however, and took a liking to her—almost in a humanistic sense—and did everything he could to win her admiration.

The captain got a little antsy after a couple of minutes of radio silence and again radioed back to the ship.

"Crew, my initial assessment of this planet is that it is quiet, barren, desolate, and tranquil in every apparent way. I see no signs of existing life. No signs of animals, insects, plant life, bacteria . . . nothing. There are no current indications of water, ice, or moisture of any kind. Nor does there appear to be any prior presence of these substances. There really appears to be nothing on the outer surface, except dirt—if that is what you call it here—and dust, and . . . and those interesting rocks that I described to you."

The crew rolled their eyes and snickered, not perceiving any significance in the rocks that so intrigued the captain.

"DAISIE, are you sure we traveled half of a light-year beyond Earth and didn't just hop to our own moon during that space-time warp?" the captain asked sarcastically.

He heard chuckles from the crew.

DAISIE humored him. “Clever, Captain, but I assure you, we’re a long, *long* way from home at our present location.”

“I know, DAISIE,” the captain responded. “I don’t see the moon developers hard at work outside my window. But this planet is just so eerily similar to our own moon.” DAISIE agreed, “*True*, Captain, very true.”

Captain Pennington was ready to get out of the SMART capsule and stretch, so he had it rolling at a good clip back toward Proximity when another odd feature caught his eye.

“Wait just a minute, guys; I’ve located some holes over here!” the captain announced, as he caught the crew off guard a bit.

Skip chimed in this time. “Some *what*, Captain?”

“HOLES!” the captain repeated. This time in an elevated and more purposeful tone.

Skip was completely unimpressed with the notion of an unexplored planet having, well, *holes* in it as the captain suggested. “Captain, this planet has been pelted with thousands of meteors over the last one hundred million years. It has been a bull’s eye for comets and who knows what other celestial collision calamities. What do we care about a few dinky holes?”

“I’m serious, Skip,” the captain responded. “I see holes, and they are deliberate, precise, symmetric holes, somehow carved into the land. Not crater-like but cut or drilled.”

Skip, half-heartedly decided to give the captain a chance to explain further. “Okay, Captain, and who or what out there is digging holes? Little space alien groundhogs?”

The captain couldn’t have possibly known the answer but offered a chuckle and a response as he captured some pictures. “Not sure, Skip, but this is seriously remarkable. I cannot determine the exact depth, but they are about three inches in diameter, and they remind me of plugs, like something we might take back home for soil sample testing. In fact, the holes are very much like the ones we have taken on previous expeditions for our own testing purposes, but I assure you we did not produce the holes that I'm looking at right now. Someone, or something *else*, did!"

The captain continued, "Make sure you thoroughly document this, Dr. Moss; we could be talking about some other form of life, which visited this very planet before us. I know it's an odd thought, but this vast universe has every chance at containing another life form beyond our own."

The crew looked around at each other, trying to conceptualize what Captain Pennington was saying. No one affirmed the thought that aliens might have already visited this planet, but everyone knew it could be true.

By this time, DAISIE had received a return message from REX. He, too, had arrived at a plausible explanation for the mysterious display of stones the captain reported. He determined that they resembled the exact coordinates and orientation of a series of stars located in a nearby galaxy. The captain was correct that their current arrangement did not occur merely by nature or chance.

REX's message read, in part: "It has been determined, with 99.999 percent certainty, that the stones in question represent a means of marking. Most probably utilized by an intelligent form of life to demarcate the planet as a waypoint as part of a lengthy journey, to be observed from great distances. Presumably in the event there was a need to revisit this planet."

DAISIE piped up and relayed REX's explanation directly to Captain Pennington, but paraphrased in her own words, "Sir, REX has indicated that those mysterious boulders you took note of previously were acted upon by an intelligent life form and serve a specific informative purpose.

Now, REX and I are not capable of one hundred percent human reasoning, of course, but could it be possible that the unusual rock arrangements were essentially markers, emplaced by an alien species, as navigational implements? *They,* whoever *they* are, appear to have taken samples, just as we are doing, and they perhaps marked this territory using the stones for future identification and a possible future return visit."

"You're reading my mind, DAISIE," the captain assured her. "I'm going to position one of our scanning and sensing camera transmitters in this area. Be sure to record its exact location on this planet."

The camera transmitter to which the captain referred would become Proximity's first left-behind node of STARS NET, the Space Terrestrial Astronautic Remote Sensing Network.

STARS NET was a network of transmitting cameras designed to be emplaced by space exploration crews at each location visited. The cameras fed images and data into a master monitoring station back at Galileo Headquarters on Earth.

The Captain made his way back to the mother ship and tethered the SMART rover within the holding compartment inside Proximity's hull. Soil samples were given to Dr. Moss for chemical analysis.

As the crew prepared for travel to its next destination, DAISIE reported encouraging initial results from the sample testing. It appeared that the planet likely contained processable raw material components. She was hopeful that this planet could be suitable for mining in the future. Perhaps it could help to replenish some of Earth's depleted resources and help sustain life as they knew it back home.

If temperatures permitted and radioactivity levels tested normal, there was a remote possibility for habitation, but water would have to be found or supplied.

Captain Pennington issued orders to his crew to prepare for flight as DAISIE mapped out their next jump sequence. Their visit to this planet generated more questions than answers. Not the least worrisome of which was what other species could have potentially visited the planet before them—and if Proximity might cross paths with them on the way to its next destination.

CHAPTER 13
Marsupan Justice

In their unique environment beneath the surface of the Earth, the Marsupans continued their struggle to exist. They lived in a world that was dark, musty, and full of natural disasters. But with the assistance of an air delivery system pumping oxygen into their lair, and a steady feed of seafood trickling in from the Hydronians, the Marsupans had made themselves modestly snug in their dirty nests.

Their emotional stability was not without vulnerability, however. Doubts about their own long-term survival crept into the minds of many, making them paranoid and desperate. Just like the commoners of the municipalities above ground, the Marsupans were susceptible to breaking the laws of the underground world. Those who were mentally weak would falter, and as a result, suffer from high violation counts. And, in a world of dwindling resources, the Venom Society periodically ordered that the population be checked back in the underground municipalities as well. That's what happened with a population of Marsupans living beneath the streets of Venom Society headquarters in Baltimore, Maryland.

In the underground Expulsion colosseums, there was only enough room for Venom Society VIPs and a very small assembly of commoners to watch the events live. Absent room for heavy equipment in the main staging area, the Venom Society employed other clever means of handling the undesirables. Sufficient lighting was supplied for viewing the celebration, and cameras captured the action so that it could be shown and viewed on large screens by commoners above ground.

Recent tremors in the area caused one of only two escape capsules in the small underground colosseum to shimmy off its rails. That one still appeared to be inoperable. A couple of engineers examined it prior to the Expulsion but left it sitting right where it was. Venom Society officers were seen exchanging bows and *V* symbols to one another as they entered their quaint VIP seating area.

This Expulsion focused on a gang of Marsupans who decided to take over a section of the tunnel network to create their own dictatorship. They held a small community of commoners captive and forced them to submit to the wishes of the gang.

Since individual tunnels below ground were largely secluded from one another, and there was no visibility into neighboring burrows, the situation went undiscovered for many months. It was a compound where no one entered or left their tunnel without special permission. These Marsupan rebels had their day, forcibly ruling over their neighbors. But soon the tables were turned on them.

Because space was limited below ground, the Venom Society devised a unique way to inject Expulsion contestants into a narrow staging area at the beginning of the gauntlet. Only one side of the cage opened, facing the entrance to the staged death run.

Kamalei began the ceremony by addressing the camera for a close up of her mesmerizing green eyes. "Welcome, *good* citizens of the Baltimore Municipality. *You* are called upon today to cast punishment upon the wrongdoers of the Marsupan communities. We are starving. We are sick. We are *dying*. We must join together as one and respect the needs of all *good* people on Earth. And yet, there are *those* who decide to commit crimes against their neighbors." She waved her left arm toward the Marsupan competitors, and the camera panned to the right and captured a view of them frantically searching for a way out of the staging enclosure.

"Today, ladies and gentlemen, we sacrifice individuals whose behavior we can no longer tolerate," Kamalei continued. "Their violation counts demonstrate that they do *not* respect the doctrine of our land. Their fate lies in *your* hands. DO WHAT YOU MUST!"

Kamalei raised both arms high in the air and signaled the staging crew to release the contestants into the main cage. Chains lifted the heavy door of the holding enclosure, and the competition began for twelve Marsupans.

Hesitant to enter the narrow gauntlet, the undesirables slowly crept their way into the dimly lit death cage. They felt a small gathering of oversized eyes levying an ominous stare upon them as what little crowd had gathered below ground watched them intently. It didn't take long for the first challenge to manifest itself.

That came in the form of a pack of hungry vorossom. Vorossom were a species of rat-like animals that lived in caves. They were not particularly large in stature but were menacing in nature. They had a voracious appetite and would eat anything, from nuts, berries, and foliage to trash and rotting animal carcasses.

What made them feared more than most mammals was the fact they were vicious hunters that attacked their prey in packs, swiftly and aggressively. A pack of vorossom could take down much larger prey with relative ease. And with most of their traditional animal prey having become extinct, they had acquired a taste for humans. And there were still plenty of those to go around.

Introduced into the death cage by the dozens, they were impossible to fend off without some sort of weapon. The vorossom were hungry, and they went right in for the kill. Cheers of excitement rang out from the onlookers above ground who appreciated the aggressiveness of these critters. With swift and agile movements and precise lunges, the vorossom separated four of the contestants from the rest of the gang. They were quickly at a disadvantage.

As the competitors received lacerations to their arms, legs, and torsos, the smell and taste of blood further excited the vorossom into a feeding frenzy. Screams rang out from the victims and that was enough for the rest of the group to cut their losses and scramble into the next chamber of the gauntlet. Chunk by excruciating chunk, the bodies of the victim gang members were disassembled. They were reduced to quivering carcasses at first, then skeletons with very little fleshy substance remaining.

In the next chamber over, one lucky contestant was able to snag an open escape capsule. He was safe, for the moment at least. The others pounded on the window in an attempt to get him back out; otherwise, they'd have one less fighter on their side. Eight was better than seven, they figured. But they quickly noticed an odd look about the man in the capsule.

His face grew lighter in color, and his skin started to ripple. Although his eyes were wide open, there was no sign of consciousness, just pure fear. And in the next moment, it became clear why that was—his head simply burst. Like an over inflated balloon, it popped. Blood spatter pelted the inside of the window and dripped downward.

The Venom Society VIPs raised their drinks in celebratory approval of the success of their clever contraption. That capsule was a trap, a compression machine designed to implode whatever was inside. Another brilliant design by the Venom Society to provide high entertainment factor for a show with limited space. It was also a reminder to the watchers to never step out of line, or they could be next.

The seven remaining gang members scurried into the last gauntlet chamber. Only one escape capsule remained. That realization meant the contestants were forced to turn on one another to try and secure themselves into the lone means of survival. All seven went straight for it, pushing, shoving, and trampling each other. Just as the first contestant was able to insert her head and arm inside the capsule, the others extracted her instantly and pummeled her for good measure.

That battle persisted for a minute, with others attempting to secure themselves inside the capsule until the Venom Society introduced the next feature of the event—chuminoids. The chuminoids looked like common bats, but these predators had three-inch fangs designed to rip and devour meat. Interestingly, they were not native to caves. In fact, they were not native to any place at all. That's because they were purely robotic. The Venom Society developed these nasty mechanical creatures specifically to elevate the game in the Marsupan tunnels.

It worked. The crowd above ground loved it. They took to their joysticks, and their collective will to kill influenced the flying robots. Until then, the chuminoids only lightly pecked at the heads of the contestants. But the wave of the will of the good to punish the wrongdoers initiated a much more aggressive attack. One that saw patches of hair and skin ripped from the Marsupans' skulls, then meat from bone.

One lucky female Marsupan survived the onslaught, though, and jumped into the last remaining escape capsule. She ended up with a few deep gashes but was still in pretty good shape overall. She slammed the capsule door shut, and it automatically maneuvered into position for its exit from the danger zone.

The other contestants paid the price for their intrusion on the good of society. They were reduced to a pile of fleshy skeletons.

A foghorn sounded, indicating the end of the event. The one working escape capsule was whisked away through an exit tunnel. No one knew its destination, but the crowd above ground cheered it on as it swooped across the big screen.

Kamalei hailed the cleanup crew to turn on the vacuum tubes so they could dispose of any remains. The locals would be given access to the killing grounds after the area was cleared. The crew mopped up the blood stains to prevent any biological contaminants from lingering, spoiling, and encouraging the spread of bacteria and disease. Once sanitized, the Expulsion grounds would be utilized by the Marsupans to set up cots for much needed boarding accommodations.

CHAPTER 14
Lava Planet

Proximity came screaming out of collider space-time transform near the crew's next target—a small planet, orange-red in color, with random dark stripes and blotches of black. Its unusual appearance was beautiful and intriguing. All of the ship's contents were once again reassembled masterfully. After regaining full consciousness, the crew began recording their present location and preparing for their approach.

Right away, DAISIE noticed high temperature readings blanketing the surface of the planet. It was obvious this planet was still searing hot in its present stage of development. Telescopic views revealed that its surface primarily existed in a molten state. Proximity searched for a potential landing site but saw mostly liquified material, churning in an ocean of lava. In some areas, volcanic activity agitated the planet's soupy surface.

Captain Pennington engaged his crew in rare form: "Well, guys, this certainly looks like a *hot* tourist destination."

Skip acknowledged the captain's attempt at humor. "Very funny, Captain." Then, he quickly turned serious. "I'm going to maneuver Proximity as close to this fireball as I safely can, but DAISIE, I'll need you to monitor the atmospheric temperature. We don't want to expose the ship to extreme heat being this far from home."

"Way ahead of you, Lieutenant," DAISIE assured him. "The temperature of the hottest parts of the surface range from 350 to 450 degrees Fahrenheit. However, the airspace closest to the surface averages only about 118 degrees—a bit much for humans, I know, but altogether safe for Proximity's exterior panels and mechanical infrastructure."

"Roger," Skip acknowledged the brilliant android.

Proximity approached the molten sphere cautiously, taking in a sensationally close view of the dynamics of its boiling surface. Seas of magma surrounded various islands of cooled solid material. A few dangerous boils spit and spattered magma into the air.

The captain offered a few thoughts about what they were observing. "I can see we're not going to be picnicking here, ladies and gentleman. However, I must wonder what potentially useful substances exist within these molten seas. Could there be valuable metals, or even unknown materials, that might be beneficial to the people of planet Earth?" he asked rhetorically. "After all, part of our mission is to discover those types of resources for our people back home. Clearly, we will not be moving anyone here to live, but perhaps these rolling masses of lava contain good raw materials, which we might be able to mine and transport to Earth."

Kassie liked the sound of that and was itching to explore the properties of the molten material more closely. She followed the captain's thought with a suggestion of her own. "We should try to obtain some samples to run initial testing on."

Dr. Moss realized this was an opportunity for her to contribute to the effort. "Lieutenant, can you position Proximity just about fifteen feet above the surface, in hover mode? I'd like to take some video to transmit back to home base. And, of course, we need to secure some samples and prepare them for transport back to Galileo's lab."

"I think I can handle that," Skip responded. "Tell me when you feel we're within reach of the surface, using Proximity's mechanical collection arms. I'll place the spacecraft in a hover, and we can begin operations."

Proximity crept closer to the surface. The crew was impressed by the planet's array of colors. The recorded temperatures were inconsistent as the infrared heat sensor scanned across the surface laterally. There were areas of lava that were completely fluid, orange and red, which registered much hotter than neighboring yellow and black areas. Also visible were small islands, which for some reason, had cooled enough to form solid masses. Some islands were tempting the crew to consider landing on them. They refrained.

"Right there's good," Dr. Moss prompted Skip to halt the ship.

DAISIE prepared the mechanical extension arms to extract lava samples, as some of the molten swirls spit lava balls into the air dangerously close to the ship. Each crew member, including the captain, fell quiet as they took pictures and jotted down some notes.

"WHOA! What was that light?" Max Gilligan called out suddenly.

"What? What are you talking about, Max?" the captain asked.

Max answered him, "Didn't you see it? There was a bright light emitting from the center point in that lava . . . there just off Proximity's port side," Max continued as he pointed in the general direction. "I guess it could have just been a bubble refracting the sun's rays in our direction, but it appeared very intense, like some sort of photonic emission from within."

The captain chose to indulge the young man. "Well, thank you for that entertaining visual, but we really need to concentrate on our sample and data-recording mission here. One false move and we could be toast."

"Sorry, Captain," Max conceded.

DAISIE continued to monitor air samples and surface temperatures as Proximity hovered over the big ball of fire. Finally, she announced to her colleagues that the mechanical collection arms were ready to deploy.

The crew watched as Proximity's sample-collection tubes dipped into the lava. They were fascinated by the thought that this planet had likely never been visited by anyone, or anything else, and that they were its first visitors. The collection tubes held up well under the intense heat and samples were successfully extracted.

Just as the mechanical arms were about to be retracted back into the underbelly of the cabin for cooling and packaging, Max's eyes were drawn back to the same area where he thought he saw the light just moments ago. He gazed back out of the window for a last, curious look. No one else noticed how his attention had gone astray again.

Unexpectedly, Max gasped, slapped both of his hands on the top of his head, and then waved them frantically, indicating for someone to come over to his window immediately. "AHHH! It's h–h–hap–ening again!" he exclaimed.

Skip scurried over to investigate what was troubling Max and confirmed what Max saw. "What in the world . . . you were right!"

The rest of the crew joined them at the window to see what the stir was about. They watched as a strong, bright light shined back at them from beneath the surface of the lava. An instant eerie feeling settled upon the crew. It was as if some conscious presence controlled the light.

"DAISIE, secure all external hardware immediately and terminate collection operations," the captain ordered, somehow maintaining a calm demeanor about him.

DAISIE responded, "Yes, Captain. I was able to package and store a couple of samples of lava so far but not all of them. What shall I do with the remaining ones that have not been secured inside the ship yet?"

"Drop them if you must. I don't care! Just make this ship tight, NOW!" The captain ramped up the urgency in his voice.

"Yes, SIR," DAISIE responded, increasing the intensity in her electronically-generated tone, as well.

"LOOK!" Max blurted out, pointing out the window again.

The crew witnessed the lava, at the source of the light, rise up on its own, without any apparent outside forces acting upon it. A strange presence materialized before their eyes. A swell of lava formed a hump or head-like crest.

"This is unreal!" Skip thought to himself out loud.

Captain Pennington's voice followed. "Incredible."

The light intensified as the manifestation spewed magma. The raised mound took on the likeness of a controlling brain or nerve center, which intensified the blinding laser light.

Horizontal protuberances formed, six of them in total, giving the impression that the manifestation had grown appendages. Then, as if it had a mind of its own, it extended one upward, making contact with Proximity, and the ship swayed slightly. The crew was paralyzed with fear.

Proximity's engines sputtered and hesitated, and the captain gritted his teeth. "Come on . . . COME ON!" he yelled at the spaceship's engines. And, fortunately, the ship responded.

Just as Proximity was about to initiate full power and lift to a higher elevation, one of the appendages, if that's what they really were, latched onto its underbelly, rocking the ship awkwardly. The crew stumbled and fell to the left wall of its interior.

Slightly confused but still fully functional, DAISIE hovered quickly over to the ship's controls and was able to right Proximity and crank up the power thrusters. She managed to separate the ship from the danger. Proximity quickly opened up a safe distance between itself and the surface of the planet.

Once out of harm's way, the captain ordered that the engines be shut down and the spaceship placed into orbit. The entire crew fell silent, trying to rationalize what had just happened.

As crazy as it seemed, the crew was sure the manifestation was something more than just a random swell of molten material. Captain Pennington asked if everyone was okay. Each individual crew member responded in the affirmative.

The captain addressed his crew. "I don't know what that was, but it needs to learn better social skills, that's for sure," he stated, again trying to put his team at ease with a witty crack. "DAISIE, is Proximity intact?" he asked the android.

"All readings are normal, Captain," she assured him. "But I'll perform a complete system inspection to confirm."

Then the captain turned toward her and assumed a very serious tone. "DAISIE, you just saved our lives. Thank you."

DAISIE, in a show of pseudo-humanistic emotion, responded, "Ahhh, it was nothing, Captain, but thank you for your sentiment. Androids do not harbor fear like humans do—well . . . maybe a *little* bit . . . we hold up *pretty* good under pressure."

DAISIE ran a multi-sensing scanner along Proximity's trail-line of escape to ensure nothing was following them and fine-tuned the ship's master controller assembly.

"Skip, radio back to Galileo," Captain Pennington ordered his lieutenant.

"Yes, sir," said Skip.

Zeller was quickly alerted and eager to hear from the captain. "Hello, Proximity, is that you? We haven't heard from you in a while. Are you okay?"

The captain responded, "Yes, Galileo, it's Proximity; we're okay, but we're a bit nervous and shaken at the moment."

"Really, Captain? What is happening there? Over." Zeller inquired.

Captain Pennington knew no other way to tell Zeller what had happened but to jump right in with the whole story. "Well, we're not real sure, exactly, but we managed to disturb some sort of extra-terrestrial presence, sir. We were in position for observation and sample extraction of a very hot planet, when some sort of . . . of . . . *beast* thing presented itself from the lava pits below. It rose up out of nowhere and made physical contact with our ship, sir. It was a swell of molten material, and it took on some form of a—a . . . thing. I just don't know how to describe it. Anyway, we managed to separate from it, obviously. Well, I should say, DAISIE was able to pull Proximity away safely. But understand, Galileo, there's *some* kind of presence within that ball of hot molten metal—a life-like creature!"

Zeller paused for a moment but answered Pennington, "Captain . . . uhmmm . . . did you say, *lava beast*?"

"Affirmative, sir," the captain confirmed.

A moment of silence overcame Zeller and his team at Galileo.

Still at a loss for the right words, Zeller tried to assure the captain that he understood his transmission and was considering a potential course of action for Proximity. "I see, well, I don't really know what to say. We're not sure what you may have witnessed, but we're glad that everything is in working order."

"It was disturbing for us all," the Captain responded. "But we're okay for now, and we did manage to secure a couple of samples for inspection before all of the excitement. DAISIE is preparing the calculations for us to make a return flight to Galileo Headquarters in the D.C. Municipality now so that we can deliver these samples to you."

"Roger, Proximity," Zeller acknowledged. "Don't forget to attempt to emplace a STARS NET camera on the planet if there is any way you can do so safely. But *don't* get too close to your fiery friend; it's not worth risking Proximity against whatever it was that you encountered down there. Your previous STARS NET camera transmissions are currently being received, and the video looks quite good. We haven't noted any unusual activity thus far, but the signal is strong. Over."

The captain concluded the communication with headquarters, saying, "We'll see what we can do, sir. There are some areas on the surface of this planet that have cooled, so we may be able to drop a STARS NET post down from a safe distance. We're going to go quiet now to regroup and test all systems. We'll be back in touch as soon as we re-enter Earth's upper atmosphere. Over."

CHAPTER 15

Life Form Experiment

Proximity appeared out of a swirling cloud of dust high in the skies over Galileo Headquarters in the D.C. Municipality. After particle reassembly, the ship assumed conventional engine power for its descent to the landing pad. Skip and DAISIE maneuvered the ship into position for entry into the launch basin.

Chief Zeller was there, awaiting the arrival of the ship. He was anxious to get his hands on the soil samples from the planet revolving around Canis Majoris, as well as the lava samples.

Proximity's safe return provided the Venom Society with an opportunity to see just what some of these distant planetary bodies might have to offer the people of Earth. The first planet the crew visited seemed more of a candidate for harboring useful materials.

The captain suggested that other life forms might have visited the planet, a theory he surmised as he collected soil samples from that planet and located holes in the surface, which seemed more deliberate than random. DAISIE had a suspicion—if non-human machines can have such a thing—that the captain was right.

Initially, DAISIE had determined that the soil contained a high level of radioactivity but also seemed to contain ferrous metals, which if mineable, could be of potential use on Earth. That was all fine and good, but for the next few hours after Proximity landed back on Earth, the more detailed process of testing the soil samples' molecular make-up was left to the highly cleared, highly-skilled, scientists at the Galileo lab. During this process, some unusual atomic structures were discovered.

Molecules, which very closely resembled what man had long known to be DNA, the blueprint of human life itself, were discovered in the samples. Chief Zeller, unsure what to make of it, summoned Captain Pennington and DAISIE to the laboratory to discuss what they found.

"Captain, we brought you in here to discuss some of the initial findings with respect to the samples that you brought back with you today," Zeller said. "Aside from confirming DAISIE's assessment of radioactivity and ferrous content, Ms. Lomaxx and our biological scientists further analyzed the materials at the microscopic and atomic levels to see if they could identify their basic chemical make-up. They noted that the raw materials are similar to that of Earth. But that's not the most interesting part. What *is* most intriguing is that we identified another substance. An organic chemical component. We believe it to be DNA."

"DNA?" Captain Pennington responded. "Embarrassingly, I've heard of it but couldn't tell you anything—"

"No worries, Captain." Zeller lightly interrupted Pennington. "Deoxyribonucleic acid."

"Deeehockahooky what?" The captain joked, making fun of the long, scientific lingo used by Zeller.

Zeller continued, "Captain, DNA is the nucleic acid that contains the genetic blueprint used in the development and functioning of all known living organisms."

The captain realized where Zeller was going with the conversation and offered a quick note of caution. "But . . . but there were no living things remotely close to this planet while we were there. And the samples we extracted were taken from seemingly undisturbed areas of the surface."

"We are aware of that, Captain," Zeller took control of the conversation again, "and that is why we needed to consult you and DAISIE—to see if there was any contamination of samples during their extraction or handling."

"*Absolutely not*," the captain assured Zeller, offended at the suggestion the crew's efforts to return unadulterated samples to Earth were less than expert. "We had sterile cut, drill, retrieve, and seal equipment, right out of the box. And DAISIE made darn sure no one had access to the materials after being brought onboard and locked in the transport vault. Isn't that right, DAISIE?" DAISIE nodded her whole upper body toward the captain in the affirmative.

Captain Pennington continued, "If you are truly seeing DNA in those samples, Chief, it is not a result of any contamination from the crew of Proximity, I can assure you of that."

Zeller wasn't one to take the first explanation as the final answer, however, so he probed the captain for more. "And during their delivery to us here on base, you don't suppose that the guards could have—"

The captain interrupted Chief Zeller in mid-sentence. "No, no way. Security doesn't allow that sort of thing to happen. What you see is what you get, and if you see DNA, Chief, there is other life out there that we need to know about."

The captain turned to go as if he was intent on rallying the team to begin planning for a return visit to the distant planet.

"*Not* so fast, Captain," Zeller stopped him mid-stride, placing his hand on the captain's shoulder to keep him from exiting the conference room before one last point could be made. "I need to inform you of an anomaly within this DNA that we are seeing. It is not a complete helix or chain of genes. It's missing one key element for it to be an effective life-sustaining formula."

"Oh? What's that?" Captain Pennington asked.

Zeller peered over at Kassie and nodded, signaling that he'd like her to explain it to the captain.

Kassie, who Zeller had already asked to join him in the lab earlier to help verify the test results, jumped at the opportunity to shine in front of the assembly of high-ranking officers. "Well, we believe carbon, sir. This . . . thing . . . this . . . life form . . . thing probably isn't going to be much of *any*thing without that last element to inject life back into it."

"How's that?" the captain inquired.

With an intent stare, Kassie reached slowly toward the captain's head, carefully identified and singled out one strand of the captain's graying hair, clenched it tightly, and snapped it from the captain's scalp.

The captain let her know exactly how he felt about that, "OUCH! What the heck are you doing?"

"You see this strand of hair, Captain?" Kassie asked him. "If I were to break it down into its component elements, extract DNA from it, and present the helix to you on a chart, do you know what the key element would be, which binds it all together into a life-giving formulation?"

"Let me guess . . . carbon?" the captain answered, unsure if he correctly remembered that from his grade school biology lessons.

"For sure," Kassie confirmed. "Without it, the Earth and all of its living creatures would be nothing. Every cell in your body is carbon-based, Captain. From the bottom of your feet to the hair on your head, you are a carbon-based life form. It is the key ingredient to all living things here on Earth, and it is assumed to be the same for other planets as well. That is, *assumed* to be."

Captain Pennington, feeling proud of himself, followed with more dry wit: "Well, thanks for the demonstrative explanation, Lomaxx, but at my age, I can't really afford to be losing any more strands of hair from the dwindling collection that I have left."

Chuckles rang out from the crew, to include DAISIE, who was intently taking in the conversation.

Kassie continued, "Let me explain quickly, Captain. Carbon falls in the middle of the Periodic Table because it, by nature, contains four valence electrons. This means that it is a very reactive element. Carbon atoms are driven to states where they maintain a full complement of electrons. This forces them to bond freely with many other elements, even itself. And when it does, it becomes very stable." Kassie continued.

"Humans, and in fact all living organisms, have a genetic makeup not too far different from one another. But one minute difference in gene sequencing might cause a frog to become a whale or a giant sequoia tree to become a day lily flower. However, the fundamental building block of both animals and plants is *what*, Captain?" Cocking her head, lifting an eyebrow, and glancing toward Pennington, so as to challenge his short-term memory.

The captain did not disappoint. "Carbon . . . but *please* don't pluck another hair from my throbbing scalp if that's *not* the right answer."

That garnered heavier chuckles, this time from the room and DAISIE.

"Of course not, Captain," Kassie assured him.

With a complete understanding from all parties in the room of what had been observed in the lab, the technicians tried to prove or disprove some origin of the genetic material. This process entailed coupling the newly discovered pitted genes with any number of possible, supplemental stabilizer elements in hopes that at least one could be identified as the key missing element of life for whatever undeveloped life form laid in their Petri dishes.

First, the scientists tried introducing the gene pool to rather inert elements, which are relatively non-reactive. They knew it was a long shot, but they wanted to begin ruling out as many elements as possible, working their way up to carbon experimentation. Everyone suspected carbon would be the missing ingredient, but no one knew what its introduction to these foreign DNA molecules might end up producing. And that scared the daylights out of them. However none of the initial experiments ended up showing any kind of chemical bonding.

Soon, it was time to explore carbon as the possible missing element in the DNA. Basically, the scientists were ready to throw carbon into the pot, step back, and wait to see what they might be cooking up. A scary proposition. But there was only one way to find out. And, so, the first experiments got underway.

Kassie was asked to oversee the testing. She had grown to become a well-respected expert in pathology and species identification. Of course, her experience was limited to all known species on planet Earth, not something potentially living thousands of light-years away. Her extensive knowledge and insight, however, became heavily relied upon by the Venom Society.

To the scientists' surprise, though, the carbon showed no better results than any of the other elements that were coupled with the DNA up to this point—a relief to some extent because there was no alien of any sort developing, nothing becoming a potential hazard or threat.

But a disappointment also in that there was still no confirmation of life beyond their planet. Still, they moved forward with experimentation. But this time, at Kassie's suggestion, the tests led them in the direction of adding silicon into the mix.

It was long hypothesized that the human race was shallow-minded in assuming that all living things were carbon-based and that other life forms, which may exist in other galaxies, might be based on a different fundamental element. A next best candidate to fill that role was silicon because of its chemical and atomic properties. Yet, it was still very difficult for humans to fathom this possibility as anything more than science fiction.

Vigorous experimentation continued however, and just a few weeks into testing the scientists had exciting news to report. One of the helix-silicon pairings exhibited a good bonding response. As a result, complete DNA helixes were generated, helixes potentially representing the building blocks of alien life.

But what kind of life might they have formulated? They wouldn't know until the samples underwent duplication and incubation, and were subjected to varying environmental conditions involving temperature, moisture, and light. Their ultimate goal was to place active cultures back on the planet from which the organism had come.

CHAPTER 16

Express Embryos

Upon receiving the news that scientists had made some progress in bioengineering potential alien life forms, Grandmaster Webb and Deputy Chulah raced over to the lab in Washington D.C. to discuss how the helixes might be useful to other scientists at the Delmarva lab. They'd allow some of the DNA helix patches to be returned to the distant planet, but they had more ominous plans for others. So, they snatched a few up and took control of them.

This is the type of leading-edge experimentation that the Venom Society tended to claim unwritten ownership of. The fact that remnants of another life form might have been discovered, coupled with the fact that the environment from which the DNA samples came might be conducive to human life, excited them.

Now, to *own* the process normally meant that the Venom Society would allow a primary team of researchers to conduct labs openly and with transparency to all appropriate oversight committees—and even the public to some extent. That served as a visible distraction to what they, themselves, planned to do privately.

In the case of regenerative sciences, the Venom Society has developed methods for accelerating the replication of cells of living organisms. That allowed them to create tissue with physical biological chemistry, and that meant they were able to engineer and produce human flesh, muscle, and bone. Essentially, they could grow extra appendages for humans whose limbs might be missing.

They could also generate human replacement organs. For instance, a patient whose kidney was failing would be a candidate to receive a regenerative replacement straight out of a Petri dish in a matter of weeks or days.

Of course, with the Earth having reached a state of maximum capacity, there was minimal incentive to actually implement any of these processes for the purpose of saving the lives of just anyone. That would upset the birth-to-Expulsion balance, which was both delicate and crucial.

Therefore, this aspect of the operation was kept secret by the Venom Society. Their doctrine was very controversial and was viewed by many as morally and ethically unacceptable. Just the science itself stirred great debate among societal leaders. If the public and other world leaders had only known the full capability of the Venom Society in this area, it would surely have incited an upheaval.

CHAPTER 17
Good Deeds

Kamalei clicked and clattered her high heels down the street at a swift pace as she headed toward the Chesapeake Municipality colosseum. She was still on the hook to collaborate with her Venom Society colleagues to satisfy Grandmaster Webb's orders to upsize the venue to be able to process more undesirables. The whole idea of creating increased space in the death cage to accommodate a greater number of kills was becoming increasingly more unnerving to her. But she was rising through the ranks quickly and didn't want to risk her good standing with Grandmaster Webb.

Rounding the last corner before reaching the colosseum, Kamalei noticed a group of vagrants camping out among a series of park benches. While the scenery was typical of the crowded, overpopulated town square, the street and sidewalks in the immediate area appeared exceptionally well-groomed.

As Kamalei was about to whisk by the group of vagrants, the reason that the section of the street was so tidy came walking out from behind a dumpster. It was Zinnia.

"Hi, Ms. Kamalei!" Zinnia called out to her, sporting a great big smile on her face. Kamalei slowed her stride to greet Zinnia properly, something she wouldn't ordinarily do for just any commoner. Kamalei noticed that Zinnia was in unusually good spirits and energetic.

"Well, well, young lady," Kamalei greeted her. "I'm glad to see you are making the best of this lovely day. You're putting yourself to good use, are you?" she asked Zinnia.

"Oh, yes, Ms. Kamalei." Zinnia responded. "I sure am! I've been working to clean up the streets for the townspeople who are in need. I'm working really hard to improve my standing in the community. I hope you still believe in me Ms. Kamalei."

"But of *course*," Kamalei assured Zinnia. "The area is stunningly tidy. *Very* impressive. I'm very proud of you, Zinnia."

"Thank you, ma'am," Zinnia responded. "To be honest, I was a little frightened after speaking with you the other day. I realized that I was in a lot of trouble and that I need to make sure that I'm always there for the boys."

Kamalei acknowledged, "Very *true*, young lady. I'll see to it that my colleagues consider reducing your violation count accordingly at our next board meeting. I'm *sure* they'll be amenable." Kamalei, delighted that Zinnia was working hard to reduce her risk of selection to an Expulsion, made sure not to seem too out of character with traditional Venom Society mannerisms.

Her facial expressions grew more serious, and she was straight with Zinnia: "I do believe you're out of the red zone now, Zinnia, but *do not* revert to old ways, or you'll find yourself in *grave* danger once again."

"Oh, that's great news, Ms. Kamalei. THANK you so much," Zinnia said. "And . . . I understand."

Kamalei returned a slight grin but shaded it from view by all passersby and placed her hand on Zinnia's shoulder. "Run along now. I see more rubbish over there." Kamalei concluded their short dialog, pointing in the direction of the sidewalk on the opposite side of the street.

Kamalei thought for a moment of how Zinnia was the epitome of courage, kindness, and hope and drew her own inspiration from that. With renewed zest, Kamalei turned and continued in the direction of the colosseum to satisfy her obligations to the grandmaster, which she considered less glorious than Zinnia's but equally necessary.

CHAPTER 18

An Intriguing Find

After navigating a narrow and treacherous road through the hills of western Maryland, Zander managed to arrive safely at the remote job site where the Venom Society assigned him to assess the damage to an underground tunnel in the wake of recent tremors there. He finagled his RV into a flat nook along the mountainside and set up camp.

It was a remote location in the Appalachian Mountains, one of the few places left in the country that had an undeveloped natural preserve. The area couldn't be built on because Earth's plates were slipping in that location and earthquakes were becoming more frequent.

Venom Society engineers instructed Zander to inspect the outer facing of the tunnel walls only, and under no circumstances was he authorized to enter the tunnel itself.

Zander knew the ruling body was secretive about its underground facilities but thought that was a peculiar demand for a senior engineer who was looking to assist them. While he had long continued to serve the Venom Society well, Zander didn't always think highly of the organization. He recently confided in Ryker that he often wondered if the underlying motivations of the elites were noble ones.

But camping was one of his true pleasures in life, so he took the gig figuring it would also offer him the opportunity to take time for himself, explore the wilderness, and distance himself from the crowded streets of the Chesapeake Municipality for a bit. He enjoyed a bit of solitude every now and then. It allowed him to shed some of the depressing thoughts about the hardships faced by society daily.

The ceiling of the tunnel at this location breached the surface of the ground and was accessible for viewing with a short hike into the bush.

Fascinated by the backdrop of the deep canyon, Zander wanted to investigate its layered formation. Maybe he'd be fortunate enough to find some interesting rocks or artifacts or even dinosaur bones. Usually, he walked away with nothing after these escapades, but he always loved searching for things.

He approached the edge of a sharp cliff, peered downward at the landscape, and was instantly gratified. The sides of the cliff appeared to be layered with stone, dirt, and minerals. Each layer contained a hidden geological story of its time in history. Curiosity got the best of him, and he made his way deeper in.

Something caught his eye along the way, though. While much of the foliage was mundane and unimpressive, a couple of plant specimens seemed unusual. So much so that he weaved and bobbed his way through the tall grass and tree branches to have a closer look.

"What's this?" he mumbled under his breath, his eyes in a squint and bottom jaw hung low. "I've seen some interesting things in the wild before, but this is a real odd-ball—a cactus growing in Maryland?" he whispered inquisitively to himself. Upon closer inspection, Zander couldn't help but wonder if it was even real.

Cautiously, he reached out and stroked the side of the cactus to sample its texture. "Well, I'll be . . ." he muttered. "This ain't your ordinary garden variety cactus. This thing is *fake*," Zander then proclaimed out loud, as if there were someone nearby to hear him. He grabbed a hold of one of its thorns and, *snap*—it broke right off in his hand. It obviously had grown brittle, being out in the elements over time.

"Why would anyone leave a fake cactus way out in nowhere land?" Zander thought to himself. He knew very few people would make their way that deep into the canyon, and yet, someone took the time to emplace a fake cactus there. Strange.

He suspected that there may be more to the fake cactus than meets the eye. Perhaps it was planted there by the Venom Society. A quick peek around the back of the cactus confirmed his suspicions. There, clear as day, was the word "STARS." This goofy, but apparently high-tech, *fake* succulent had to be part of the Venom Society's STARS NET communications link. An apparent receiver for incoming intergalactic signals. Probably used to capture transmissions for further processing in the underground facility.

Zander never actually worked on the STARS NET project during his years with the secret organization, but he had heard about its capabilities.

After dropping the prickly prop in his backpack, he continued deeper into the canyon, still curious about its geological features. It was getting late, though, and before long, he would need to reverse course and get back to camp to get some rest. He had to get up early and make a day of locating and assessing the damage to the tunnels as he had promised his Venom Society bosses.

Parched from maneuvering about the steep cliff-side, Zander rested his hefty body on a boulder and grabbed a swig of cold water from his canteen. He took in a few deep breaths and got to thinking about what the morning might bring. Then, tired and lethargic, he gazed around the nearby ground and spotted a circular pit where there should have been grass. This pepped him up a bit. It was about two feet in diameter and only a few yards away from him. It was a good thing it wasn't dark yet, or he might have wound up losing his footing in the hole.

He allowed his rear to slide off the rock, and he landed on his left hip. A quick pivot of ninety degrees and an awkward roll to his side allowed him to see right down into the hole. Underground, a cylindrical pipe appeared uniform and symmetric in both directions. "Holy smokes," he whispered to himself, "that's exactly what they were thinking might have happened."

It was a topside breach of a Venom Society underground tunnel. The circumference and surface material of the inside walls, along with a set of carry rails, appeared to have been constructed to serve the specific function of underground high-speed transport. He lay there a moment admiring the sight.

Then, shockingly, he heard echoes of wailing voices coming from the depths of the tunnel, and it frightened him. Clearly, the cries weren't just audible calls from bats or rats or any such thing. They were human. It sounded like a human distress call. He panicked, believing someone was suffering and needed help.

But he fought the urge to jump down into the tunnel and follow the noise. The Venom Society elites had strictly prohibited him from entering, and these cries were most likely the reason why.

Alternatively, he dangled his husky torso precariously over the side of the hole in the opening and captured a few photographs of its interior walls. He probably wasn't supposed to do that either, unless the pictures were strictly to supplement his damage report. Then, as if he sensed someone watching him from behind, he jerked his torso up and out quickly and assessed his surroundings to ensure he was still alone. He didn't want his low violation count to increase. Nor did he want a pinprick to the back of his neck. He decided to get the heck out of there and head back to camp.

Zander needed to catch a few winks before drafting a scope-of-work proposal for the Venom Society. But first, he sent a text to his buddy Ryker at the Museum for Human Evolution, describing what he had found in the mountainside. He didn't hear back from Ryker before he drifted off to sleep.

He awoke early in the morning, still shaken by his experience the night before. Not knowing what he stumbled upon inside the tunnel, he decided to pack up his camp and cut his stay short. He'd seen—and heard—enough. He still hadn't heard back from Ryker, though.

It was eerily quiet in the canyon, a far cry from the crowded lands Zander was used to. He hated the fact that he couldn't just stay there forever, in reprieve from the disheartening reality of the harrowing metropolis to which he was heading.

Ryker, after examining the curious images he received from Zander, remembered attending a deep space exploratory convention where he met a security guard who described a similar situation. It was Jett. The two men shared a connection because Jett traveled with Venom Society VIPs as a chaperone, and he had seen Jett hovering around their headquarters in the Baltimore area at times.

Ryker befriended Jett at the convention and picked his brain a little bit about the progress the Venom Society was making in the science of particle point-to-point transfer. Jett told him a little about what he knew, but he couldn't say too much.

It had been a while since they had spoken to each other, but Ryker felt compelled to dig up Jett's phone number and give the old guy a call. He had been wanting to check in with him anyhow, to catch up. But more importantly, he needed to inform Jett of Zander's discovery.

Ryker had to fumble through a bunch of drawers containing piles of papers and books and junk from years of clutter build-up. But before long, there it was, scribbled on a flyer from the convention, Jett's name and number. "Ahhh, I hope this still works," Ryker thought to himself.

It did. The call was made, and after just a few rings, a raspy voice came on the line. "This is Jett, can I help you?"

Ryker responded nervously, "Yes, sir, um, my name izzzz Ryker Meadows. I live in the Chesapeake Municipality, and we met at a convention last year. I kept your number after we spoke at one of the breakout sessions. I had hoped to contact with you again regarding my latest research on animal-to-human virus transmission. Do you remember who I am, sir?"

Jett thought for a second and realized who was on the other side of the line. "Why, yes, I sure do. And how have you been, Ryker?"

"Very well, sir, thank you, and I hope this call finds you well," Ryker continued. "Sir, a friend of mine is currently traveling through a remote part of the mountains in Western Maryland where the population has not yet spread. It is still quite desolate there. The Venom Society assigned him to the location to assess underground tunnel damage, and he's been studying the geology and unstable landscape there. However, he stumbled upon some very intriguing things on site, and he sent me some images and a description of what he found. I was mystified, and I simply had to speak with you because the scene is reminiscent of something you described to me last year."

"I see," Jett responded. "Go on."

"Well, you see, sir, my friend, Zander, described this cactus as something totally out of context, which had pointy extensions on it . . . that appeared to be antenna receptors of some sort. Of course, there are no cacti growing in this part of the country. It was an obvious fake."

This caught Jett's attention, and as Ryker continued to describe Zander's findings, Jett began digging into some notes of his own until he found just what Ryker was referring to. Jett, not to be rude but to save Ryker a breath or two, interrupted him and indicated he knew full well what Ryker was talking about.

"What else ya got," Jett asked Ryker.

Ryker went on to indicate how Zander spoke of some frightening noises coming from a hole in the ground and described the tunnels from which the horrible sounds seemed to emanate. In a very indirect way, Ryker was offering Jett an opportunity to join him in a deeper investigation of the matter.

Jett knew right away that he had to talk to these guys in person. "Listen, let me schedule some time with you in a couple of days," Jett proposed to Ryker. "I'll be in the Annapolis Municipality preparing to assist the Venom Society in an upcoming Expulsion there. We can meet at the Chesapeake Town Square, go over these findings in detail, and decide on a course of action from there. Would you be open to that?"

Ryker was, of course, excited about that and urged Jett to get back with him soon to finalize the details. He also asked Jett if a colleague of his from the museum, Savanna WhiteEagle, could tag along. Savanna had worked at the museum for much longer than Ryker and knew more about the Venom Society's underground development. Ryker suggested that she would be able to provide more valuable background to their discussion. Jett was fine with that.

Jett expressed his thanks to Ryker for contacting him, and he assured Ryker that he would be back in touch in the next few days to finalize the details of the meeting. Jett also hinted to Ryker that Zander wandered perilously close to one of the Venom Society's highly secure labs, which was used for secret experimentation.

Jett knew full well that Zander could be in grave danger if he got caught snooping around an area like that. He advised Ryker to radio back to Zander and warn him to watch his step there. He told Ryker that he couldn't speak about it further until they met in person.

CHAPTER 19

Journey Back in Time

Proximity cautiously entered the atmosphere of another planet that was Earth-like in appearance. Parts of it appeared as blue regions, likely blanketed by water. Other parts flaunting various natural landscapes. Upon approach, Captain Pennington called for Skip to steady the ship into a slow descent toward the beautiful sphere.

Mechanical arms collected air samples of each layer of the atmosphere as Proximity neared its target. DAISIE confirmed oxygen and nitrogen levels and temperatures and noted that the readings were strikingly similar to those of planet Earth. She and Dr. Moss prepared to take soil samples once the ship had safely landed. They were optimistic that this planet contained materials useful for Earth. Whether or not its habitat was amenable to human life remained to be determined.

Confident of the suitability of the airspace surrounding the planet, Proximity entered hover mode, close enough to the planet to take soil test samples. The surface of the planet directly beneath them was tan, brown, and red in color. It contained barren tundra, not that different from what they might find in the hills and valleys of Earth's arid western states.

The shrubs were not very leafy, some downright prickly. The trees were few in number and dry. The crew was ecstatic that they found a planet that resembled, may even be a close relative of, Earth.

Anxious to land Proximity and begin preparations for exploration, Skip asked DAISIE for the results of the initial soil testing. Her response sent chills of adrenaline down his back. "All soil sample testing results fall within safe levels for human and animal habitation," DAISIE assured him. "The metals that are present are also found in Earth's soil. Percent hydrogen (PH) levels are in the safe range for plant life. Microscopic organisms and the planet's chemical and molecular blueprint closely mirror that of Earth."

Satisfied with DAISIE's report, the crew prepared to exit Proximity—this time on foot, without the aid of spacesuits. Each crew member quietly and anxiously conjured up their own images of what could potentially happen when they entered the unexplored territory of a planet 150 light-years away from home.

The fear of what awaited them back home, should they fail to discover new habitable land, drove the captain to trip the release hatch on the main exit door. The door lowered and contacted the dusty top surface of the planet. The pressure neutralized comfortably inside Proximity. A ladder was extended out and downward from the floor of the craft.

The crew breathed an initial sigh of relief once the ladder was set, but no one was quick to be the first to climb down it. DAISIE, most confident in her own material sampling analysis, decided she'd lead the crew to the ground. She was a brave android, to begin with, but was also likely at little risk, physically, to any potential harmful atmospheric conditions that may have gone undetected.

Captain Pennington followed DAISIE, and then his crew trailed behind him. No words were spoken. The only sound was the creaking of the ladder's rungs under the stress of the weight of the crewmembers.

One by one, the crewmembers successively stepped foot on the ground and backed away from the ladder, clearing space for the next. They carried sophisticated measuring and gathering equipment with them. They were awestruck by the fact that they could be the first humans to ever stand on the surface of this Earth-like planet.

Not in need of any artificial breathing apparatus, they were relieved that DAISIE's initial assessment of the air's oxygen content was accurate.

Patches of greenery occasionally interrupted the view of the sparse landscape, which suggested that those plant species had ample nutrients from the ground to sustain them, and presumably water from somewhere. Kassie Lomaxx added that the plant life appeared to be receiving adequate levels of sunlight, if, in fact, the green coloration of the foliage was indicative that photosynthesis was taking place.

Conditions were hot and dry where the crew had landed. Max Gilligan noted that the temperature where they were standing was about ninety-nine degrees Fahrenheit, and that was in the shadow of the spaceship. He conjectured that the sun, which carried this planet, could be many times larger than Earth's. Either that, or this planet revolved unusually close to its sun.

Both properties just happened to be easy calculations for DAISIE, though. She spoke up, confident and proud, and announced the mass of the planet's sun and also the precise distance the planet sat from it. She had already run the numbers through her sophisticated processors, unbeknownst to the very impressed Gilligan.

The sun hovered menacingly large and high above them. The light from its extreme flaming gases felt as if it was searing the crew's faces but, oddly, did not seem to harm them. Deep breaths through their noses yielded clear, pure, unadulterated oxygen, fresh and free of impurities.

Initial inspection of the area was amazing, albeit quiet and uneventful. But soon, Kassie detected a movement in a nearby bush. Startled, she signaled to the crew to listen quietly for a second. Everyone stood frozen.

Kassie guardedly strolled over to the crop of bushes where she thought she had heard something. She leaned over and pulled aside a patch of droopy leaves. What she saw next was astonishing.

It was a living animal. Kassie jumped back but, as frightened as she was, could not generate a vocal yelp. Her fellow crewmembers came to her side to see what was there. Kassie moved the bunch of leaves aside one more time for her colleagues to see. It was a small dinosaur-like creature. Or perhaps it was a lizard. Whatever it was, it swiveled its head around and fixated on the crew as the rest of its body froze in its position.

It didn't take long for the crew to observe the creature before they decided to retreat and take cover behind Proximity's landing gear. The dino-lizard, for lack of a better term, scampered to the safety of a nearby boulder.

Gilligan fumbled frantically with his recording equipment and began documenting the event to share with the scientists at Galileo Base Station, who might otherwise not believe the story the crew would have to tell.

A few moments later, the lizard appeared next to the spaceship, attempting to satisfy its curiosity about the new visitors to its planet. Then, with surprising calm, Kassie was able to coax the little critter into a breathable glass container.

The crew rambled haphazardly back up the ladder and into the bows of Proximity to have a closer look at the animal. It was an unusual-looking specimen—unlike anything they were accustomed to seeing on Earth, particularly since dinosaurs were extinct there. This creature had six legs, a diamond shaped head, which it held high and erect while carrying u-shaped horns just above its thinly slit eyes. Vertical plates projected up from its lateral surface and traveled all the way down its back. The tail was medium-sized and split in two at the end. Its mouth contained snake-like fangs, yet it had not wielded them at the humans in any kind of aggressive manner. Actually, its disposition was one of tranquility and trust. It appeared to be quite friendly.

Kassie recalled that paleontologists on Earth had uncovered similar fossilized remains of a dinosaur believed to roam the Earth some 600 million years ago while they excavated during skypod construction in the Arizona desert. She noticed peculiar similarities between the two specimens and suggested the crew contact Galileo Base Station to report their findings for comparison.

She theorized that any apparent connection between the specimen found on Earth and the critter in the glass container would amount to tangible evidence that two very distant planetary bodies, in two different locations of the universe, could have developed from the same set of building blocks, in the very same manner. And that over billions of years, two different planets could have ended up developing the same types of life forms.

Captain Pennington radioed back to home base over a weak signal and a bunch of static. "Proximity to Galileo Base Station, come in Galileo," he said. "Proximity to Galileo. Do you read me?"

Fumbling for the microphone was an evening shift flight-support officer at Galileo who went by the name of Diego Slater. With no one else around, he was dozing off and was startled by the unexpected call.

"Proximity, this is Slater at Galileo communications control room. Transmission received. Connection is weak, but I hear you. Over."

The captain leaped right into why he was calling. "Proximity requests immediate assessment of recently discovered dinosaur fossil remains. The specimen currently resides in a vault at the Venom Society Biological Recovery Center in Arizona. The remains were discovered near there during the excavation of the dessert flats amid the construction of skypods. We need you to retrieve all online records, descriptions, pictures, autopsy results—anything you can find regarding this species. Once you can adequately describe the specimen to us, radio back immediately on this frequency. Over."

Confused at what the captain's motivations were, Slater hesitated but assured the captain that he would honor his request. "Roger that Proximity. I can have a response to you in approximately twenty minutes. Over."

Proximity went silent while Slater went diving into the Recovery Center's databases.

Just a few moments later, breaking up a light chatter among the crew of Proximity, the radio sounded. Static momentarily filled the voice transmission channel before Galileo control center was able to clear it and issue a summons.

"Galileo to Proximity, this is Slater. I have returned on air. Do you receive?"

Anxiously awaiting the call and almost interrupting Slater's voice, Kassie perked up and intently took over communications.

"We're here, Slater; we're here. Did you retrieve the information about the specimen as requested? Over."

"Better than that, Kassie. The remains of the dinosaur are here with me. I had them collider-transported to this location immediately so that I could complete a first-hand examination myself. Exactly what is it you want me to do with it?"

"We need you to prepare for visual examination of its bodily features," Kassie informed him.

Slater responded in an inquisitive tone, "But . . . what are you expecting to—"

"*Please* Slater, just do as I ask, and we'll answer your questions momentarily," Kassie interrupted, pleading with him.

Slater agreed. "Roger. Awaiting further instruction."

Kassie continued, “Slater, describe for us the exterior covering of the specimen. Over.”

Slater responded, “Its skin is very scaly, like that of a present-day reptile, scales are large and coarse.”

Kassie took some notes and continued, “Slater, describe the head and neck features to us, please.”

“Roger,” Slater responded. “I’m trying to figure out how to describe it. The head appears to have been carried high on a thick neck, perpendicular to its body when standing in a fully upright position. Umm, perhaps to be able to see over tall grasses or rocks or something?” Slater seemed to question his own elementary paleontological analysis.

Kassie assured him he was on target. “Roger, Slater. Go on; you’re doing just fine.”

Captain Pennington and Skip looked around the ship and found blank stares on the faces of their fascinated colleagues, who by this time were pondering the implications of the possible discovery of identical life forms in two distant locations in the vast universe. To them, this meant mankind might be able to begin traveling to this location at some point, easing the burden of overcrowding on Earth, which was the ultimate goal of almost every mission they flew.

Kassie needed more information to make any confident preliminary decisions on that though. She continued, “What sorts of external features make up the specimen’s general appearance?”

Slater responded, “It’s eyes, Proximity . . . they’re very thin, and its pupils stretched parallel to the ground, conducive to optimal lateral, peripheral scanning. And it has horns . . . there are u-shaped horns, like that of an Angus bull.”

Kassie noted the eerily similar appearance of their captive dino-lizard, and the crew shared an elevated level of intrigue.

Captain Pennington chimed in, "Thank you, Slater. Please continue."

Slater obliged, "Roger, Captain. But . . . um, can anyone tell me what is going on there?"

Captain Pennington was quick to keep the officer focused on answering their questions. "We need your cooperation, Slater. You must trust that we have everything under control. Please understand that, for now, we need you to not ask questions and simply give us—"

The captain was abruptly cut off by Slater, who decided it was best to continue to pacify the crew rather than question anything. "*Six* legs . . . I understand the procedure, sir . . . my apologies. This specimen is showing six scaly lizard-like appendages, each bearing four toes with sharp pointy claws. This might be one of the weirdest creatures I've ever laid eyes on. It has a crocodile-like rear structure with thin vertical plates spanning the distance from the back of its neck to the end of its seemingly powerful tail."

Slater was a bit awkward and cumbersome in his appearance and mannerisms. Obviously highly intelligent but minimally physically skilled. He fumbled over the examination table as he flipped the specimen over to assess its underside. He continued, "Proximity, its belly has rippled layers to it like you might see on the underside of an alligator. Given its outward appearance, I'd say this ferocious little guy could hold its own with some of its larger opponents."

The crew of Proximity confirmed their suspicion—they had discovered Earth-like life, light-years from Earth. They had made the first inter-galactic connection to their own planet. They were holding astounding proof that there was a means for man to exist beyond their own planet. For that, they were elated.

By this time, Kassie had allowed her new-found friend out of the jar. It climbed up her arm and perched on her right shoulder, just as a pet iguana might. And the little dino-alien showed his appreciation by licking her cheeks with its gritty, coarse tongue. The crew could do nothing but watch in disbelief.

Slater, unaware of what was going on in the spaceship, continued to describe what he was seeing, "Proximity, I don't know what you are doing or where you are, but I know one thing, I'd hate to wake up in the middle of the night with this menacing thing at the foot of my bed!"

The crew of Proximity broke out into symphonic laughter, realizing that what appeared to Slater to be a terrifying, dangerous, unknown creature, was turning out to be a cute—in one's own opinion—mild-mannered, friendly specimen. A new friend to the crew of Proximity, but more importantly, a symbol of hope for mankind.

Captain Pennington cut the conversation short, "Thank you very much for assisting with this, Slater. We're going to go silent now. We'll connect with you with an update once we complete our initial exploratory protocol. Over." The captain ended the connection with Galileo.

"Well, everyone, I don't know how we're going to explain this one to the folks back home," Pennington said, projecting his voice throughout the cabin. Then, he disrupted the elation of the crew with a sudden serious question. "Wait a minute . . . do you all hear that?" he said. "A rumbling sound off in the distance, in that direction," he said, pointing out the window over Skip's shoulder.

The crew quieted down, offered the captain a nod, and took a cautious look through the windows to see if they could determine what might be creating the noise.

Approximately 300 yards away, they noticed a small valley cutting through the hillside. Kassie indicated that she thought she could see movement in the distance. Peering in the direction of the valley with a look through his binoculars, the captain witnessed a most incredible sight. It buckled his knees momentarily, and Max motioned as if he were going to break the captain's fall should he continue toward the ground. But Pennington held his balance.

"What's the matter, Captain? Are you alright?" Skip asked.

"Take a look . . . there, just beyond the western rim of the hillside. Bear witness to the most incredible thing you've ever seen," the captain answered him.

The crew followed the captain's orders, and what they saw in the valley was almost enough to stop their hearts—a herd of massive dinosaur-like creatures making its way along one side of the valley. Each individual animal likely weighed several tons. It looked like a pack of apatosaurus. In awe of the view, the crew clamored to the closest windows, watching intently. Kassie recorded video to document the moment.

In a short time, however, the crew had come to realize they were far outnumbered and a bit of panic set in. While they took comfort in the surrounding double-walled shell of Proximity, they realized that if the alien dinosaurs happened to venture in the direction of the spaceship, it could become a dangerous situation.

Captain Pennington decided it was time to make a quick exit from the planet. He ordered Kassie to release the small dino-lizard before having Skip retract the ladder and close the main door. Prior to securing everyone inside the ship and firing up the engines, Skip remembered to place a STARS NET camera on the ground beneath the spaceship.

CHAPTER 20
Zinnia's Revenge

The population of the Annapolis Municipality, adjacent to southeastern border of the Chesapeake Municipality, had reached an alarming state, which caused an imbalance between the number of humans living there and the means to sustain them. That compelled the Venom Society to conduct their next Expulsion there.

Both municipalities were reeling from repeated robberies perpetrated by the citizens of a rogue skypod, 51A. The local population experienced great suffering as a result, including Zinnia, Xion, and Dalton. Eighteen inhabitants from that skypod, once productive, law-abiding citizens, chose a path of crime causing their violation counts to rise dramatically. They were shackled and escorted to the Expulsion staging area.

Kamalei stood before the crowd and delivered her ceremonial opening message.

"Welcome, *good* citizens of the Annapolis Municipality. I am Kamalei Ricinulei, Master of Expulsions. Our population is in the red," she reminded them. "We are starving. We are sick. We are *dying*. We must join together as one and respect the needs of all *good* people on Earth. And yet, there are *those* who decide to cross their neighbors." She waved an arm toward the undesirables as she peered at the holding cage deliberately and menacingly. The crowd of watchers responded with heightened applause.

"Today, ladies and gentlemen, we sacrifice individuals whose behavior we can no longer tolerate. Their violation counts demonstrate that they do not respect the laws of our land. Their fate lies in *your* hands. DO WHAT YOU MUST!"

Kamalei, both arms held high in the air, signaled to the staging crew that the event was about to begin. Laser lights and pyrotechnics filled the colosseum, indicating the start of the Expulsion.

The undesirables were presented to the crowd, and their charges were displayed upon the big screens. The massive mechanical arm and steel claws began snatching up undesirables, and, one by one, they were loaded into the death cage.

They scampered around the arena, fending off their competition, trying to find an escape capsule to jump into. But the capsules would not be had easily. The watchers were intent on avenging the thieves. They quickly zeroed in on one young male, in particular. It was TeeJay, who was known to have committed most of the robberies around the Annapolis Municipality. He was the ring-leader. His thievery had cost lives. If he got too close to a killing device, there would surely be enough disdain among the crowd for him that the device would be activated. And that's exactly what happened.

As TeeJay scurried for safety, he spotted an escape capsule hidden in a bank of boulders located precariously at the top edge of a climbing wall. To get to the top, he'd have to scale the rocky wall by hand. He was tough and athletic, but he didn't have any rock-climbing experience per se. But he was an Astronian, and they were all naturally good at negotiating heights by hanging and swinging aloft. TeeJay was confident he could gain access to the escape capsule unscathed.

He didn't notice, however, a series of crossbows hanging from the top of the cage, aimed directly at the top of the rock formation. An obvious method for a kill, should that be the will of the audience members, collectively.

TeeJay demonstrated just how good a climber he was. That triggered memories for the watchers, who realized that he had scaled the tower supports of their skypods much the same way—unannounced and unwelcome—in the middle of the night, taking their food and goods from them. They snapped at that thought. And just as TeeJay's right hand reached the peak of the wall, a surge of electronic influence from the watchers' joysticks was more than enough to trigger the master control modules of the crossbows. Executioners wasted no time in deploying the devices.

In an instant, TeeJay's body was riddled with arrows, and he fell to the ground, a lifeless shell. That drew a hearty cheer from the crowd. It felt good to get back at an undesirable who had harbored so little respect for others.

And there was TeeJay's partner in crime, Mo. He was an enforcer-type. He had scoped out the locations the gangs wanted to hit. And when the hits went down, Mo made sure no one interfered. Without Mo, TeeJay would have been caught and terminated a long time ago.

Mo threatened to kill anyone who stood in the way of the gang. Two weeks ago, he led a series of gang raids in the Chesapeake and Annapolis Municipalities. He savagely beat a girl in an orphanage who was a hundred pounds lighter than he for doing nothing more than threatening to call the authorities. That victim was Zinnia, and that was disgusting. But he didn't care. He was selfish and under the influence of TeeJay. He took what he wanted from the orphanage, including Xion's reserve of food and medicine, and had no care for the boy's wellbeing.

The incident sent Xion into a downward spiral, and his health deteriorated beyond recovery. Zinnia nursed him intensely with the extra rations donated to her by the others at the orphanage, along with the stashes that she secretly received from Kamalei, but it was to no avail. Xion had very little appetite.

Zinnia spent a couple of days cradling and comforting her brother, who grew increasingly weak. She could do nothing more for him but to remind him how special he was and how much his family loved him. Eventually, Xion became incoherent and then nonresponsive. His breathing slowed, and his heart nearly stopped beating altogether. At that very moment, Zinnia saw a scorpion scurry across the floor and through the door. A prophetic sign. Her brother passed in her arms, and his spirit left the room. Sadly, Xion died just three days after the savage raid on the orphanage.

Zinnia was devastated having to live through another tragedy early in life. She had lost her mother and father in tragic fashion as a young child. Now, losing her only brother was almost more than she could bear. But she grew stronger as a human being with each struggle. And she still had good reason in life to remain a positive and productive citizen. Namely, Dalton.

Zinnia was bitter for her loss, though. And that led her to attend the Expulsion this day. Now, it was Mo's turn to pay, and Zinnia, her heart full of anger, was looking for a way to take him out.

Many of the observers in the crowd were from the Chesapeake Municipality. They, too, wanted nothing more than to make Mo pay for his misgivings. Mo knew this, but he was savvy. He lasted for quite a while without putting himself in danger's way. But it meant he couldn't focus on securing an escape capsule for himself. The onlookers were relentless in their pursuit to avenge, though, so he was forced to take some chances to try and outmaneuver the rest of the competitors.

He charged past a pack of executioners, who had not yet received enough will to kill from the onlookers to attack him. They took off after him, though, to keep the heat on.

Mo fell from a ledge and into a large crevice between two rock walls. A bit stunned, he staggered to his feet, thinking to himself, "God, let there be a capsule around here somewhere!" And to his luck, there was. An unoccupied one.

It was only about fifty feet away, but Mo was badly hurt from the fall. He could only limp his way toward the capsule. The executioners peered over the ledge, wondering if they should go in after him or not. And then the walls surrounding the crevice rumbled and moved slightly.

The onlookers quickly figured out that the valley Mo was in was actually a trap. And their collective will to kill him was enough to create a tremor when they leaned on their joysticks. But it wasn't enough to squeeze the walls completely in on him. Not enough, that is, until Zinnia stood up, faced the crowd, and reminded them of the ruthless ways of these robbers.

Kamalei, now with very mixed feelings about her loyalty to Venom Society mission and a growing inner sympathy for Zinnia, saw what Zinnia was attempting to do and ordered that the main camera be directed at her in a show of support.

Zinnia appeared, close-up, on the big screen. She pulled a necklace and locket from her shirt pocket. She held the locket facing the camera for all in the crowd to see. She opened the cover to reveal its contents. It was a picture of Xion. A heartfelt reminder of the consequences of the rath of the skypod gang. Instantly, the crowd noise increased twofold, and the crevice walls began to converge on Mo again, faster this time.

Mo knew he had to either get to the capsule immediately or turn around and go back out of the crevice and find a different way. After hesitating a moment, he decided to go for the capsule. It was only fifteen feet away now.

"Remember my brother, Xion, and DO WHAT YOU MUST!" Zinnia called out to the crowd, raising both arms up high, urging them to eliminate the dissenter who had caused Xion's death and hurt so many others along the way. And it worked.

The mobile walls kicked into full motion. The fear on Mo's face was pronounced. He had regained some of his mental faculties and that allowed him to pick up his pace slightly. But he needed to really get moving or else he'd be crushed in a few seconds.

It looked like he might actually reach the escape capsule before the walls could sandwich him. But then, from the end of the valley behind him a swarm of large scorpions appeared. They were moving much faster than Mo and far outnumbered him. Worse yet, they were in attack mode.

Zinnia wasn't sure whether this was another kill tactic triggered by the watchers or a supernatural act from Xion, but the scorpions were real, and they were on Mo instantly. They took him to the ground just a few feet away from the escape capsule. In agony, he lay there screaming, trying to drag himself closer to the capsule as the venom started eating away at his insides. Zinnia watched with a cold, blank stare.

Finally, the walls made contact with Mo's limp body. He quivered, then ended up as a mash-up of flesh and blood spattered on the rocky walls. The crowd cheered at the elimination of this despised dissenter—more out of happiness for Zinnia's retribution than for anything else.

That was all Zinnia could handle emotionally. It was a difficult time for her. She turned and walked toward the exit, conflicted once again about whether or not the event she had just witness was justified.

Jett, who happened to be assisting security at the event, reached into the deep pocket of his left pant leg and grabbed one of his business cards with a notion to offer it to Zinnia. It dawned on him that he had just recently foiled her attempt at breaking into a storage facility, but he remembered seeing something special in the young lady that day. Jett asked her how she was doing before she had a chance to exit.

"Oh, hi, Mr. Jett," Zinnia responded. "I'm doing okay, I guess. Thank you for asking, sir."

"That's good to know," Jett said. "I'm sorry to hear about your little brother. He was an inspiration to so many of us. You're a very brave young lady."

Zinnia thought in her mind to thank him for his condolences, but a swell in her throat prevented her from vocalizing it to him. All she could do was lightly nod to Jett as she worked to keep from breaking down.

"It's alright, Zinnia," Jett continued. "Things will be okay." He paused and thought for a moment and then decided that he, as a concerned adult and one who Zinnia looked up to, must encourage her to continue to work hard, to do good deeds.

"Look, something's bothering me," he said to Zinnia. "I'm worried about you. I've been hearing some strange things—some rather disturbing things—about the Venom Society. It has to do with what some of my colleagues believe has happened to the Expulsion winners. I can't go into a lot of detail right now, Zinnia, but I wouldn't feel right if I failed to impress upon you just how important it is to keep your violation count low. I believe you are an extraordinary human being, and this world can really profit from individuals like yourself."

Zinnia was able to thank Jett this time, verbally, and on top of that, she gave him some reassurance. "Don't worry, sir. I will be just fine. Thank you for your concern." She turned slightly as if to go, but then doubled back, looked at Jett again, and said with confidence, "Mr. Jett, I plan on saving this world one day!"

Then, Jett leaned over and gave her a hug, opened the door to the exit way, flashed his business card, and encouraged her to go and get some rest. She looked up at him, smiled, grabbed the card from Jett's hand, and went on her way.

Armed with Jett's contact information, Zinnia now felt empowered to start her own investigation into some of the strange behaviors of the Venom Society.

As fate would have it, Zinnia filed in line behind an entourage of Venom Society officers who had also decided to make an early exit from the colosseum. They were lightly aware of Zinnia's presence close behind but thought nothing of it. After all, what sort of threat could an innocuous, unassuming teenager be to them?

On their way out of the exit tunnel, they casually discussed some of the biological experimentation that was taking place underground, which some of the townspeople had caught wind of and expressed concern over. Townspeople, that is, who mysteriously disappeared any time the topic came up uninvited.

The venom Society officers grew a little uncomfortable that Zinnia was lingering nearby but still felt confident that she was not paying them any attention. Their voices decreased in volume, but they continued their conversation.

But Zinnia was paying attention. She knew something was up, and that sparked her into action. She continued to follow the Venom Society elites outside and into an alleyway, acting as if she was simply attending to the homeless and cleaning up trash and debris from around them, as Kamalei implored her to do.

The Venom Society officers traded accolades first, then notes about what they had observed at the Expulsion. During the exchange, a junior member of the Society accidentally dropped a thumb drive on the ground. Not he nor any of his colleagues noticed. But Zinnia did, and her eyes lit up.

As she collected waste and placed it into a garbage bag, she edged her way uncomfortably close to the polished leather shoe of the Venom Society officer who had dropped the thumb drive.

There, glistening in the late-day sun, was the small metal device. Zinnia didn't have time even to think. She snatched it up instantly, along with some spent syringes and used gauze. She did get a look from a couple of the Venom Society officers, but she ignored them and kept her composure.

Zinnia casually increased the distance between her and them, staying on-point with her clean-up facade, until she could turn and make an unassuming departure from the area.

Jett wasn't finished for the day either. The Expulsion hadn't ended yet. And Petra, the final dissenter, was about to enter the death cage. The mechanical arm and claws whipped her around as her violation count and charges were displayed on the big screens. Then, she was forcefully injected into the death cage.

Petra was another gang member who worked for TeeJay. She was easily the most despised female of the day's participants. She would be the next target of the fury of the crowd. And she didn't even have to go "looking" for a killing device. One found her instead.

It came in the form of a robotic body-stretcher, one that was disguised to look like a large plant. But one with serious kill capability. With the assistance of an infrared tracking system, the branches of the fake plant, which appeared harmless, would pinpoint the victim's hands and feet, latch on to all four extremities, and begin a slow, excruciating separation of limbs from body.

This machine was nimble and tracked its prey with precision accuracy. If a competitor was especially fast, they might be able to outrun it on a short sprint, but it would eventually catch up with them. Petra was actually pretty peppy herself. But not that fast.

As soon as she saw the mechanical plant coming at her, she headed for the center of the cage, thinking she could climb a support column to where the device couldn't get to her. She didn't quite make it there before the killer plant had her in its shackles.

The distinguished Venom Society members that remained to watch the end of the Expulsion sat in the VIP seating area right next to where Petra was bound, and they found this very entertaining. Some of the commoners, a bit squeamish, turned their heads when they realized what was about to happen. Others watched intently because they were part of the collective will, the influencers, that had caused the robotic plant to hunt down Petra.

It only took about ten seconds, and amid a death screech, they watched her body lose one limb at a time as each snapped away from her torso. Her shredded body dropped to the ground and bled out quickly.

With that, the last remaining contestant claimed the third and final escape capsule, and a cheer filled the air. That was followed by the ceremonial foghorn and extraction of all escape capsules.

Jett opened the exit gates and ducked out quickly, before the heavy crowd began its egress. He wanted to get home and figure out a way to find out more about the frightening noises in the underground tunnels that Ryker had told him about.

CHAPTER 21

Surprise Swarm

After rationalizing the potential impact of what they had already encountered during their prior planetary visits, the crew of Proximity grew even hungrier to locate more human-friendly planets, free of danger. Still, it was unclear if the ideal planet even existed. Captain Pennington and his crew were determined to find out.

DAISIE and the rest of Proximity's crew focused their attention on their next target in a galaxy believed to contain a potentially lucrative solar system. Having just witnessed live dinosaur-like beings roaming a distant planet, they knew the possibility of discovering safe, habitable land was now greater than ever.

Skip ensured all systems were in order and warned the crew that he was ready to commence deep space travel. "Everything looks good, team. Take your positions and secure your seating as I prepare the ship for space-time transform."

Captain Pennington assured Skip that the crew was ready to go. "Roger that, Skip. You may initiate the travel collider at your discretion."

"We will enter into space-time travel transform in approximately sixty seconds, sir," Skip responded. Just a minute later, Proximity vanished into thin air.

Although the spaceship was traveling a great distance on its next jump sequence, it pulled out of space-time transform just minutes after collider activation. As part of the cargo molecular disassembly process, the crew had no sense of time while they were in transit.

They regained cognitive capacity when the ship and its contents were completely reassembled. Their journey was another success, and they began to get a bearing on the direction and distance of the target solar system. The jump put them within close range.

Proximity resumed standard combustion engine power as DAISIE worked to identify a specific planet to visit.

One orb stood out as unique. It was a planet, light blue, with obvious aquatic features, as well as small land masses. The crew was anxious to give it a closer look.

Proximity entered the atmosphere surrounding the planet, and DAISIE began recording its temperature and chemical make-up. Readings were generally spaceship-friendly, with just a couple of spikes in the percentages of oxygen and helium but nothing so dangerous that it prevented further approach. Proximity entered a slow trajectory directly toward the planet and prepared for initial surface electro-optical scans.

The crew searched for an area that might prove conducive to landing. Cameras panned the shallow blue-gray skies above the seemingly quiet planet. Proximity was still in dark space as it orbited, but the planet was well lit by the center star, which governed the solar system.

As Proximity eased its way through the upper atmosphere, it drifted into a thick layer of clouds. The crew lost visibility of the planet as a result, but DAISIE was able to capture atmospheric samples, and she ran some initial tests on them. Indications seemed safe, but the foggy conditions continued to worsen, and an eerie feeling overcame everyone on board.

Captain Pennington asked the obvious question. "Skip, what is all of this cumulus activity indicative of?"

Skip responded, "Well, sir, I'm not a meteorologist, but I presume it is a build-up of moisture, which has formed some sort of weather event. Most likely a process of evaporation, condensation, and precipitation cycles, similar to what we experience on Earth. The microscopic discharge from our exhaust might serve to seed water droplets, which could lead to the formation of rain as we navigate through it."

The captain continued, "Kassie and I noticed this layer as we approached, but it didn't appear to be anywhere near this dense and inhibiting. Seems strange."

"I agree, Captain. It's almost as if it baited us in," Skip conjectured, half-wittingly.

DAISIE confirmed for Captain Pennington that the clouds remained high in both oxygen and helium gas.

"Thank you, DAISIE," the captain showed his appreciation to her.

The captain and Skip leaned closer to the main window to capture some partial view of the target planet. To their astonishment, they detected movement a short distance out. It was a floating mass. A presence. A being of some sort. And it was animated, moving in a slow, flowing manner. It was distinct from the clouds and seemed to relish the dense fluff of white that surrounded it.

The captain said nothing but placed his hand firmly on Skip's shoulder, holding the first mate firmly in place. This was the captain's way of saying, without words, "Stay calm. I see what you see, but don't show any fear. Remain still and act natural. I don't want to alarm the others." Skip heard no voice but knew exactly what the captain was trying to tell him. He formed a statue-like pose and remained speechless. His back was turned to the others. And his jaw trembled.

The two men witnessed the being floating, or drifting somehow, amidst the mysterious clouds. It was large, twelve to fifteen feet from top to bottom, and resembled what the men knew as the common jellyfish in Earth's rivers and seas. Its body was oval but constantly morphed into circular and elliptical variations.

Slow-moving and cumbersome, it sported tentacles that covered all aspects of its body. Slight twitches in its muscularity seemed to cause the tentacles to propel the creature slowly and methodically along. Its flesh was translucent, and it didn't appear to have appendages—or anything that might be considered a head. It didn't notice the spaceship. Or, at least, it didn't care that the ship had infiltrated its environment.

Captain Pennington issued his colleague an order under his breath, "Skip, snap some shots of this thing quickly as I alert the crew to what we are looking at."

"Yes, sir," Skip responded.

The captain called over the loudspeaker to the others, who were busy documenting the event, "Crew, I know you are all awaiting final approach to this planet. I also know that you are hoping to discover a planet conducive to human life for our compatriots back home. Well, we have a bit of a situation here. Skip and I have spotted unusual activity out the main window. It is in the form of . . . well, ummm, of . . . a jellyfish, I believe. *Now*, I don't want everyone to stir at once. *Please* just remain at your positions and ensure all systems remain intact. I need you all to prepare to revert to distant orbit observation of this planet. We're backing off for now. There's been a change in plans, folks."

In light of the events that we've witnessed during our previous planetary visit, and given what Skip and I just saw outside the spaceship, I resolve that it is safer for us to perch high above the atmosphere and observe thoroughly and cautiously at a distance before considering further approach."

Skip loudly interrupted the captain's announcement: "CAPTAIN, it's right outside our window now, sir, and it's NOT ALONE!"

The crew heard Skip in the background of the PA system, and there was clearly an urgency to his voice. However, they continued to carry out the captain's orders, despite what was going on outside in the murky clouds.

The captain spun his chair back around, peered out his window, and saw dozens of jellies navigating about the perimeter of the spaceship. None of them appeared at all harmful or threatening, but the sheer numbers were unsettling. The captain ordered DAISIE to immediately move the ship to a safe distance from the planet. She, too, sensed the urgency in the captain's voice. And Proximity made a hasty retreat.

CHAPTER 22
Aquapod Expansion

Clank. Screech. Rumble.

An all too familiar clamor filled the air as the daily build for survival raged on. The Chesapeake Bay grid of aquapods was expanding. The Venom Society was ramping up the number of Expulsions taking place in the Delmarva Peninsula, but that wasn't enough to bring the supply of food into balance with the recent population growth for this region. The proliferation of aquapods would help ease the hardship of the local population to some extent.

But it also taxed the environment. The more aquapods the Society added to the bay's surface, the more sea life perished as a result. Locals continued to watch the situation in the bay deteriorate—not because they enjoyed the slow death of a once-thriving aquatic habitat. Not because engineers mindlessly built more dwellings for selfish reasons without caring about the environment. They continued to build masterful sky-piercing aquapods because they had to do so to survive.

By 3022, undeveloped land was scarce. Precious areas that had not been built upon were maintained as versatile havens, utilized in the production of food and other resources and for the disposal of waste. Man was eventually forced to move into the water and adapt to its harsh discomforts.

An almost constant *crash* and *bang* melody permeated the landscape as hundreds of tons of steel pressed together. Engineers worked tirelessly to connect the network of beams supporting the newly constructed aquapod, located in the Severn River, a tributary stemming from the northeastern flank of the bay. Much of the river's perimeters were already covered with a layer of aquapods.

The steel used to produce the assembly beams was derived from materials far beneath the Earth's surface. Man had pitted the crust of the Earth over the last thousand years, bringing a considerable portion of its bounty topside for use in skypod construction. This did, however, allow for better underground maneuverability by the Marsupans. At the same time, however, it increased the risk of Earth's tectonic plates becoming more vulnerable to slippage.

Still, led by Venom Society engineers, human construction crews built on. They had no choice in the matter.

As the aquapod barge was slowly positioned into place, ready to be attached to the existing network, the inhabitants of the existing aquapods braced for a controlled impact. Dozens of barges towed the megaton structure carefully toward its desired resting place. Engineers used cranes to interleave the connecting hinges into their precise locations and readied them to complete the union. Once the new aquapod barge was situated, the massive connector pins would be seated into the hinges, finalizing the bond between the new aquapod and the existing structures. The community was ready to take on another piece of its grid.

It came at a cost, though. More sunlight would be deflected before reaching the ocean. A view from the satellites overhead showed a steel crust surrounding much of the Earth's surface already, steadily growing and engulfing more of the planet each year.

As the barges pressed through carcasses of perch and rockfish, the sea captain flashed a bright light, signaling all tugboats to come to a halt. The huge, steel connector pins hovered over their intended hinge guide holes.

Finally, the signal came in from the port tower to drop the pins into position. Most hit their targets with precision, but several proved a bit stubborn. No human-built super structure was too big for the ocean currents to move. And slight offset was all that was needed to inhibit some pins from seating properly.

The surrounding aquapod community let out an initial cheer for the crews for what they believed was a successful expansion. However, they soon realize there was more work to be done before the job would be deemed complete. With lubricant and a clever maneuvering of the barge slightly left and right several times over, the final few pins were coerced into their hinges, and at last, the Severn River aquapod grid had grown.

It was a humble success. To complete the job, a supply of electricity, a means to produce sanitized water, and sewage hookups would all have to be installed and operational.

One of the first undertakings for newly attached aquapods was to establish transport from the water's surface to the habitable portion of the pods themselves. One of the primary solutions came by way of a super elevator. These high-speed, high-ascent tubes were skillfully designed to endure long runs and carry heavy loads while keeping humans safely hunkered inside. They were strung from the most durable, scientifically-engineered nano-carbon cables available, the formula for which was still a protected secret of the Venom Society.

The new aquapod was not a finished product just yet, and the crowds who lived in the existing adjacent pods grew impatient. They wanted out of their current harsh, overcrowded conditions. So much so that they eventually overwhelmed the construction crew's attempts to calm them and keep them at bay.

Once the first crossing bridge, connecting the new aquapod to the existing mesh, was firmly in place, the Hydronians bull-rushed the engineers. Like a herd of buffalo, the frenzied commoners infiltrated their new space. Finishing touches to the super structure would simply have to take place around them.

CHAPTER 23

Tensions Boil Over

The newly added aquapod tower on the Severn River was now firmly in place, and it reached capacity quickly with the overflow of tenets from the existing mesh. It took days before amenities, such as electric and water, were functional. The new inhabitants were hot during the day, cold at night, and didn't have any means for self-hygiene.

And, under the extreme duress of not always knowing if their next delivery of rations would arrive on time, a fractured group-think mentality got the best of them. They questioned whether the surface-dwellers were making a sincere effort to accommodate the engineers who seemed delayed bringing the new living space up to code with electricity and water feeds. That became a source of strained relations with the commoners below.

Like any neighbors might, the two groups were bound to have disagreements, but at the end of the day, they needed to sustain their symbiotic relationship. Anything less was detrimental to the survival of the entire community . . . and the larger municipality. The surface-dwellers provided the upper level with an ample supply of seafood. The upper level returned the favor by ensuring enough sunlight reached through, to the waters below to fuel the growth of green plant life. For instance, algae oil had become an important source of biofuel for all species, while seaweed was a fundamental staple of nutrition. By all regards, the two groups worked diligently to respect the needs of each other.

Unfortunately, bliss didn't last forever under the rigors and stress of living on and above the water, and tempers eventually flared. That's when things came crashing down, in a most literal sense.

It all started when the inhabitants of the upper layer, without consulting the Hydronians below, began building a network of additional out-coves and bridges to negotiate the gaps that existed between pods. The extra construction was not part of the original scope of work for the additional barge, and that became a source of consternation.

The newly-built bridges were extensive and came at a high cost in manpower and raw materials. The upper-layer engineers had not anticipated the detrimental effects the bridges would have on the communities below them.

The extra construction was poorly planned in terms of how much sunlight would be blocked from the water's surface. The Hydronians were highly dependent on a steady dose of natural light to satisfy the daily environmental requirements. Without it, key elements of survival would be negatively impacted.

It only took a week for the waters to feel the effects of the new construction. As more bridges were established, the shade covering the waters increased. This initiated a chain reaction whereby aquatic plant life experienced reduced photosynthesis, and oxygen levels in the water decreased dramatically. An increased number of dead fish began to appear at the surface, as did gobs of dead algae and seaweed. The entire ecosystem had taken a big blow.

The surface-dwelling Hydronians found themselves in quite a predicament. Their primary food source, not to mention an essential food source for their neighbors above, was dwindling, and people would end up dying unless something changed. They summoned representatives from the upper layer community to the surface to address the situation.

Jaxx, a local municipality representative who lived high above, spoke on their behalf: "We do understand that our presence overhead has impacted your resources, Shakiya. We're here to work through this so that your people do not experience an unexpected hardship."

Shakiya, the leader of the surface-dwelling community responded in earnest, pleading her people's case. "That's right, Jaxx. It appears your community has overstepped its bounds. The extended physical infrastructure overhead was not built to code, and it has caused us a substantial loss in natural sunlight, and that is a disparity that our ecosystem cannot sustain."

"I see," said Jaxx. "Well, then we shall provide you with a ten percent increase in the bounty of our fruit and vegetable harvest to help reduce this burden. It will weigh on us greatly, but we're willing to do our part, Shakiya. That will supplement your losses and keep your people nourished."

"That's not enough, Jaxx," Shakiya responded. "The impact of the expansion of your superstructure will amount to significant losses of life for us if you continue to shade the river this way. We'll be forced to withhold a portion of what we're now providing to the Marsupans below ground and also what we're providing to your people. It isn't just us who will suffer from your indulgence, but all species are at risk."

Jaxx thought for a moment as he devised a rebuttal. "But my people cannot survive in lesser conditions above. We were at a breaking point. We needed to expand quickly. So we did and found some reprieve from severe overcrowding in our existing aquapods. But the electric and the water—they never came. And our daily sustenance was lower than we anticipated. So, we began assembling bridges to import rations from our friends up high, and out coves to generate more area for establishing fruit and vegetable growing crates. You understand, don't you, Shakiya?"

"I do," Shakiya assured him. "But your survival now comes at the expense of ours. I am sympathetic to your immediate needs, but I cannot let my people suffer and die as a result of your people taking your own liberties overhead."

"What are you asking us to do, Shakiya?" Jaxx asked her.

"Sever half of your bridges and drop them into the ocean immediately. This will restore enough daylight to adequately sustain life in these waters. That, in turn, will reinvigorate our primary source of sustenance and allow us to avoid a fatal imbalance. You may not realize it, Jaxx, but your build-out is threatening us all with mass death. I know it's not what you want to hear, but it's the only way."

Jaxx, unconvinced, let out a frustratingly anxious laugh and rebuked the suggestion. "*No*, it's not what I want to hear, Shakiya. I cannot destroy any of our bridges now, or many of my people will die. There must be something else we can do to ease this burden on you."

Shakiya was offended by Jaxx's less-than-kind sentiment and became more direct with him. "Eliminate the bridges, Jaxx, or we'll eliminate them ourselves. I cannot be any clearer than that. I'm sorry."

Jaxx adjusted his posture upright and employed a more imposing demeanor so as to convey his point more adamantly this time. "I will not! The bridges will stay! Don't bother asking my people to return unless you're willing to negotiate on other terms. Everyone, return to your quarters!" Jaxx signaled for his entourage to go.

Emotionally-charged sidebar conversations erupted from the upper-level inhabitants as they retreated into their elevator. Its steel cage doors slammed shut behind them, and the group headed skyward. Jaxx remained with Shakiya and her people. He could see the frustration building within them. He thought he might be able to win them over if he appeared alone and less threatening.

Shakiya immediately tried to calm her people, who were clearly irritated by the lack of cooperation of the upper inhabitants. "Everyone, *please*, hear me. Remain calm until our guest can rethink his stance on the matter. I have faith that he will see things our way." Shakiya turned to Jaxx and gave him one last chance to consider her request.

"You can see that my people are hurting. You can see the destruction and damage we've incurred. Now, I ask you once again, Jaxx, to listen to me and stand down your expansion efforts. Adjust your living quarters accordingly, and give us reprieve."

Jaxx knew he could not honor her request, and he searched for the right words to stall for a bit longer while he pondered the consequences of his stubbornness. "But, Shakiya, as I've already told you, your demands are not reasonable. The bridges shall remain intact. We can supplement your rations for a short time. Beyond that, I'm afraid you're on your own."

That was enough for Shakiya to realize that elimination of the new aquapod was necessary. Someone was going to have to die, and she didn't want it to be anyone in her community.

In a fury, she called her people to arms. "TAKE DOWN THE TOWER!" she cried out to them.

The surface-dwelling Hydronians didn't have easy access to the overhead bridges and out coves that Shakiya wanted to eliminate. They were too high, which made them easy for the upper layer to defend. However, the base of each aquapod terminated conveniently on its barge located at the surface of the water. That meant an entire aquapod structure was vulnerable to structural sabotage.

Sounds of jackhammers, drills, and saws immediately permeated the area, and a frenzy of determined Hydronians began to chip away at the bases of the legs of the newly erected aquapod. Shakiya's goal was to topple at least the newest structure, maybe more, before the upper community could mount an offensive of their own. Jaxx scurried to confront the commoners, begging them to stop, but they paid him no attention.

The sky-dwellers caught wind of what was going on down below, and they quickly devised a plan of their own. There was an inherent advantage to being located directly overhead of an advancing threat: gravity. As long as they had material possessions to dangle precariously over the rails of the aquapods and release, they might be able to counter the aggression and would likely maim or kill anyone in the way of falling debris.

They formed assembly lines and funneled to the ledges any items that could be utilized as vertical projectiles. Their intent was to pelt the humans below with so much debris that they would be forced to either retreat from the immediate area at the base of the aquapod or be crushed.

Almost instantly, a slew of material items went flying over the aquapod's perimeter rails. Some upper-level inhabitants even decided to jettison their personal goods, such as canteens, spoons, and tools. Those things were not designed for combat, of course, but they were good enough to clobber unsuspecting attackers down below.

Dropped from such heights, even a dull butter knife could gain enough speed and momentum to sever a hand from the arm of a victim. And a small gold ingot could become a bullet-like weapon, entering the skull of the enemy and lodging itself somewhere in their torso. Shots at the attackers below were imprecise, at best, but brutally effective when they hit their target.

Although the surface-dwelling Hydronians sustained some human losses from the implements raining down on them, they were able to weaken the supporting structure of the tower. As most skypods stood balanced on four curved support legs, taking out just one or two would easily be enough to cause it to topple.

Shakiya, ready to witness the tower's collapse, waved her walking cane to the sky and ordered everyone to clear the area in the open waters on the east side. That is where the tower would fall. That is, if they executed the demolition precisely and were able to control its angle of plummet.

They did, and just like a great sequoia tree might do once it's cut, the aquapod came falling down, crashing into the river. Its inhabitants leaped from the structure, but that was a futile attempt at saving themselves from the horrible crash. A rousing cheer erupted from the commoners below.

A huge splash and wave pushed out from the impact zone. The sheer power of the wave rocked the surrounding barges. A few unfortunate surface-dwellers were unable to flee the immediate area in time and became casualties themselves.

But the aquapod's inhabitants were the ones who paid the greatest price in this fight. They had nowhere to run and went down with the tower.

Jaxx stood there, terror etched on his face. He thought the towers were indestructible and would withstand much greater forces than a few angry neighbors. That was not the case, though, and more of his neighborhood's towers were in serious danger.

Shakiya pointed her cane directly at the next tower over as an indication that it would become the next victim of the fury of her community and shouted at Jaxx, "I gave you a chance! NOW, WE'RE TAKING CONTROL!"

The sounds of jackhammers, drills, and saws again ramped up, and the angry mob approached the support columns of the next aquapod. Just as they were about to reach the legs of the structure and begin demolition, a female Venom Society officer appeared and ran toward the chaos. It was Kamalei. She had rushed to the site of the conflict, having seen the events unfolding on camera feeds back at Venom Society Headquarters.

Kamalei immediately took charge of the situation. "Shakiya, call off your people! Let me speak with Jaxx."

Shakiya, after a short and intense glare at Kamalei, turned to her people and shouted, "Stop the destruction!" The ambient noise level fell to near silence as the banging and sawing came to an abrupt halt.

Kamalei laid out her orders: "*Good* citizens of the Severn, I implore you to come together in earnest to resolve your differences. Destroying one another is not going to make it better for any one of us. The imbalance of production that you create through the loss of life could have a catastrophic effect on all of us. You both know that you are completely dependent upon each other. Losses for *you*," looking at Jaxx, "and losses for *you*," turning and looking at Shakiya, "mean losses for everyone in this municipality. It could lead to years of continued death and disease and a slow painful recovery for all of us. A *wiser* decision would be for you to come together and negotiate resolve in the best interests of mankind. If we listen to and respect each other, we can minimize our collective losses. HEAR ME, my friends, and lay down your arms."

Shakiya and Jaxx steered their attention away from Kamalei and engaged in a stare-down. Each waited for the other to show the first sign of compliance, of weakness. Shakiya broke first. "Okay, we'll stand down. But you *know*, Jaxx, that we cannot allow your current infrastructure above us to remain intact, as it is now. You must help us!"

Jaxx sensed defeat and tapped into his humble side when answering Shakiya. "I know, Shakiya. I know. I will lose some of my people, as will you, but I will release enough bridges to allow for the waters here to flourish again. Please, just give me twenty-four hours to identify the areas where we can roll back and sustain the least negative impact. I'm sorry to have caused your people harm. Forgive me."

Shakiya peered at the surrounding waters and saw human bodies floating about. Some were her own close friends. A sad consequence of the dispute between the two communities. With an eerie silence in the air, everyone realized the magnitude of what had just happened.

The surface-dwellers laid down their tools of destruction and reverted to communal survival mode. They needed to clean up the dead before they began to decay and spread disease. The bodies would be introduced into the human body vacuum tubes for disposal. Normal operations for producing food and potable water would commence immediately.

Although there were some losses of life that day—and more would follow in the coming months before they could fully recover—it could have been much worse. Kamalei bid them farewell and walked away. She needed to make her way over to the infirmary to prepare the weekly stash for Zinnia.

CHAPTER 24

Secret Passageway: Security Leak

Jett had not been sleeping well at night after speaking to Ryker about what Zander stumbled upon while assisting the Venom Society with damage assessment of an underground tunnel in western Maryland. He needed to dig deeper. He had suspected for years that there was a dark backstory to the secret tunnels of the Venom Society. And after hearing from Ryker, he was determined to figure it out.

He devised a plan to prod a former acquaintance of his who was in a position of growing authority as a member of the Venom Society and, as a security guard, spent a lot of time patrolling the underground. A couple of years back, they worked together as gate guards for space launch operations at the Virginia Beach launch site and had become fond of each other.

Although officers in the Venom Society were forbidden to involve themselves with commoners on a romantic basis, the two of them did manage to discreetly share dinner and drinks on a couple of occasions. Some viewed their professional interactions as flirtatious and modestly inappropriate, but nothing adverse ever transpired.

Always an out-of-the-box thinker, Jett suspected that if he could reestablish close contact with her again, gaining her confidence, he might be able to use her as a "target" for inside information about the tunnels.

The target's name? Ivy Breez. Ivy, a budding Venom Society officer, was recently cleared to supervise the Venom Society's secure building construction and maintenance operations. As such, she received credentials to move freely into and out of heavily guarded areas.

Having provided security services to the Venom Society throughout his career, Jett was privy to the existence of the secret passageways, but he was never permitted to enter them. He had posed a few questions to some of the Venom Society elites during casual conversation, but he was smart and cautious enough not to risk being viewed as probing. And he never crossed any forbidden lines on his own volition by exploring areas, which were off-limits to him. He didn't want to end up like old Ginny. That's where he thought Ivy might be able to help out.

Jett and Ivy's social encounters never amounted to anything when they used to work together, but the two had lightly kept in touch over the web since that time. Ivy found him attractive and somewhat intriguing in his capacity as a high-profile commoner in the security business. And even more so now that he was a consultant to the Venom Society. So, it was quite natural for her to accept his invitation to meet with him again at the next public space launch, which was taking place in an aquapod grid along the coast of Virginia Beach.

Jett did not wish to make the trip alone, though, so on Ryker's recommendation, he asked Savanna WhiteEagle to accompany him. She agreed.

Savanna had a reputation as someone well-versed in the developmental history of the Earth and space. She has attained a strong standing in the scientific community for her notable written works, which documented relationships between ancient civilizations and modern-day space discovery. But she was interested in learning more about global underground development efforts. Ivy recognized and respected that.

The three arranged to meet up at a canteen located on the base level of aquapod Unit 3375, situated right next to the main boardwalk at the beach, the day before the next scheduled public space launch. Ivy was not particularly excited to learn that another woman would be there with Jett, possibly competing for his attention. But she couldn't resist her desire to reconnect with a commoner who had made such a stark, positive impression on her a couple of years ago. So, she rationalized Savanna's presence in her mind as purely in the capacity of assisting Jett with his continued studies in the space-science arena.

At first sight, Jett was impressed with Ivy's appearance. It took him quickly back to the time he first met her, when he felt attracted to her.

After settling the butterflies in his stomach, he approached Ivy and offered her a friendly embrace and introduced his friend, Savanna. Ivy intently, but silently, scrutinized Savanna's appearance from head to toe but smiled politely and shook her hand. Ivy noticed that Savanna did not have the fancy hair or voluptuous figure that she, herself, had—a minor relief to her. But Savanna was still a very attractive woman in a natural sort of way—mildly discomforting to Ivy.

The trio proceeded to make their way to a table inside the canteen where they could quench their thirst and begin catching up a bit.

Ivy led off by describing her role in security within the Venom Society organization and that she had to be very careful not to abandon the protocol established by her superiors by becoming too social with them. She made it clear that her time would be limited with them in public, and certain classified topics were not open for discussion. However, she would be glad to talk about the latest ventures in human expansion efforts, in general, unclassified terms.

Savanna felt slightly awkward having to interact with the Venom Society elite on those terms and didn't wish to dwell on that. Instead, she jumped right into highlighting a couple of her recent publications, which spoke volumes to her own professional accomplishments. She described her latest piece that documented the linkages between ancient hieroglyphs and symbolism from past civilizations and how they related to the configurations of the stars and planets—a piece that won her national acclaim. Ivy felt slightly intimidated by Savanna's success but maintained some measure of confidence in her ability to impress Jett.

Meanwhile, Jett was silently mulling over ideas for exploiting Ivy's knowledge of the Venom Society's secret passageways. "How can I relax this woman's guard a bit over the next day or so?" he thought to himself. He realized she may be a difficult nut to crack.

Jett broke his silence with the idea that the three cohorts move to a more private setting where they could exchange ideas without being overheard. The trio stood and walked out of the canteen, only slightly more comfortable around each other than when they walked in. They made their way across the boardwalk to the visitor's center, which was vacant except for the lone receptionist. There, the conversations continued.

Jett turned the topic to the reason he set this rendezvous in the first place. "So, Ivy, I've heard reports of unexplained hallways and doors that appear to mask a network of underground tunnels," he said. "The areas are always cordoned off and highly guarded, and commoners are discouraged from asking questions about them." Savanna nodded in agreement, indicating she had heard the same thing. "I must admit, I've been rather curious about what lies down below," Jett added. "I'm heavily involved in researching best practices in security, and I might benefit from learning more about the protocols that are in place to deter unwanted visitors from accessing the tunnels. Can you tell me about them?"

Ivy stuck a grin on her face as if she knew all about the tunnels. "Well, you're right, Jett," Ivy said. "They are quite heavily guarded. I'm part of the security force that's responsible for enforcing that. There are good reasons that the Venom Society wishes to keep those areas off-limits. But I should remind you, I cannot go into any details about that." Having privileged knowledge gave Ivy a feeling of meaning and power, and she hoped that might help her in her bid to win Jett's admiration.

Ivy shifted the focus back to Savanna to learn more about her and to duck any further probing questions from Jett. "How about you, Savanna? What sorts of things have been keeping you busy lately?"

Savanna thought for a moment and recalled that she'd been reporting on an incredible case that involved the remains of a dinosaur on Earth and a connection to dinosaur-like life on a distant planet, the remarkable similarities.

Ivy's eyebrows arched over the top rim of her dark glasses as if she were interested in hearing more about that. Savanna sensed she had struck a chord with Ivy, but also sensed that Ivy was slightly jealous that Jett held her in such high regard. Savanna resented that to some extent but knew she had to maintain a pleasant demeanor and continue to play into the hands of Ivy if she and Jett had any chance at getting her to talk about the secret passageways. Having piqued Ivy's interest, Savanna excused herself to go make a phone call.

With Savanna away from the table, Jett decided to play Ivy's jealous nature against her. He asked Ivy about her personal life to deliberately give her the impression that he might be interested in more from her than a straight professional relationship. Then he followed with another hard question about the contents of the secret tunnels.

Ivy immediately felt torn between trying to satisfy her ego of winning Jett over romantically and trying to keep the secrets she was sworn to protect on behalf of the Venom Society. She knew if she got caught leaking information, her Venom Society superiors would pull her aside, like they did Ginny, and have a little "chat" with her.

But Ivy found Jett so intriguing that she knew deep inside, she would give into him. With Savanna out of sight, Ivy seemed ready to talk, and Jett continued to press her.

"So, tell me, Ivy, what exactly *are* those mysterious passageways?" he asked.

"Well, *ahem* . . . you see," Ivy hesitated and then edged a bit closer to Jett, lowering her volume. "They are secret entranceways to a network of highly protected tunnels that only the Venom Society has access to. Only Venom Society elites and some essential engineers and mathematicians are authorized access to them."

"I see," Jett responded. "Well, what on earth do these tunnels lead to?"

Ivy giggled softly and responded, "Well, if I told you that, Jett, I'd have to—"

Jett quickly leaned into Ivy, making slight contact with her hair at the neckline, and sampled her perfume, cutting Ivy off in mid-sentence. Then he asked the question again, very emphatically. "*You* were saying?"

Savanna caught the tail end of the flirtation from across the room and kept her distance for a bit longer.

Ivy could hardly speak after the sudden, pleasant surprise, but she continued. "The passages and tunnels are all networked together, forming a fantastic underground grid. Some of the tunnels act as high-speed carriers of humans from municipality to municipality. Some lead to special deep-space launch sites. And still others lead to classified research labs. I really can't say more than that."

Jett, having gotten some of what he wanted, indicated to Savanna that he was making progress with a coy grin and a quick nonchalant wink as she returned to the table. Savanna got the hint that he had matters well in hand. She suggested that since it was getting late, the three retire for the evening and link up again the following afternoon a few hours before the public space launch. Ivy agreed.

Jett and Savanna made their way out of the visitor's center and into the busy streets of Virginia Beach. Jett conjured up his next move, which was to try to convince Ivy to give him access to one of the secret tunnel entranceways. A tall order, no doubt. But he had until tomorrow afternoon to figure out how to make it happen.

CHAPTER 25
Horrific Revelation

Ivy awoke in a cold sweat, breathing heavily. She tossed and turned throughout the night, knowing she had said too much to uncleared individuals. But she was too awestruck by Jett to care and wanted to meet with him again.

Ivy wasn't the only one looking forward to continuing their conversation, though. Excitement grew within Jett and Savanna as they entered a boardwalk pub just outside the entrance to the space launch facility. Ivy was already posted at a tall, round table, nursing a martini. She looked dashing in her long white slacks, a vest, and dark glasses.

After exchanging greetings, Savanna excused herself to head outside and over to a set of bleachers where she set up her camera and tripod to record the lift-off. Jett took the opportunity to catch up with Ivy one-on-one. Ivy was very receptive to the idea of having a few minutes alone with Jett and pulled the bar stool out and signaled for him to sit down.

Jet squeezed his large frame between the table and stool and eased into the seat. Realizing his attraction to Ivy was quite real, he thought to himself, "This woman . . . I'm really beginning to like her more and more."

"What?" asked Ivy.

Having accidentally mumbled something audible, Jett snapped out of his self-talk and right into a discussion with Ivy. "Sorry, I was just thinking to myself. Hey, listen, I'd like to talk more about what we discussed yesterday."

"That's fine," Ivy assured him, which was encouraging to Jett.

"Oh, but . . . I wouldn't want to waste too much of your time here, together, if you have no intentions of . . . well, you know, helping me out with my research," Jett said, dropping a hint that he was ready to delve into some pressing matters.

Ivy sat back in her chair and contemplated but for only a second, then she blurted out, "Try me."

This was Jett's cue that it was safe to press for more information about the tunnels. He moved Ivy's drink aside so that nothing separated the two of them. Then, he took on a serious tone and fired some difficult questions at Ivy. "Look, it would really help me better serve the Venom Society as a ranking security guard if I could just take a little peek inside the entryway to the underground tunnels. I don't need a detailed tour, just a quick look at the design and architecture. I know you're troubled by the idea of allowing a commoner to access the tunnels, but I assure you, my intentions are genuine."

Ivy, without saying a word, touched the end of Jett's nose with her pointer finger and grinned ear-to-ear as if she were thinking "Nice try, big boy, but I can't go there." Ivy assumed this request was coming, but even so, she could feel her heart pounding as she pondered how she had allowed herself to get into this uncomfortable situation. But the whole thing was just too exciting to walk away from.

Ivy broke. She decided to give Jett what he wanted. "Well, you know I could get into a lot of trouble with the grandmaster for even considering your proposition," Ivy reminded him. "However, I'm impressed with your resume. You're quite determined, and I respect that. If you promise not to say a word to anyone, I'll see to it that you have a brief look inside."

Jett gave the Venom Society officer a reassuring nod and struggled not to outwardly display his delight.

Ivy wrote down the access code to the cipher lock of a hidden passageway located just down the street and handed it to Jett. He reciprocated with a lengthy and comforting embrace before the two of them exited the pub and joined Savanna in the bleachers.

A thirty-minute countdown appeared on the large screen off to the right of the launch pad. Savanna, Ivy, and Jett took their seats among the spectators and carried on a light conversation for a few minutes. Ivy's pager rang, and she motioned to the others that she needed to answer it. Jett told Ivy that he and Savanna would be happy to give her some time to respond.

Then, Jett turned to his friend and said, "Savanna, why don't you and I go for a stroll and do some sightseeing while we're waiting for the ship to launch. I understand the local landscape here is—well, rather intriguing, and I'd like to explore a bit while we have a few minutes."

"That sounds wonderful," Savanna responded, acknowledging the hint from Jett's facial expression that he had other ideas in mind.

Ivy was still unsure of her decision to give into Jett, but with an adrenaline rush, she renewed her drive to win Jett over and quietly offered her wish for them to enjoy their venture around the complex.

A short two-minute walk from the aquapod, down the boardwalk, had Jett and Savanna staring at an unsightly and seemingly abandoned alleyway, one littered with trash, vagrants, shopping carts, cardboard boxes, and most certainly, a few happy rodents. The nook was no place that anyone would want to wander into for any good reason. That was no deterrent for the duo now, though, and they stepped over limp bodies and rubbish until they reached a door at the back of the alley, hidden by a cluster of spider webs. It was exactly as Ivy described it to Jett in the pub just a short while ago.

Jett located the cipher lock and keyed in the series of numbers that Ivy had given him. The rickety, dirty, but oddly high-tech door unlatched, released and swung open. "Pretty good," Jett thought to himself, raising his eyebrows and peering over at Savanna. The two then snuck inside, and Jett pulled the door closed. It sealed tightly behind them with a heavy clamor.

They got an eerie sense that the place was equipped with advanced technology, even though it appeared dark, dirty, and inhospitable. A set of spiral stairs led downward into the tunnel system that drew them there. Jett took Savanna by the hand and led her down the stairs and around the corner and saw that the tunnel opened up to a large chasm—an underground colosseum of sorts. They made their way quietly to the end of the tunnel and peeped around the edge of the wall. What they saw next was stunning.

It was a large network of highly advanced computers and other heavily guarded equipment. A team of scientists worked, evidently preparing for a high-profile event, but it was unclear exactly what that could be.

"Over there," Savanna muttered softly. She tapped Jett on the shoulder, indicating he should look over to his right. There sat the most incredible spaceship that they had ever seen. A deep-space travel craft, huge in size and diamond-shaped. It was already in hover mode, not resting on the ground or on any sort of launch base. But oddly, they heard no sound nor noticed any air disturbance.

"How can that be," Jett thought to himself?

In order not to draw any attention to themselves, Jett and Savanna contained their fascination enough to create the appearance they were part of the team of scientists. They were of the mind they must pretend to belong in the tunnels, so they acted comfortable, sure of their movements and actions. Once they had taken on this professional demeanor, they chose a tunnel to begin exploring.

The complexity of the web of secret tunnels became evident to them as they navigated a dimly lit corridor. They came upon a section that was roped off but unguarded. "The capsules," Jett exclaimed. "*Just* like they have at the Expulsions."

They were about the size of a fifty-gallon drum, egg-shaped, and just large enough for one person to hunker down in for a solo ride. Each capsule appeared to operate via collider technology. Jett was vaguely familiar with that since he had been hired by the Venom Society to guard collider facilities in the past.

"I wonder if this is a drop-off point for Expulsion winners," Jett said, rhetorically. "This must be how they get around from municipality to municipality," he added. "Ivy told me about these things. Come on, let's go!"

Jett grabbed Savanna's arm, and they ducked under the rope. He wanted to go for a ride. Savanna was reluctant, but she wasn't going to be left behind by herself. They each got into a personal capsule and agreed to engage the exact same sequence of buttons on the dashboard to select a preprogrammed destination, so they would not get separated.

As they strapped themselves into the seats, the top-lift doors closed automatically over them.

Soon, the mini colliders kicked in and in a fraction of a second, the small capsules were transported to a location somewhere in the western portion of Maryland. "Boy, if we only knew about these cool real-time travel capsules before our trip to visit Ivy," Jett thought to himself, giggling under his breath and shaking his head in amazement.

The doors to the capsules lifted high overhead, allowing them to hop out. Immediately, they heard shrieking noises coming from a tunnel just off to their left. Savanna turned to jump back into her capsule, but Jett grabbed her and insisted she stay put. Jett recalled that Ryker had told him about distant cries, which Zander described in the same basic location that Jett found himself standing with Savanna.

"Wait right here; I'm going to see what that is," Jett told Savanna.

"But you could get hurt—or killed! I'm scared!" Savanna replied.

"It'll be okay," Jett assured her. "I've got to see what's going on down there. We may never get another chance to enter these tunnels. Wait for me right here, and we'll return to the launch site shortly. Trust me, Savanna."

Jett walked off into the tunnel from which the cries seemed to resonate. He followed the sound until he was able to pinpoint the source. He spied a door with a sign posted overhead: "Keep Out, Unauthorized Personnel Strictly Prohibited." With no one in sight, Jett seized the opportunity to enter.

He switched the light on and quickly determined he had entered a laboratory. To his immediate right, there was an assortment of test tubes with some sort of fleshy blobs in them. They were under a specially designed light—something that might be used to grow and cultivate vegetation.

With a glance to the opposite wall, he saw a number of tables lined up in neat rows. Each table was equipped with a rack of tools, which appeared to be surgical in nature. But this was unlike your traditional hospital arrangement of implements. They seemed more experimental in nature. This struck him as odd.

Jett noticed a large glass cubicle just ahead with a door sign, which read: "Biological Materials: Facial Covering and Uniform Required." Jett didn't take the time to grab scrubs as the sign suggested; he just rushed right in. The light in the cubicle popped on automatically as the motion sensor detected his presence.

"Oh my," he sighed under his breath as he took in the sights around the enclosure.

Lining the walls and filling most of the square footage of the cubicle were racks of shelves, each full of large jars that appeared to contain human body parts.

Adjacent to them were other, even larger aquariums occupying a different array of shelves. In them appeared to be some sort of actual living beings, unlike anything he'd ever seen before. He cautiously approached them to have a closer look. There was something lurking inside one of the glass cages that appeared to be human appendages attached—or growing from—a center torso of some sort. Jett jumped back, becoming erect.

He realized his jaw had physically dropped, and he pulled it back into normal position. He had to remain calm. If he lost his composure and attracted attention to the room, as an uninvited intruder, he and Savanna would surely die right there on the spot.

"Savanna," he thought to himself. "I've got to get back to the capsules and get us out of here." He turned to go but noticed some oversized jars to the right of the lab's exit. As he got closer, he recognized their contents. Human heads! But they were not simply shriveled and discolored, like ones that might have been housed in a museum of natural history centuries ago. These heads bore animated expressions and seemed full of life. Their eyes were open; they appeared to have an awareness, or consciousness, about them. Some of them were growing appendages from the bottom of their necklines. Jett realized the gravity of the situation.

The Venom Society was experimenting with humans in ways that were completely unethical, even if the Earth and its population were at extreme risk of extinction. And even more shocking—they were the heads of many former Expulsion winners. "What has the Venom Society done with them?" Jett asked himself out loud. Some were obviously transported to this location for use in biological experimentation. "This was their reward for coming out on top?" he thought to himself, becoming frightened.

Jett scampered toward the exit but stumbled and tripped over the leg of one of the shelving units, sending it crashing to the floor. Several of the aquariums did not survive the crash, the glass shattering into hundreds of pieces. Human heads rolled across the floor, now free from their containers of liquid preservative.

Horrified, Jett recovered from his tumble and dashed out the door. Peering back into the room, he saw the fleshy beings flailing around on the floor and was momentarily paralyzed. "Oh, my . . . what have they done?" Jett whispered to himself.

Before the liquid puddle on the floor could reach his feet, he charged into a full sprint back toward the collider cars.

He wasn't sure he should let Savanna know about what he had just witnessed. He didn't want Savanna to come unglued and ruin their chances of getting out of there undetected. Savanna sensed he was upset and started asking a bunch of random questions without giving him time to answer any of them.

"*Listen*," he exclaimed as he grabbed Savanna's shoulders and brought her close to him, quite literally face to face. "I'll explain everything later, but we must go quickly!"

It had been twenty minutes since they had left the launch pad, and they didn't want to give Ivy any reason to begin wondering what they were up to—or give her any reason to confess her misgivings to the grandmaster.

Jett and Savanna hopped back into their collider capsules and commanded them on a course back to the aquapod in Virginia Beach. It would only take a second to get back there.

The public space launch was about to get underway. They hopped out of their capsules and briskly made their way toward the exit, being careful not to stroll too close to anyone who might question who they were. A short walk to the mysterious doorway and a double-tap on a touch-screen's "Open Door" button had them right back in the midst of the dreary alley scene.

Ivy stood at the end of the building, leaning on the wall, seemingly unhappy with the amount of time the two were inside the tunnels. She knew darned well that Jett took Savanna deeper into the tunnels than he said they would, and Ivy warned him not to do that. Still, in the comfort of the plan to strengthen her personal rapport with the man she truly admired, she said very little about the matter.

CHAPTER 26

Asteroid Rocks Aquapods

While aquapod engineers were developing new dwellings to allow man to continue to exist on the surface of the water, there was a troubling threat looming overhead—way overhead. It would eventually spell disaster. Venom Society astronomers at the Galileo Center for Space Exploration were planning asteroid-chase operations aimed at evaluating a cluster of stray asteroids, which had been identified as an imminent threat to the northern hemisphere of planet Earth.

The crew of Proximity was tapped for the assignment since they were already in deep space searching for additional habitable land and useable resources.

Just hours after receiving messages from Captain Pennington about the dinosaur planet and floating jelly life forms, Chief Zeller made the hard decision to request assistance from Proximity for the purpose of observing the asteroids in question. He made a call right back to the ship to explain to the captain that he needed the crew to delay their next planetary visit and divert course to the location of the asteroids, putting them in harm's way, despite their unsettling recent encounters. Zeller instructed Pennington to find the asteroids and position themselves to make a determination about the likelihood of their affecting

Earth. Zeller ordered the captain to call him back immediately once he had a plan in place.

The captain obliged, and DAISIE was right on top of things. In just a couple of minutes, Proximity was able to transport to the asteroid belt, located in Earth's solar system between the orbits of Mars and Jupiter. With the ship's distance observation telescope and DAISIE's keen sense of direction, they were able to capture a visual of the cluster of asteroids at the precise coordinates Zeller gave them. From their current vantage point, the crew would be able to accurately assess the speed, size, number, and trajectory of the asteroids in question.

Captain Pennington returned Zeller's call as ordered: "Galileo, come in Galileo. Do you read me? Over."

"Affirmative, Captain; we receive. Over." Zeller responded.

The captain gave Zeller an initial assessment of how he planned to proceed. "Copy that, Galileo. Just a quick check to test our communications channels and to let you know that we have a visual on the asteroids in question. Soon they will be passing by our location . . . well, within 1000 miles of Proximity. We'll be able to make an initial assessment of the path the asteroids are on and transmit the results to you promptly. Here's hoping that we can report to you some very good news. Over."

Zeller was satisfied with that and closed out the conversation with, "Roger, Captain. We await some *good* news. All systems are a go on our end. We will hold this frequency open and dedicate it to your transmissions only. Over."

Soon, the cluster of asteroids became menacingly clearer within the optics of the ship's powerful telescope, heading in the direction of the spaceship. This made the crew uneasy. However, DAISIE assured everyone that none of her calculations indicated that Proximity was at risk. Nonetheless, instrumentation sat at the ready.

The crew caught their first glimpse of some tiny flares, small yet easily visible to the eye. They were nothing more than space dust, which surrounded the truly larger and more ominous structures yet to come. These little racers posed no threat to Earth because by the time they pressed through Earth's atmosphere, there would be almost nothing left of them. They'd burn up and become harmless little embers. However, lurking right behind them were larger and potentially destructive asteroids.

Before the crew could settle snugly back into their seats after viewing the space dust, Skip called the captain over to the telescope. "Sir, come quickly; take a look. Do you see the line beginning to form on the lower left?"

The captain responded, "Of course, what do you suppose that is?"

"That's *them*," Skip said. "And according to DAISIE's calculations, they will be passing right alongside us in about ninety seconds."

The captain immediately called out over the loudspeaker: "Be prepared to make a comprehensive assessment of our first asteroid fly-by. Our friends back on Earth are depending on us. Please remain calm and stay focused. Let's hope these things prove harmless."

The crew scrambled to their posts and prepared for observation and recording.

ZOOM!

The first asteroid came and went. Everyone was busily working to adjust the cameras and recording equipment. DAISIE went into full compute mode, and her silence turned into a myriad of flashing lights and beeping sounds. It was her job to discover the exact trajectory of the fireballs, and she was preparing her initial report for Pennington.

"Captain, you can relax for a bit. The first three sizable asteroids are of absolutely no threat to the people back home. They will be racing by Earth at a speed of 54,000 miles per hour. They will be 20,000 miles overhead. I can assure you they will not make contact with Earth. Nor will there be any major effect on electromagnetic fields, gravitation, or the atmosphere. They might actually make for a good conversation piece for the people if the skies are clear."

The captain calmly responded to her, "Well, that certainly *is* good news, DAISIE. Galileo will be glad to receive your report. Keep up the good work."

The crew continued to monitor a flurry of asteroid activity for the next hour, all showing positive results—for Earth. The instrumentation gave them exactly what they needed to make a thorough assessment. And DAISIE continued to interpret the data into terms the crew and those at Galileo could understand.

Unfortunately, just before the observation ended, DAISIE recognized several asteroids coming into view of the telescope on a slightly different vector.

As a super-computing android, DAISIE seldom felt or displayed humanistic emotions, but she soon realized this formation of asteroids was problematic. A couple of small chunks were on course to enter Earth's upper atmosphere and burn away to nothing, but one was medium-sized and on a direct collision course for the planet. She quickly summoned the captain.

"Yes, DAISIE, what is it?" the captain asked.

DAISIE was frank with him. "Well, sir, I'm afraid to look closer at the next small pocket of asteroids. Their trajectory is not currently favorable. During my observations this evening, I have identified a certain 'critical area' in the optic. Asteroids traveling through this area would most definitely pose a threat to Earth. So far, nothing has even come close. However, the next cluster of activity is worrisome."

DAISIE spoke almost as if she lacked confidence in herself or was hesitant to tell the captain something.

Pennington sensed that and assured DAISIE that she needed to give him every detail available, even if the news was not so good. "Well, I understand this is unsettling, DAISIE. It's not easy for any of us, and you are at the forefront of it all. But understand, it is your assessment that could lead to forewarning our friends that a major event might be imminent. If you feel that your calculations indicate that Earth is in danger, you must report that to me . . . and to Galileo. They need to know right away if an asteroid strike becomes a reality."

DAISIE responded, almost instantly, "That's just it, sir, I already know it's a reality. I just didn't know how to tell you."

The captain froze, a blank stare plastered on his face. He hoped that DAISIE had miscalculated something and that she would correct herself and come back with a more favorable prognosis. And so, he quietly asked the question: "So . . . it's true? This one is heading right for them?"

"I'm afraid so, Captain," DAISIE confirmed. "One asteroid, twenty-five meters in diameter, is on course to strike Earth. My computations have it impacting the south Arctic Ocean, in the Beaufort Sea, directly north of central Alaska."

Captain Pennington asked DAISIE to verify her calculations and communicate them in human-friendly terms, to include its exact trajectory, estimated mass, speed, day and time of entry into Earth's atmosphere, and most importantly, the approximate coordinates of its predicted impact point. He began to generate a warning message to send back to Earth.

Ten minutes later, a message from Proximity was received at Venom Society deep space launch site in Staziak, Alaska. The message read:

"This is the crew of deep space mission PROXIMITY. This message requires your immediate attention. DAISIE has confirmed that there is an asteroid traveling near our position, which is on a direct course for Earth. We regret to report that Earth is destined to sustain an asteroid strike approximately forty-eight hours from the time you receive this message. There are four asteroids in question. Three have been deemed likely too small to survive the flight through Earth's atmosphere and are expected to dissipate through frictional burnout before impact. However, there is one that is twenty-five meters in diameter and an imminent threat. DAISIE has calculated that the speed and trajectory of this asteroid have it entering Earth's atmosphere and impacting the southern sector of the Arctic Ocean, in the Beaufort Sea. It is likely to impact an area of little development where only a small number of aqua skypods have been erected. Therefore, catastrophic damage due to immediate impact is expected to be minimal to moderate. However, an event of this magnitude will pose disastrous after-effects in the form of atmospheric-born water particles and massive tidal waves in multiple directions. Authorities must brace all ocean skypods for oceanic swells. Wherever possible, all humans should move well inland from the ocean's shores. We will forward more exact impact coordinates to you once we have them. God bless—End of Message—"

With this news, astronomers began a frantic stir to sound the sirens for emergency evacuation of the Beaufort Sea Municipality. This would entail the movement of a multitude of human colonies away from the predicted impact location. Because of the massive overcrowding on Earth, there was very little lateral mobility for humans, so movements would have to be smooth, calm, and deliberate.

There was little time to gather belongings or ration food supplies. Any lack of sustenance would largely have to be dealt with after the fact. In and around the impact area, rescue crews were activated. Forty-eight hours was not a lot of time to move the commoners.

At this point, authorities fully expected that the population would sustain casualties, but human instinct drove them to try to save as many lives as possible. For centuries, mankind had fought a laborious battle for survival due to the physical limitations of space and provisions on planet Earth. This next fight for survival, however, would be a very different one.

Preparations were in place, as much as they could be on such short notice. The human population surrounding the predicted impact area had dispersed as best they could, given the crowded conditions. Land-dwellers mustered together into all available spaces far inland to make room for the Hydronian exodus.

An air of quiet panic set in when the forty-eight-hour warning came and went with no asteroid in sight. Hunkered down as tightly and securely as possible, the masses awaited word of the impending impact. And heading into the forty-ninth hour, the terror began.

A cry rang out over the mass notification system for everyone to ready themselves for impact. Within seconds, the speeding planetoid entered Earth's lower atmosphere. The sky lit up with a fiery streak. But only for a second. A still silence was interrupted by a chilling shriek and a bone-crushing sonic boom. An unavoidable, massive crash followed. Disaster had struck.

The asteroid hit precisely where DAISIE had predicted and an enormous swell of seawater encircled the point of impact, marking the beginning of tidal wave activity. Dead center in the destruction zone, a secondary swell leaped skyward, reaching a quarter mile into the air. Six aquapods near the impact were obliterated, destroyed within seconds. Then, a secondary array of twelve aquapods disappeared under the rolling super wave. The occupants had nowhere to run. Although adept to the influences of seawater, most did not survive.

Within minutes of impact, the huge swells made landfall. Humans not fortunate enough to have found space inside skypods further inland became the first victims. A few of the older, weaker skypods succumbed to the forces and were toppled. Others showed impressive structural integrity. They leaned with the momentum of the initial push, but they did not give way. Terrified occupants clung desperately to the steel bars of the massive structures, some dangling precariously above the surge. Some slipped and fell and were swept away. With Earth's massive overcrowding, human casualties were unavoidable. There were simply too few places to run and hide.

CHAPTER 27
Heart to Heart

It was getting close to bedtime for Dalton, and Zinnia had just given him the last protein bar that Kamalei provided them last week. This week's stash from Kamalei was likely ready for her to pick up, so Zinnia tucked Dalton into bed and dashed out of the orphanage to retrieve it.

Zinnia liked to wait until after dark to go because that provided good cover. She made her way down the street and around to the spooky side door of the infirmary. She held the electronic fob close to the cipher lock, and its small screen lit up with the familiar prompt for a password.

Zinnia keyed in the combination, and the door cracked open. As usual, she began to tip-toe her way over to the supply closet where she normally found the stash, but the profile of a shadowy figure stopped her in her tracks. Someone was there, leaning against the wall.

The ambient light of a nearby window cast the shadow of a tall, slender body onto the floor. Zinnia was terrified. She couldn't move.

Then, the figure separated from the wall and strode toward Zinnia. Her heart started beating heavily. As the figure entered into the open walkway where the light shone brighter, Zinnia saw their face. It was Kamalei.

"Oh, Ms. Kamalei! You frightened me," Zinnia said. "But I'm glad it's you. I just fed Dalton our last protein bar, and I came to see if you had provided us with more."

"*Good* to see you, Zinnia," Kamalei responded. "Of course," she continued, "your rations for the week are right over there," she said, casting her right arm in the direction of the closet. "You'll be pleased to notice that I've added a wholesome share of fruit to your stash this week. And, actually, I decided to wait for you to arrive because I have something that I want to say to you."

"Oh, gosh, Ms. Kamalei," Zinnia responded. "I don't know quite how to thank you for your generosity and guidance. You know, with feeding us extra and helping me reduce my violation count and—well . . . I don't know what you did to ensure that I was not selected for the last Expulsion, but . . . I'll never be able to repay you."

"*You* don't have to thank *me*, Zinnia," Kamalei assured her. "In fact, I came here tonight to thank *you*." Kamalei took a few more steps toward Zinnia. She wanted to make sure Zinnia could see and appreciate the sincerity in her facial expressions. "I've learned something from you, Zinnia. A life lesson, if you will. Things I never previously valued as a Venom Society officer. Your determination, your perseverance, your dedication, and your *love* for others. I admire that. You're an amazing human, Zinnia."

Kamalei took a final step toward Zinnia and continued, "I've come to realize that your compassion for life and your goodwill are contagious. As a ranking officer in the most powerful organization in the world, charged with eliminating individuals who no longer serve the community well, I'm not trained to embrace those qualities. But you've enlightened me, dear girl."

Zinnia didn't quite know how to respond to all of that and was clearly humbled by the sentiment of the Venom Society elite. "Well, thank you very kindly, ma'am. And Xion, if he were here, I know he would thank you, too."

"About Xion," Kamalei continued. "I am sorry for your loss. I wanted to assure you that his death would not have been avoided with a second dose of the antivenom. I knew from the minute I saw him that his prognosis was grim. His condition had already deteriorated beyond saving him. I just didn't know how to tell you. Giving him a few extra weeks to be with you was about all I could do for him. You understand, don't you?"

Zinnia let her head drop and didn't say a word but nodded in agreement. The two shared a moment, both remembering the little boy. Then, Zinnia sobbed heavily. Kamalei held her composure but did feel a tear or two welling up in the corner of her eyes.

Then, Zinnia looked up at the tall, beautiful woman and asked her something that had been eating at her for weeks, "Ms. Kamalei, I know what happened to Ms. Ginny. You didn't help her like you helped me. Why?"

Kamalei thought for a second and responded, "I suspect you don't quite know what to make of me, do you, Zinnia? I'm afraid sometimes I'm not sure what to make of myself. I'm sworn to uphold the objectives and desires of the grandmaster. Anything less, and I, myself, might be the next victim. But sometimes, people aren't always on the inside who they appear to be on the outside. Let's just say, I'm learning a lot about life, Zinnia. Just like you are."

Kamalei asked Zinnia to grab her stash from the supply closet and encouraged her to get back to the orphanage to check on Dalton. She wanted to make sure that Zinnia got out of the infirmary unnoticed. Zinnia sneakily exited the door, turned to Kamalei, thanked her, and offered her the traditional show of respect: "Thanks be to the Venom Society!"

CHAPTER 28

Found Alive

The crew of Proximity felt helpless and saddened about the asteroid strike. They knew many lives were lost, but there was nothing they could do about it. DAISIE maneuvered the ship to a safe location where they could calm themselves. Captain Pennington wanted to allow his crew to destress and reenergize before their next jump.

After a short time, Captain Pennington knew he had to rally his team and keep them focused. They had a clear mission to sustain. They ploddingly regrouped and shifted their attention to their next planetary target.

The captain sat busily recording his own notes about what had just happened. As much as he could with a shaky hand, at least. The crew hadn't prepared themselves for all of the events of the last couple weeks. In retrospect, though, there probably wasn't any way to even do so.

DAISIE ran the control room equipment through the standard test sequencing. She wanted to recalibrate the communications command center before the next jump. She sprayed out a series of transmissions—short bursts of electromagnetic energy designed to confirm that the transmitter and receiver were in good working order. What DAISIE chirped out into space, the crew had heard a hundred times before. What they heard in return was completely unexpected.

"Hellllp meeeeeee," came a weak, rusty voice in English. The captain and Skip both heard it. Proximity had not left the Milky Way, so it was possible that this was a voice transmission from Earth, bleeding into outer space.

Now distracted from his notebook, the captain looked up, and his eyes immediately engaged the android as he called out, "*Stay* on that frequency, DAISIE." He then slid his bucket seat into a position much closer to DAISIE. "Spray another test message, please," he asked her. "Same frequency." DAISIE complied without even responding to the captain.

Almost instantly, they got a second return, "Hello, hello—I hear you! Can you hear me? Help us. PLEASE HELP US!"

The captain leaped to his feet, astounded. His notebook and pen hit the floor. "That's Banes!" he shouted. "THAT'S BANES! OH, MY HEAVENS! IT'S BANES!"

CHAPTER 29

The Rescue

As the crew of Proximity tried to fathom what they'd just heard, DAISIE was smothered by the captain who was immediately focused on establishing a communications link with the voice he believed belonged to Captain Byron Banes. The captain ordered DAISIE to track the strength, direction, and distance of the transmission. She busily blinked and beeped as she worked to isolate the properties of the signal. Finally, she was able to identify the carrier frequency, and she attempted to establish an asynchronous communication.

If the captain was right, and it was Banes, that would confirm that at least someone from space exploration ship Curiosity survived their ill-fated mission. If so, the next question would be, can they be saved?

In short order, DAISIE delivered. She informed the captain that she believed she had successfully established a connection. Pennington called out over the link, "COME IN! Anyone. come in. This is deep space mission Proximity. Is anyone there? Over."

He got a return. "Hello? Hellooo?" said a fading voice.

Captain Pennington pepped up loud and clear, "YES. YES. We're here. HELLO! BANES, is that *you*?"

In a raspy, withering voice, another return came through. "Oh, Pennington—thank goodness, it's you."

Bursting out in euphoric laughter, Captain Pennington shouted: "BANES! I KNEW IT WAS YOU! OH MY GOSH. . . Banes, *don't* worry—we're here . . . we have a track on your location, and . . . we're coming to *get you*, my friend!"

He turned toward DAISIE for at least some assurance that she believed she could safely guide Proximity to the location of the lost ship. DAISIE gave the captain an android nod, which was essentially an upper half-body tilt, letting him know she had the exact coordinates of the lost crew.

Captain Pennington ordered that everyone strap in and remain silent and still so that DAISIE and the Lieutenant could initiate a collider space-time jump. The crew of Curiosity had been missing for weeks, and time was of the essence.

In a flash, Proximity was transported to a location within a few nautical miles of the lost ship. The exterior body of the ship was clean and didn't show signs of stress or structural damage. Curiosity appeared to be essentially intact but was floating around like a lame duck. Obviously, the ship had no power, and there was nothing around it but the freezing darkness of space. Captain Pennington feared the inside could be critically cold, to the point where even the crew's thick puffy suits would no longer provide adequate warmth for survival.

Docking with Curiosity and creating an unobstructed throughway from the gut of one ship to the gut of the other would be fairly straightforward because the new line of space travel vessels was equipped with a standard connector tube assembly designed for multiple units to lock ends seamlessly, albeit with a bit of skillful pre-positioning. Even so, the crew needed to approach the coupling carefully by establishing the proper distance and orientation. That would take a little time.

DAISIE and Skip drew upon their expertise and experience, and as a team, they maneuvered Proximity into the perfect position. Captain

Pennington called to Curiosity and warned them of the approach. He received only a short, belabored reply from Captain Banes, "We're here, Captain. Help us."

This was cause for concern to Pennington, who was hoping for a more enthusiastic reception. The crew now feared what they might find inside the vessel, but they pressed on.

The two ships came to within inches of one another, and their connector tubes began to press together. Max deployed the stabilizer clamps to hold them in place, and the process of securing and sealing the entryway was complete.

As the two ships coupled, an eerie silence fell over the crew of Proximity. Not because they were despondent in their thoughts, but because they were still in shock that their comrades, once thought to be lost forever, were just a couple of titanium panel doors away from reuniting with them.

The screech of sticky door hinges breached the silence abruptly as the connecting tube doors slowly opened. The captain's mouth hung open as he wondered what the scene would look like onboard Curiosity. His heartbeat was detectable through his thick spacesuit. Trying to reconcile mixed emotions of both fear and excitement rendered him speechless. But then, it all kicked in again—his years of training and a good rush of adrenaline.

And there they were, strewn across the ship's cabin, four listless bodies. Thus, began a hurried investigation by the crew of Proximity to determine exactly what condition their colleagues were in. After an initial emotional greeting with Captain Banes, they noticed that he was the only crewmember moving or speaking. He appeared very thin and weak.

Chaz Knightly was curled up on the floor over by the ship's command center. Skip rushed to his side, but when he went to turn him over to check his condition, rigor mortis had already set in. There was no saving him.

Harris Tungsten and Katrina Strange were also lost. Their bodies were never reassembled correctly by the collider. The scene was much worse than the crew of Proximity had expected.

Dr. Moss, Kassie, and Max dragged the bodies of the three dead astronauts across the connector tunnel into the belly of Proximity and stowed them in the dry ice chamber to prevent decomposition.

Captain Pennington knelt beside Banes to assess his condition. Banes fell in and out of consciousness.

CHAPTER 30

Ultimate Secrets Exposed

Realizing that Captain Banes was nearer to death than he originally thought, Captain Pennington wanted to squeeze what he could out of him regarding their ill-fated excursion. He propped Banes's head up with his backpack, offered him a drink of water, and began a conversation with him right there on the cabin floor of Curiosity.

Banes responded with every bit of strength he had left in him. He indicated that the Venom Society had ulterior motives. He said that his crew found life on a planet located 4.37 light-years away from Earth, a fact the Venom Society has known about but has not divulged.

He was referencing Alpha Centauri, the nearest solar system to Earth's solar system. Banes told that captain how his crew, on their own accord, identified a planet that might be a viable option for human life. This was, of course, exactly what the crew had set out to do. What they found there, though, would change the course of their lives forever.

Banes explained, "We took position in a hover over the surface of the planet, when a living colony of beings came into view. We couldn't believe what we were seeing. They were real aliens, Pennington—real, live, aliens. But not the kind you're thinking about. No, these were people—humans—just like us, Pennington. Just like us!"

Then, Banes lost consciousness for a few seconds, and his head fell to the side. That scared Captain Pennington. He poured water on Banes's forehead and shook him to see if he could bring him back around. It worked.

With his energy dwindling, Banes went on to explain to Captain Pennington that they were able to identify some of the subjects as past Expulsion winners.

"WHAT?" Are you sure? How is that possible?" Captain Pennington asked Banes.

"We asked ourselves the same question," Banes said, "and we had to find out for ourselves." Banes went on to describe how he felt comfortable setting the ship down in a nearby clearing. The crew sat quietly and observed the humans for a few minutes. Then, feeling comfortable that the humans were not showing signs of aggression or disease, Banes exited Curiosity and approached them. "They appeared to be in good health but were agitated and desperate in their communications and actions. I asked them how it could be that they were there, standing before us. They explained everything to me."

Captain Pennington offered Captain Banes another drink of water. "Go on," he urged.

Banes took a deep breath and painted a grim picture for Captain Pennington. Their leader was a man named Leyton. He was a dominant Expulsion winner from several months back. He explained to Captain Banes that Expulsion winners were exploited by the Venom Society for nefarious reasons. Some were whisked away to secret underground laboratories. Some were transported to the distant planet, along with a thirty-day supply of food and water.

Banes was losing strength and deteriorating rapidly. The crew of Proximity was unsure of just how much longer they could sustain him. But as he lay there taking quick, shallow breaths, he was still coherent enough to provide more details.

The planet was littered with an alien plant called the Venus Giganta, the species from which the Venom Society extracted acitaneum. That was man's answer to killing zaraseptosis, the single worst disease threat to mankind. The undesirables were charged with harvesting as much acitaneum poison extract as possible, processing it into medicinal form, bottling the derivative, and preparing it for transport back to Earth. If they survived the harsh conditions of the planet and supplied the Venom Society with at least one vile per day, over thirty days, the Venom Society would spare their lives and transport them back to Earth.

The task of producing acitaneum was not an easy one. The Venus Giganta stood over ten feet tall and, like its ancestor, the Venus Flytrap, was ever ready to impale its victims if they stimulated its sensitive feelers. Oddly, once triggered, their barbs popped up suddenly from underneath the surface of the ground. A victim could be positioned well away from its stalk and leaves and still get stabbed. If death didn't occur instantly, the enzymes coating its daggers worked quickly to infiltrate its prey's bloodstream. The victim would dissolve into a liquid, which was then absorbed through the plant's root system.

Banes struggled to project his voice any longer and was reduced to whispering. "My crew was attempting to make a hop back to Earth to stage rescue operations, when the collider onboard Curiosity malfunctioned, killing Tungsten and Strange and leaving Knightly and me dangling helplessly in space," he muttered.

Captain Pennington was not sure if Banes also knew that Knightly had perished but didn't say anything to his colleague about it.

With a few of his last shallow breaths, Banes made sure that Pennington knew the approximate space-time coordinates of the planet that contained the undesirables. Then, his body fell limp. Pennington slumped over his friend, dropped his forehead to his shoulder, and sobbed. Banes was gone now.

CHAPTER 31

Is This Really Happening?

After getting Dalton fed and settled for the night, Zinnia made time to look at the thumb drive that she recovered outside of the colosseum after the last Expulsion. She was anxious to see what it contained.

Zinnia pulled the drive from the bag of trash that she collected from the alleyway. She wiped its casing clean of the mustard sauce that had leaked from a spent can of sardines and began to examine it. It was different from the standard, general use thumb drives she was familiar with—a bit larger with a tiny LED screen. Zinnia was unsure of how it worked.

Dalton saw Zinnia fiddling with it and noticed right away that it used the same wireless communications technology as some of the toys he played with. While Xion was still living, he and Dalton were the gamers in the orphanage. The Venom Society didn't mass produce and distribute electronic gaming components due to the associated cost in raw materials, but they did provide a few toys for terminally ill children. Offering them a way to happily pass their remaining days was considered a kind and charitable gesture. Xion had been the recipient of their goodwill and Dalton, as a result, became proficient in operating small electronic components.

Almost without thinking about it, Dalton pointed to the side wall of the thumb drive and said, "magic screen." Zinnia knew this was his way of telling her that the small screen display would activate automatically if a compatible device came within close proximity of its magnetic receptor.

"You're *right*!" Zinnia exclaimed. "I bet one of Xion's old toys can trigger the thumb drive to activate." She grabbed a pair of virtual reality glasses from underneath the bunk bed and positioned them end-to-end against the thumb drive.

Instantly, the device's screen lit up, looking for instructions from the set of glasses. Zinnia and Dalton hopped up into the top bunk and explored what was on it.

An obvious "play" button appeared in the middle of the screen prompting the user to initiate a video. Dalton pressed the "play" symbol, and the video started.

An unidentified and unseen videographer was holding a camera and recording as they walked through a narrow hallway. There was audio with static but no voices. The recording captured the tubular shape of a series of passageways, and it was clear the video was taken in the underground tunnels. This could be very enlightening to Zinnia with respect to her investigation into the secret activities of the Venom Society.

For a couple of minutes, things seemed rather innocuous. The camera panned around the halls while it shimmied up and down as if to follow the natural rhythm of the footsteps of its owner. They were mundane but were included in the shot to give the viewer a chance to follow the path the cameraperson was taking.

The footsteps stopped, and the camera steadied as a closed door came into view. Above the entrance was a sign that read: "Keep Out. Unauthorized Personnel Strictly Prohibited in Lab." The cameraperson gave the door handle a tug, and the door separated from its frame and cracked open a few inches.

Whoever was recording did not enter the room right away. It seemed as if they were hesitant to even go in at all. Zinnia had the sense that the cameraperson was taking an initial look around the room to assess their own safety before making a commitment to enter. Then the camera edged slowly forward.

With the audio silent, the video rolled on, and the camera began to capture the inside of the lab. The walls were lined with an extensive grid of shelving units of various sizes. The camera drifted toward the left side of the room and zoomed in on a rack of shelves.

They were full of containment tanks designed to accommodate specialized contents, presumably animals of some sort. The label on the shelf facing read: "Extremities." Zinnia thought that was odd, but without time to even ponder what it could mean, the camera zoomed in.

"Are those fingers?" asks Dalton.

Zinnia turned and looked at him but didn't say a word. They both trained their sights on the tiny screen. Dalton sunk into the mattress a little bit closer to Zinnia as they continued to watch.

Panning to the right, the camera took an angle toward the lowest shelf of a different rack. Another sign centered itself in the frame. This time it read, "Limbs." Dalton didn't have a clue how to read it, and Zinnia did not inform him. Both kept watching.

In an oversized tank lay human arms and lower legs. "Oh, my g—," Zinnia started to belt out in reflex but stopped herself from finishing her exclamation.

Dalton's eyes filled with fright, and his body became rigid. Zinnia hurriedly stashed the thumb drive in her pocket so that it could no longer be seen and coddled Dalton with both arms. "I'm not going to let anything happen to you," she whispered.

In her own mind, she silently continued, "This is an atrocity. The Venom Society elites are not who they say they are. I've suspected something for a while now, but I just couldn't figure out what was going on. Now, I think I know! Well . . . I know they are not being truthful with us. They are not telling us everything!"

"What's going to happen?" Dalton asked.

Zinnia stopped her inner monologue and responded to him: "NOTHING! *Nothing* is going to happen to us," as she brushed his bangs from his eyes.

"Are they going to hurt us?" Dalton asked.

"No! They're not going to do anything to us, Dalton. Stop talking like that," Zinnia told him emphatically.

Dalton teared up. He was still too young to grasp the impact of it all, but he understood that something was just not right, and that scared him.

Zinnia held him tightly and whispered, "Don't worry. I have some friends who I believe can help. I'm going to contact them. Now, you must swear not to tell anyone about this. You understand?" Then peering deeply into Dalton's eyes, she assured him, "We're going to be alright. I promise."

Zinnia asked Dalton to join some children a few rooms over in a game of checkers to take his mind off the video. She reminded him of how important it was to continue to stay positive and free from worry. He indicated his agreement with a simple nod, slid down off the bunk bed, and darted down the hall.

Satisfied that Dalton was occupied, Zinnia couldn't help but wonder what the rest of the microchip contained. She sat backward against the wall and set the video in motion again. It didn't get any better.

The camera moved forward and focused on the bar that ran along the right wall. The video skimmed past the sign above it so quickly that Zinnia couldn't make out what it said. The optic focused on the top shelf, and that's when the situation grew worse than Zinnia could have imagined.

A distant view of a glass container revealed an elongated object suspended in a gel or liquid. As the camera zoomed closer, Zinnia could see some sort of pupa growing inside. It was reminiscent of a human embryo in the developmental stage. It had appendages, but they were far from fully developed. It had a head, which was also not completely formed. Every few seconds, it twitched and squirmed as if to comfort itself in a slightly different fetal position. "What is that?" Zinnia thought to herself. "What is going on?"

The camera panned slightly to the left but remained aimed at the same rack of shelves. Another large jar appeared, one containing another pupa. It twitched and flinched just as the first one did. Zinnia's cheek muscles tightened and pressed upward, and her eyes squinted at the sight of the things, but she remained fully attentive to the video. She had to try to understand what all of this meant. It seemed so surreal.

The camera zoomed in on the fetus, pulling it right into the full frame of view. Zinnia immediately identified the main torso of the pupa and its appendages. As the camera followed along the curvature of the body and drifted toward its left profile, the side of its skull came into view. Its body was covered in pale, wrinkly skin. "This is unbelievable," she thought to herself.

The camera held steady in a fixed position for a few seconds, and Zinnia picked her head up and looked around the room to make sure no one had wandered too closer to her while she was viewing the video on the thumb drive. No one had.

Reluctantly, Zinnia continued watching the video. The scene moved to the next section of the laboratory. The camera honed in on a countertop offset from the wall, covering an island of cabinets in the middle of the room. The cameraperson hesitated a bit, as if they were unsure of whether or not to proceed.

The camera edged forward. There was one large cage sitting on top of the countertop. The cage formed a complete cube with four walls, a floor, and a ceiling. It was clearly built to restrict the contents.

There was a specimen in the cage, one about two feet tall. It was a bipedal animal with no fur growing on its wrinkly skin. Its back faced the camera, and it sat in a crouched position. The head faced away from the cameraperson.

The camera view abruptly angled toward the floor. Zinnia could tell that the person recording the video had bent over to pick something up. It was a measuring stick.

The camera centered back on the holding pen, and Zinnia could see the stick being poked through the metal bars. The cameraperson took steady aim and gave the subject a swift poke in the back. Then quickly jumped back, apparently thinking they'd get some sort of a reaction from the specimen. Nothing happened.

Zinnia could see the measuring stick once again poking through the bars. This time, it was aimed right at the back of the specimen's head. With another poke, the cameraperson fumbled the camera and jumped back away from the cage. Still, the specimen sat motionless. It must have been asleep. Or perhaps dead.

That was somewhat of a relief to the cameraperson—and Zinnia, as well. In a greater show of comfort and courage, the cameraperson moved in for a closer look, and at the same time, edged to the side a bit. The specimen reacted.

In an instant, and with a half shriek, half-hiss, the creature turned its head directly at the camera in a confused rage. "AHHHHHHHH-HHHHHHHHHH," was all Zinnia heard. She followed with a shriek of her own, which garnered light attention from some nearby residents.

The camera fell to the ground but was still powered on. For a few moments, it sat steady on the floor, recording nothing but a bare wall through hairline cracks in its glass lens. Zinnia could hear someone breathing heavily and fumbling in the background. Then the video went dark.

Zinnia was stunned. She dropped her head to her knees. Her heart was pounding, and she found herself breathing fast and heavy. She made no eye contact with the residents and sat silent until Dalton returned.

Zinnia helped Dalton into the top bunk and underneath the covers and said a prayer with him.

Then, she grabbed what was left of a box of crackers and a canteen of water and stuffed them into her backpack. She had already decided that she needed to see the underground labs for herself. And, if she were clever enough not be spotted and killed by the Venom Society, maybe, just maybe, she could capture a little video of her own.

CHAPTER 32

Lost in Deep Space

The crew of Proximity knew they needed to act quickly on the revelations of Captain Banes if they wanted to have any success locating and rescuing the undesirables. Proximity executed a swift space-time jump on course to find the planet.

Once the jump was complete, the ship reassembled its engine compartment, body, and fuselage before reassembling the astronauts themselves.

Captain Pennington asked DAISIE to assess their current situation, "DAISIE, how long until Proximity's combustion engines can take over flight?"

"In ten seconds, sir." DAISIE counted down for the captain, "Nine, eight, seven . . . three, two, one."

"Skip, go ahead and power-up the engines," said Captain Pennington.

Skip responded, "Done, Captain. Space-time warp transform was successful, and we are completely under conventional power at this time."

"DAISIE, what is our present location, vector, and distance from the target planet?" Captain Pennington asked.

DAISIE hesitated, not answering the captain's question immediately as she normally did. She was in full-compute mode, and the display panel on her stainless-steel shell appeared overly busy with flashing lights. She, in her own android way, seemed bewildered or concerned about something. She remained silent.

Skip followed up with the android on the captain's behalf, "DAISIE, the captain asked what our present—"

But DAISIE cut Skip off in mid-sentence, "I *received* the captain's inquiry, Chief," She responded. "I was trying to recalculate a number of complicated Fourier mathematical equations because the initial result was a bit puzzling." DAISIE continued, "Captain, I'm afraid the ship may have delivered us off the mark with respect to the coordinates Captain Banes gave us."

"Well, that's okay, DAISIE," Pennington assured her. "We've been fairly spot on with our collider travel up to this point, and we've traveled a long, long way. Proximity has held up well thus far. I suppose a little bump in the road is to be expected once in a while."

"Actually, Captain, it's a little bit more than a *bump*," DAISIE suggested to him.

A wrinkle across his forehead accompanied a silent pause from the captain as he stared at DAISIE, wondering what she was trying to tell him.

"Go on, DAISIE," he encouraged her.

DAISIE continued, "My calculations have us traveling beyond our original destination; however, we appear to be on the proper vector. For some reason, the collider space-time transformer propelled us much further than we had programmed in."

"Really?" the captain responded. "So, we will need to backtrack a bit at an opposite heading?"

"Yes, sir," DAISIE said.

Skip asked the android for some clarification, "DAISIE, is this a trek that we can accomplish under Proximity's conventional engine power or do we need to retransform via collider?"

DAISIE didn't answer Skip.

This time, the captain spoke up and compelled the android to answer, "Skip asked if this is a trek that—"

DAISIE, cutting the captain's comments short this time, responded, "*It's a very long* way, gentlemen. I don't know how to tell you this but—" DAISIE paused yet again.

"*Just* lay it on us, DAISIE," the captain demanded.

"Ten thousand light-years, sir," DAISIE said.

That brought silence to all members of the crew. They looked around at each other, fear apparent on each of their faces. The fear of being lost in deep space, not knowing exactly which way to go.

The captain sighed and wiped a bead of sweat from his forehead. Then, he tried to calm his crew down a bit, "Okay, okay. They told us this sort of thing might happen. Nobody panic, please." He turned to DAISIE and questioned her in a calm, soft voice, "What do you suggest we do now?"

DAISIE seemed relatively calm, not having an actual facial expression of her own to share with her colleagues. She sensed the rest of the crew was upset and decided to cut the tension with a bit of sarcasm, "May I suggest a little cappuccino and a good book?"

Skip, not in a joking mood and clearly agitated at this point, burst out at the android, "Will you be serious, you cantankerous tin can!" He moved impatiently toward DAISIE in an imposing manner.

The captain, knowing DAISIE had matters well in hand, spoke up, "Easy there, Skip. Have a sense of humor, won't you?" chuckling at DAISIE's humanistic wit.

DAISIE took charge of the situation, "Relax, Chief. I'll get us back on course; I just need to get a bearing on the nearest Galactic cluster or celestial belt or star—*something* that I lock onto as a point of reference. Then, I'll adjust our collider travel coordinates back to our intended target."

The crew gazed out of Proximity's windows. There was nothing but darkness.

DAISIE's ears, which were nothing more than tiny holes in her metallic head, became filled with concerns from the nervous crew. But she was capable of tuning all of that out when she needed to. She heard, but ignored, rumblings from her colleagues as she worked to reprogram the collider navigational unit.

"I don't see anything in this direction," Max said.

"It's totally pitch-black out there," Dr. Moss added.

"How can there be . . . just . . . *nothing*?" Kassie wondered.

However, DAISIE was not at all anxious and calmly interjected, "Kassie, out of your window, to the lower left, look very closely. Do you see a faint collection of slightly flickering lights?"

Kassie responded, "Well, actually, yes, there is a line of lights stretching—"

DAISIE cut Kassie off in mid-sentence to get right to her point, "*Stretching* left to right, all of the same low intensity, except for one, the leader of the pack, which is significantly brighter than the rest, and of a slight orange glow. Isn't that right, Kassie?" she asked.

"That's right, DAISIE," Kassie responded. "Do you have these . . . these . . . stars, or whatever they are, in your database?"

"Of course, I do," DAISIE assured her. And with no arms, just a tap sound and an awkward upper body forward lean, DAISIE wittingly pretended to pat herself on her own android back, as if she deserved some of the credit that no one else was ready to offer her.

DAISIE continued, “Now, if you will all take your seats in your travel chambers, strap in, and just relax, I’ll get us on our way.”

The crew was a bit more at ease now and placed their confidence in the android’s ability to recompute and recover Proximity’s proper heading. Captain Pennington sighed in relief as he melted back into his launch position.

Skip powered down Proximity’s conventional engines and prepared the collider for a transform to their original destination.

CHAPTER 33
Edge of the Universe

Relieved that Proximity was back on track but concerned with what just happened, Captain Pennington wiped the remaining few beads of sweat from his brow and prepared a word of advice for his crew. He walked over to the main window and peered out into the darkness.

Then, in a very serious tone, he began his soliloquy about how vast the universe is. He opined that with one minor mistake in calculation, the collider could blow them right out of existence.

"Let this be a lesson to all of us," the captain said. "If we're not extremely careful, things could end up much worse for us next time. Think about it. We are neophytes, perhaps taking for granted the true capabilities of this ship. I do not want us to end up millions of galaxies from home, unable to find our way back. You saw what happened to Curiosity. Space travel is a dangerous undertaking. Let us never take our good fortune for granted. Our people are depending on us for answers to our long-term survival."

The captain continued, "Allow me to present you with a very interesting concept," he said. He went on to explain that the universe is composed of an uncountable number of galaxies. And that one single galaxy contains billions of solar systems (stars surrounded by planetary bodies). Distances across and between these behemoths are measured in billions of light-years. He reminded the crew that one single light-year is defined as the distance that light travels (at 186,000 miles per second) in one year's time. Staggering statistics.

"So, just how vast is the universe?" he asked the crew. "Is there a theoretical limit to it?" He challenged their imaginations by asking them: if they could travel fast enough to reach the edge of the universe, what would it look like? Would the atmosphere ahead of them appear completely black? White, perhaps?

"What lies beyond, as you peer forward into a time that hasn't even theoretically begun yet?" he asked rhetorically, knowing no one had an answer for him.

Not having any answers for himself either, the captain finished his thought and quickly put his mind to more pressing matters—the lost undesirables. "I'm befuddled, as you probably are, too. But don't let that diminish the point I'm trying to make about how careful we must be while we carry out our mission. Now, may God allow us to complete our current mission—that is, to rescue the humans out there who need our help. Let's go *find* them!"

CHAPTER 34
Human Heads

With fire in her eyes, staring straight ahead, Zinnia speed-walked her way down the street toward the schoolhouse, sidestepping a profusion of much slower-moving commoners. She had always believed she was born to save the world one day. She even casually mentioned that to Zander and Ryker at Market Day a while back. And now, she sensed this was the genesis of her life's mission to do so.

"My conversations with Mr. Jett, the interrogation of Ms. Ginny, the thumb drive, it's all beginning to make sense now," she thought to herself. Zinnia synthesized enough information to produce a mosaic of events that suggested unthinkable things were occurring in the underground labs. She was determined to find out for herself what it all meant.

It was after normal school hours so all doors were locked, but some of the windows were left open so the science professors could fumigate their rooms. This provided Zinnia an opportunity to get into the schoolhouse. She was small in stature so reaching her perch on the topside of the windowsill was not particularly easy for her but slithering through the crack in the window was a piece of cake.

After entering in the science department, Zinnia made her way toward the gymnasium where the locker banks hid the secret passageway door. Except for the new head janitor, there was no one around, so she didn't have to worry about being spotted. However, there were cameras mounted to the ceilings. She hoped they were not actively recording hallway activity at this hour, or she risked being identified.

An eerie feeling overcame her as she approached the locker banks that obfuscated the door that led to what might reveal the Venom Society's ultimate secrets. Not because she was afraid of getting caught—well, maybe a little bit because she was afraid of leaving Dalton alone. But more because she remembered what happened to old Ginny as a result of her willingness to breach the very same door a few weeks ago.

She still had the vivid image of the interrogation in her mind. It was almost as if she could hear Ginny's friendly voice, emanating from the walls, saying to her, "No, don't do it." Zinnia shook it off though.

Zinnia's violation count had improved lately but was still not stellar, but the thought of extending it back into the red zone didn't stop her. She bent over to peek around the backside of the last row of lockers and spotted the precarious door.

It was hidden behind the end of the locker bank itself. No one could enter the door without it being moved out from the wall a short distance. That was not easy for Zinnia, given her small frame, but she managed to get it done. She took one last look around the hallway to ensure the place was still empty and then manually poked the security code into the cipher lock.

For a second, she flinched, not knowing exactly how the door would react. She stared intently at it, waiting for it to move, but it didn't. "That's odd," she thought, "I thought I wrote the combination down correctly." She tried the number again, thinking perhaps she mis-keyed it the first time. Still, nothing. "What the heck," she whispered to herself. She hesitated to try it a third time, as that could potentially have triggered a tampering alarm, but she couldn't help herself. The thought of demystifying the activities of the Venom Society was exciting to her.

She tried the number a third time. Still, nothing happened. That deflated her. She let out a heavy sigh and turned to squeeze back out from behind the rickety old lockers. Just then, her armband came within inches of the cipher lockbox. As she began inching to her left, she heard the screech and squeak of the automatic door as it cracked open. That spooked her.

Whatever data transferred from Kamalei's key fob to her armband back at the infirmary must have included an automated secure door entry code and transmitter signal. "Whoa!" she exclaimed.

Zinnia inched back the other way and noticed that the secret door was ajar. She was reluctant to enter right away, but she knew she didn't have much time to think about it. The door was likely timed to automatically close within seconds, whether anyone had entered the premises or not.

After a short hesitation, she made her split-second decision. She lunged through the opening, landing on her hip inside of the doorway, narrowly avoiding her feet getting pinched as the door closed forcefully behind her. She wasn't hurt, just shaken.

Zinnia found herself alone in unfamiliar territory where members of the most powerful organization in the world roamed—a scary proposition, even for someone with a courageous personality like hers.

She was vulnerable, and that meant she had to take all precautions against being spotted. There was little reason for a teenage girl to be wandering around in these tunnels. If she were to be discovered, she'd risk her violation count soaring into the red zone, possibly instant death.

Zinnia was conflicted in her thoughts. On one hand, she had strived to trend her behavior in the direction of lawful obedience. On the other hand, she couldn't help but risk her life by giving in to the temptation to investigate the dark side of the Venom Society.

Conjuring up images of the video from the thumb drive in her mind, Zinnia began snooping around the halls of the tunnels beneath the schoolhouse. According to Jett, at least one of the labs was located not from her current position. She knew to look for the "Keep Out" sign above the lab door and was nervous about what she might encounter beyond it.

She moved along at a lively pace. Her light footsteps were nearly silent as she scurried toward *something*—she didn't know exactly what yet. She began to hear voices off in the distance. She slowed down but didn't stop.

As she approached an intersection of tunnels, the voices grew louder. Then, a couple of security personnel walked by, chatting and giggling amongst themselves. Zinnia was able to duck into a small nook in the wall. It was tight, but Zinnia was small enough to disappear from their sight. Her heart was racing. "Shew, that was close!" she thought to herself.

Within minutes, she came to a point where the tunnel met a large open area. It was a holding platform for a deep space exploration ship, although it happened to be empty at the moment. And the transport capsules that Jett described . . . they were there, too. "Wow," she muttered under her breath. After making sure no one was around to see, she made a bead for the nearest capsule.

She hopped in and the overhead door automatically closed. Her adrenaline kicked in high gear, and she figured out how to program the unit to take her for a short trip. She keyed in the coordinates she had written down from the video on the thumb drive, and the capsule transported her there in a flash.

Zinnia looked around in all directions to see if it was safe to exit. There was no one in sight, so she jumped out of the capsule and began looking for the sign. A fast-walking Venom Society guard shot across the hallway just ahead. Stone-faced, the guard didn't even offer a glance in Zinnia's direction.

Just beyond the guard, she could see a sign that read, "Keep Out, Unauthorized Personnel Strictly Prohibited," posted above a door. "*That's it!*" she thought, careful not to make a sound. She slowly side-stepped her way down the tunnel, glancing back and forth from front to behind, until she made it to the door. It was exactly what she was looking for.

She rotated the handle, and the door cracked open slightly. Zinnia just stood there for a few seconds. Then, she found the courage to peek inside with one eye, but it was quiet and dark.

The smell of preservatives permeated the air. The stench almost caused her to gag. She pushed through, though, and flicked on the light. As her eyes adjusted, she relaxed her squint to a clear view of her surroundings.

"Oh, my word," she thought. "The shelves—they're just as Jett described. Full of jars and everything." She took a minute to size up the room from a distance.

Recovering from the initial shock of it all, she decided to take a slow walk around. This may be the only time she'd ever be able to do so. She shivered, not knowing what she might find.

She came upon blobs of fleshy material that were suspended in jars. They appeared to be embryos—some kind of experimental biological creations. But they had not matured into any recognizable form yet. Her knees buckled slightly.

She made her way to the back-left portion of the lab where there were more shelves. These shelves held much larger glass tanks. They contained objects that appeared round and hairy from a distance. Zinnia approached with caution, getting close enough to see them clearly.

"*Heads*!" she shrieked loudly, before quickly putting her hand over her mouth. Fortunately, no one was nearby to hear her. She stumbled backward into a long stainless-steel table and knocked it sideways. The table carried a second tank, which went crashing to the floor. She stood there in silence, stunned by the morbid scene.

Zinnia snapped out of her trance after noticing a rumbling sound coming from the other side of the table. She continued to stand motionless, shivering, and taking quick, shallow breaths.

Then, she slowly crept around the end of the table to see what was making the noise. The source of the disturbance came into full view.

"AHHH!" Zinnia screamed. She grabbed her face with both hands to shield herself from the terrifying sight. She was so paralyzed with fear that even if she had tried to run, she wouldn't have been able to do so. She remained glued to the floor, a safe distance from a head that was now free from its holding tank. And it was alive! It exhibited facial expressions. Zinnia recognized the head as one of the winners of the first Expulsion she had witnessed. Appendages had grown from its underside. Zinnia almost got sick, but she remained put.

She could see the appendages moving as the head lay on the floor. She tried to get a picture of it but couldn't hold her hand steady enough to manage the shot. And then the head turned toward Zinnia and looked her in the eyes.

"AHHH!" she shrieked again. The creature used its appendages to propel itself across the floor, lunging at her. Zinnia reflexively kicked the head, sending it for a tumble. But it immediately righted itself, staring in the opposite direction of her.

The head slowly turned to its right as it scanned the room for movement, and then it locked its eyes on Zinnia again. She bolted for the door, slipping in the preservative along the way. She was able to make it out of the lab, but the head scrambled on its appendages, intent on going after her.

Zinnia ran down the hall without a care in the world about who might see her. She had to get back to the collider capsule. It wasn't far away, but the head was right behind her. Zinnia dove into the capsule and forced the door shut, just as the reanimated head-creature slammed into the window.

Zinnia was terrified, but she navigated back to the collider depot nearest the schoolhouse, where she had entered the secret passageway. She was shaken but needed to get back inside the schoolhouse without being detected.

She slammed the door to the tunnels behind her, squeezed past the lockers, pushed them back in place. Then, she scurried through the nearest schoolhouse exit, back into the familiar, busy street. Once she was in a safe location, she sat on the ground to catch her breath.

"Jett!" she mumbled to herself. "Oh, my gosh. I need to tell Jett!"

CHAPTER 35

Hydronian Justice

Located in the Assateague Municipality, just north of the Maryland-Virginia border, a communal cluster of aquapods spiraled into turmoil when the inhabitants of aquapod 42V formed an alliance and sponsored a rash of gang activity. With a group-think mentality, their collectively poor decisions sent them down a dubious path. They formed a new gang and called themselves the Black Tide. They dedicated themselves to a life of extortion, theft, and abuse against their neighbors.

The Black Tide started out as a normal aquapod community. Most tenants had carried low violation counts for many years. They committed their fair share of manpower and resources to the surrounding area by assisting in construction operations, harvesting food and nutrients from the waters, and ensuring that quantities of rations were evenly distributed among neighboring aquapods. Unfortunately, that changed over time as the local population boomed and the strain on resources in the municipality grew heavy.

With the proliferation of aquapods in the municipality, local food resources harvested from the waterways dwindled. In part, due to greater consumption from an increased population, and in part, due to the environmental impact the massive towers had on natural aquatic resources. With a widening imbalance between sustenance and mouths to feed, the Black Tide made the poor decision to take matters into their own hands.

Echo and Skye, two heartless sisters, established themselves as the primary leaders of the gang. They had a knack for getting their own crony to do whatever they wanted them to do. The commoners of aquapod 42V, once honorable and trustworthy, now followed the sisters' lead because they knew it meant more bounty for the entire colony, and that was too enticing for them to ignore. But satisfying their greed came at the expense of others.

The sisters maintained a psychological influence over the gang members. They were so well practiced at looting their neighbors that on a moment's notice the gang could assemble quickly and efficiently. All Echo and Skye had to do was provide the target, the day and time for the hit, and a motivational diatribe to initiate a heist. Then, the sisters sat back and watched and waited for their clan to return with a bountiful take from unsuspecting victims.

As much as the surrounding aquapod communities tried to fight back, they couldn't. They were too weak. Once robbed of their nutrition, most were subjected to famine and a slow, rigorous physical recovery. A recovery that never completely occurred.

A number of commoners ended up dying as a result of Black Tide invasions. The victims fell into a downward spiral of becoming the weaker population, and they remained at the mercy of the Black Tide. That is, until the Venom Society unexpectedly stepped in and declared that an Expulsion would take place, an event dedicated solely to Black Tide undesirables.

A group of Venom Society commandos, led by Trent Chulah and aimed at carrying out special tactical operations, swooped in and overwhelmed the rogue aquapod. Echo and Skye never saw them coming.

They converged upon the aquapod with jet skis and hoverboards. An impressive show of stealth and authority from the Venom Society played out. Their mission was to place all gang members under arrest, shackle them, and transport them to the nearest colosseum.

With unrivaled precision, the SWAT team quickly moved in and locked down the aquapod. In no uncertain terms, Chulah informed them that they were selected to participate in the next Expulsion for the Assateague Municipality.

But the SWAT team was met with cackling laughter as Echo peered at Chulah and challenged his authority. "How dare you enter our premises unannounced, Chulah!" Echo said. "Be gone. You have no business here."

Chulah let that go in one ear and out the other. "Get down on the ground, now!" he ordered.

"Chulah, you don't really want to do this, do you?" Skye asked him, taking over the conversation on behalf of her sister. "We're your most productive aquapod in this entire municipality. We've provided the lion's share of seaweed, fish, and squid to the surrounding communities and even to the Venom Society—for years now. Surely you can look past our little squabbles with our neighbors. Why don't you go and give someone *else* an earful?!"

"Your self-serving behavior has upset the balance of survival in the entire Delmarva Peninsula, Skye," Chulah responded. "You've pilfered food and medicine from the weaker community without considering the consequences. The communities that suffered increased the demand on our reserves and that has caused us undue hardship. We must execute another substantial Expulsion to regain stability with our resources in this region. Your entire aquapod must participate. Now, turn around, and put your hands behind your back."

Just as Chulah went to place Skye in cuffs and shackles for transport to the Expulsion colosseum, one of her faithful followers lunged at him in an effort to back him away from the ringleader. A big mistake, that was. With a lightning-quick prick to the back of the outlaw's neck, he dropped to the ground like a wet towel—reminiscent of the way Chulah took care of Ginny after her interrogation.

Chulah looked down and admired his work as the gang member lay lifeless at his feet. He then turned his head toward Skye, righted his dark sunglasses on his face with his forefinger, and once again asked calmly that she obey his orders.

Echo knew Skye was overmatched and urged her to comply. "Do as he says, sister. We'll go with him peacefully. When Grandmaster Webb hears of this, he'll see things our way. Surely, *he* hasn't forgotten about our generous contributions to the Society."

The two miscreant ring leaders knelt down to be bound and transported. Twenty-eight other gang members watched in fear, thinking they would be next. Chulah raised his arm, pointed at them, and admonished them. "The rest of you: remain in place. Do not attempt to evade or you will be terminated immediately. A transport unit will arrive shortly. You will all board calmly, and we'll proceed to the colosseum."

Then he turned and issued an order to his SWAT team. "Hold the undesirables here and await transport." In less than an hour, the entire gang was shackled, extracted from the aquapod, and hauled away.

They didn't have to travel far, though, as there was a specialized aquapod, extending from the east flank of a nearby band of pods, built specifically to accommodate Expulsions for the Hydronian community.

As the transport unit pulled up to the base of the Expulsion aquapod, Kamalei was seen raising the heavy entry gates. The staging area was ready to receive the competitors and the enormous mechanical arm, with its claws, was already in position.

A total of thirty undesirables were being entered into the Expulsion.

Locals made their way into the colosseum to secure their seats for the event. Many were lethargic from being deprived of their normal course of food and water as of late. But they were intent on reaping revenge on the gang members.

Moving the prisoners from the water transport vessel up onto the base of the aquapod and into the staging area was difficult. A heavy chop on the ocean's surface made for an unstable bridge. Some of the prisoners realized this and tried to take advantage of it. They pushed several crowd-control officers aside and made an escape attempt. Like seals gliding off of a slick iceberg, ten undesirables slid down from the bridge and made entry into the water.

This was their native habitat, so their egress was swift and natural. The Hydronians were born swimmers. And while that was a strength of theirs in the waters surrounding their own aquapods, it would be of little use to them this time. The Venom Society was well prepared to handle the situation.

A dozen skilled SWAT team members mounted their jet skis, which were made in the likeness of giant water-scooting mosquitos. They were equipped with laser guns that, when discharged, effectively exploded whatever the laser hit.

In this case, the targets were the heads of the undesirables. The Hydronians could hold their breath underwater for minutes at a time but not forever. They had to resurface periodically to catch their breath. The SWAT team sat and waited for the undesirables to breach the surface of the water, and . . . *ZAP!* . . . in an instant, they were vaporized. The little red pools in the water cleared up in short time, and the carcasses provided good feeding for hungry scavengers.

This little mishap didn't faze Chulah and his crew, though. They had things well in hand. The twenty undesirables who remained willfully followed orders and were loaded into the staging area of the colosseum.

Kamalei signaled to the Expulsion stage crew that the event was about to begin. The big screens displayed her peculiarly stunning beauty up close. Kamalei stared directly into the camera with her bright green eyes and captured the fascination of the audience. She then started into her well-rehearsed opening remarks.

"Welcome, *good* citizens of the Assateague Municipality. I am Kamalei Ricinulei, master of Expulsions. Our population is in the red. We are starving. We are sick. We are *dying*. We must join together as one and respect the needs of all of the *good* people on Earth. And yet, there are *those* who decide to cross their neighbors."

As she had done a hundred times prior, Kamalei peered over at the holding area deliberately and menacingly. The crowd erupted with a collective heckle. Kamalei continued, "Today, ladies and gentlemen, we sacrifice individuals whose behavior we can no longer tolerate. Their violation counts demonstrate that they do not respect the laws of our land. Their fate now lies in *your* hands." Then, Kamalei faced the camera, raised both arms high, and shouted, "DO WHAT YOU MUST!"

Kamalei signaled to the stage crew that the event was now underway. Lights, lasers, and pyrotechnics ceremoniously prompted the loading of the competitors into the Expulsion cage.

One by one, the undesirables were snatched from the staging area by the mechanical arm and claws, displayed upon the big screen along with the charges against them, and forcefully injected into the huge death cage.

Three escape capsules placed strategically around the colosseum indicated that mercy would only come to those contestants who located them and secured themselves inside. The others would die.

In the opening minutes of the contest, the undesirables took a team approach and refrained from attacking each other. Their first obstacle was a fiery rope bridge suspended precariously above the first section of the colossal cage. All but four contestants scaled it completely, avoiding injury. The four who were the last to attempt to cross, plummeted to the ground when the rope snapped. They died upon impact.

The sixteen remaining contestants moved swiftly to the next challenge where they encountered the swim of death. They had to cross a shark-infested mote to get to the area containing the escape capsules. There was no way around it. The water was murky, and nothing could be seen beneath the surface, so the contestants simply took their chances and jumped in.

Sleekly and quietly, the undesirables slithered into the dark water. They hoped that if they managed not to cause a disturbance at the water's surface, they might just get by unnoticed by the sharks. A clever attempt that was . . . but not terribly effective.

While it was only a thirty-second swim to the other side, the sharks hadn't eaten in weeks, and as soon as the prey entered the water, they were under attack. The first six undesirables to enter the water made it across unscathed. Echo and Skye were among them. That gave hope to their followers.

But in a split second, hope turned to terror. One shark took a middle-aged woman that was readying herself to exit the water. She was gone in an instant. The onlookers watched as a whirlpool in the water turned red with blood. An uptick in the volume of chatter was heard around the colosseum.

Next, two teenage boys were able to reach the platform and exit the water to safety. Looking behind them, they watched in horror as an elderly man was dragged below the surface A swirl of blood again filled the void. The crowd let out a cheer once they realized the sharks were in full attack mode.

The smell of blood ignited a feeding frenzy. The interesting thing about the hungry predators was that the onlookers didn't even have to engage their joysticks to make these kills. The sharks needed no coaxing and were completely self-sufficient.

Over the next several minutes, the mote turned into a blood bath. Screams from the six remaining victims in the water could barely be heard over the boisterous crowd. They were all taken by the sharks.

Eight capable undesirables made it through the death swim and remained in the competition. That led them to the last section of the cage, which was dry and contained the three escape capsules.

That section was fitted with a huge array of manmade steel stalactites that hung from the ceiling. Before the undesirables could even survey that area of the colosseum, several of the big spikes dislodged from the ceiling and fell to the ground. Some onlookers had already spotted them from their seats and had waited anxiously, with joysticks in hand, to electronically levy enough collective will upon the electronic control modules to allow the executioners to drop them.

As a majority of onlookers followed suit, the ceiling spikes fell in bunches. There was nowhere for the contestants to go but forward to try to occupy one of the escape capsules located fifty feet away. The crowd leaned heavily on their joysticks. The more will to kill collectively generated by the onlookers, the more spikes began to fall.

The prisoners scurried toward the three escape capsules, and they were quickly occupied by the fastest competitors. Echo got one of them for herself. Four of the remaining five contestants, who were not quick enough to secure one, were impaled by the spikes. Two in the shoulder and upper torso. Two right through the skull.

The crowd was aghast at first but quickly grew to appreciate the efficiency of the kills. They felt some sense of satisfaction, having lost loved ones at the hands of the gang members-turned victims.

One dissenter was still alive, though. It was Skye. As a leader of the Black Tide, she was a target that the audience had been looking to avenge from the beginning. They were about to get their chance.

She took cover behind some padded baffles, which stood about five feet tall and were strategically placed to obstruct the undesirables, making it difficult to evade the falling projectiles.

Posted around the perimeter of the cage's top were executioners armed with flaming harpoons. Skye knew she was their only target now, and she'd have to dodge shots using the baffles as shields. The onlookers were intrigued by the idea, and they once again leaned on their joy sticks to watch the attack play out.

The ability to trigger each flaming harpoon was granted to its executioner as the collective will of the watchers increased. One by one, the safety locks freed the triggers.

Skye successfully shielded herself from a few harpoons, which pierced the baffles, but her back remained a clear target. As soon as a harpoon trigger was released to the control of an executioner located behind her, she would be immediately in their sites and likely taken down. She could only hope that the shooters had bad aims.

After about half of the staged harpoons zoomed past her head and body, Skye made a bold move. She stepped out from behind the baffles and faced the executioners, who had not yet deployed their weapons. She peered into their eyes and scalded them, "WHY? *Why* must you take your frustrations out on *me* this way? I tried to feed my people the best way I knew how. Your friends—" She pointed hastily to the gathering of onlookers around the colosseum. ". . . They are *weak*," she said. "Had we not taken from them, *they* would have taken from *us*. We simply reacted *first*. Spare me this fate today. GO HOME! ALL OF YOU!"

Skye then scanned the VIP seating area, looking for the Venom Society elite who had shackled her and brought her there. "*Spare* my life, and I shall never step foot in this municipality . . . EVER AGAIN!" She spoke as if to elicit conflicting emotions and receive forgiveness.

It didn't work. The crowd stood, burst into an uproar, some raising their joysticks in the air and shaking them at the bitter gang leader. Collectively, they provided more than enough influence to active the remaining weapons.

Skye received two harpoons right through her mid-section. The impact knocked her back a couple of steps and slammed her against one of the baffles. But she remained upright for a moment.

With a look of sheer terror, Skye slowly lifted up her head, looked toward the Venom Society elites, and delivered her final message. "You'll rot in eternal damnation for this, Chulah!"

It was something of a prophetic statement by Skye in that her voice became muffled by the swell of flames that engulfed her. She slid down the baffle to the floor, and her eyes rolled back in her head as her body became limp.

Kamalei signaled the end of the Expulsion, and the ceremonial fog horns sounded. The three escape capsules zoomed out of sight. The Venom Society elites exchanged praise among one another and offered their appreciation to Kamalei by presenting their right thumb and forefinger in the shape of a "V" against their chests. Then, they formed a single file line and made their exit.

CHAPTER 36

Surprise Visit

The thought of nearly becoming another statistic of lost missions was a sobering one, but the crew of Proximity knew they needed to continue their search for the planet where Banes said they could find the lost undesirables. DAISIE calculated the space-time travel sequencing and initiated the ship's collider. But suddenly the ship lost power.

Proximity had been extremely reliable up to this point. For the ship to just fail altogether was strange. The captain was puzzled.

DAISIE was not, however. She recalled that Venom Society engineers had programmed into the ship's navigation system's specific coordinates, which were off-limits to Proximity. Any attempts to visit these locations automatically caused the ship's power supply to stall until fresh coordinates were entered. It was a measure put in place to obscure the whereabouts of the Expulsion winners. That was also the likely reason Proximity's first attempt to locate the planet failed. Webb, Chulah, and the Venom Society elites strove to keep that planet inaccessible by anyone other than themselves. It was a clever design on their part, and it appeared to be effective.

The captain glanced over at DAISIE as if to ask her for the solution; without even saying anything, DAISIE knew. She was built by, and for, the Venom Society. She paused for a second and then explained the situation to Captain Pennington.

"Sir, what is happening is this: we do not have access to the planet in question. The master navigation control unit has been pre-programmed to avoid those coordinates."

Captain Pennington didn't understand what the android was getting at, so he asked for clarification. "What does that mean, DAISIE? We simply want to visit the location where the undesirables were placed. We need to determine if they are still alive. And if so, we must attempt a rescue."

"Yes, I understand that, Captain," DAISIE replied. "But . . . the Venom Society leadership . . . they do not want us to visit the planet. They've taken steps to guard against discovery and disclosure of their activities concerning the Expulsion winners."

Captain Pennington continued to stare at DAISIE, at a loss for words, deflated by her revelation. DAISIE seemed conflicted about the matter in her own artificially intelligent way.

DAISIE did follow up, though, with some good news for the captain, "*However*, Captain, I know the keying sequence that can unlock this restriction and allow Proximity to proceed to this location."

With that, Captain Pennington rose from his chair, rushed over to DAISIE, and addressed her face-to- . . . well . . . android-face, "DAISIE, you've *got* to help us. You've got to help . . . *them*. *Do* what you *must*!" the Captain pleaded to her.

Then, touched by a flash of humanistic reasoning and emotion, DAISIE realized what the right thing was. As an android, she was programmed to obey only commands that were in the best interest of protecting the secrets of the Venom Society. This time, however, she resolved to go against those instructions in an act of humanity.

The captain and crew grew quiet and watched DAISIE, wondering how she would respond. Without saying a word, DAISIE edged over to the ship's master navigation control unit and began transmitting a series of light and sound pulses. Within seconds, the power kicked back on inside the spaceship.

With that, the captain ordered a swift and aggressive departure. He again approached DAISIE face-to-android-face and sincerely thanked her, as if she were somehow human.

Soon they found themselves approaching the planet where the undesirables were abandoned, the topology of its surface coming into view. It was a small planet with a basic blue and brown coloration. Cirrus clouds floated in its upper atmosphere, which indicated a rain cycle existed.

DAISIE ran a check on the components of the air space blanketing the planet, and it was much like that of Earth, but the nitrogen content was slightly higher, the oxygen count a hair lower. Readings were still in the safe breathing range for humans, however.

Proximity orbited the planet for a few hours as there was no initial sign of life or activity. Finally, though, the crew spotted movement on the surface. There they all were, milling about. The Expulsion winners that Captain Banes had spoken about.

Skip took control of the ship under conventional engine power and searched for a safe landing area. The humans noticed the spaceship approaching and collected themselves into a tightly packed group, gazing up at it. They were probably anticipating a fresh delivery of food and supplies.

"It's them," Captain Pennington assured his crew. "We've found them. Banes was right."

While the ship began its final descent, Captain Pennington considered how he might address the undesirables. After all, they were probably not expecting a crew of astronauts who were ill-equipped to provide them sufficient nutrition or supplies. Proximity carried a supply of food onboard commensurate to what the crew of five would consume during their mission, but that wouldn't sustain the undesirables for long.

Most importantly, however, the crew brought a good and honest intent to rescue the undesirables, so the captain felt confident he would not be met with resistance.

A difficult decision for the captain to make would be who he would take back to Earth first and in what order the rest would follow. The undesirables had been traumatized over the last couple of months. The Expulsion and deportation had likely taxed them emotionally. They all probably wanted out of there as soon as possible.

Captain Pennington sunk into his chair with an inquisitive look about him, pondering exactly how he would negotiate a collectively agreed upon, calm exit plan, one where no one felt the need to fight for a spot onboard. And hopefully, no one would get hurt or killed. After all, that was a mentality the prisoners had developed within themselves.

CHAPTER 37
The Plan

It was implausible to bring the undesirables back to Earth and then continue on with the deep space exploration mission. If the Venom Society caught wind of the fact that Pennington and his crew had discovered the excommunicated Expulsion winners and learned they were being used as pawns on a distant planet, they'd be swiftly eliminated to prevent any leaks.

Pennington didn't want to believe it at first, but it was clear that the Venom Society had ulterior motives that were secret and sinister. While some of their actions appeared noble and sincere on the surface, a darker side had seeded within them and had grown stronger with time. They didn't really care about the welfare of the commoners as they led everyone to believe. It was all a cover story for their morbid, self-serving abuse of others and power. It had gotten out of control, and now Pennington realized it. He saw no other way but to revolt against the regime and replace them with the truly good people of Earth.

But how could they possibly overthrow such a powerful and deeply embedded organization?

The captain's plan was a clever one. Extract all Expulsion winners from their current predicament, surreptitiously return them to Earth, and nurse them back to full strength. Then, train and organize the group into a fighting force, leverage their prowess and resentment, and arm them against the Venom Society.

But they could not simply walk up to Venom Society Headquarters and expect to breach the gates and launch a successful offensive against them. The compound was too heavily secured. They'd need to lure the entire regime out of their safe haven and into a more vulnerable situation. That would require help from the inside, though. The Venom Society wouldn't take the bait without a small push from a trusted source.

"Jett!" Pennington thought to himself. "I need to contact Jett immediately."

Jett's association with the secret organization in recent years, while respectable, was not without some angst. He was slow to gain respect from the Venom Society, and they never seemed to have enough confidence in him to place him on the more prestigious assignments. That nagged at him late in his career. But his discontent may also lessen his apprehension to bring down the evil ones.

Being heavily involved with Expulsion security operations, Jett was in a good position to coordinate an offensive operation. He'd have to fabricate a plausible story to lure the Venom Society into an unassuming situation, though. And perhaps tap one of his Venom Society colleagues for authoritative assistance to make it work.

Going on the information that Captain Pennington fed him, Zeller had already passed word on to Venom Society leadership that the crew of Proximity had made exceptional distant planetary discoveries recently and that there was promise for harvesting more acitaneum and other precious resources. That was quite enticing to the egocentric elites.

Webb, Chulah, and other top leaders of the Chesapeake Municipality had good reason to attend the next "special" Expulsion. But Jett knew he had to influence someone on the inside to play along. Ivy Breez was Jett's obvious choice. He had gained her confidence at the last space launch and knew he could leverage that fact. Surely, he could convince Ivy to encourage her supervisors to attend the next Expulsion.

It was now or never. The fate of mankind appeared to come down to this one event. All of the pieces were falling into place, and it was up to Jett to anchor the operation.

With the shock of what he and Savanna encountered in the underground tunnels and having received an urgent cry for help from Zinnia, Jett didn't think twice. He landed a gig as a security guard for the next Expulsion. He had no say as to who the Venom Society selected to participate in the Expulsion, but he was prepared to utilize the competitors to carry out the plan.

CHAPTER 38

Awakening

The Venom Society prepared the colosseum in the Chesapeake Municipality for the upcoming Expulsion and loaded the event's undesirables into a long bus-like hover craft with boarded-up windows. Most were silent, with the exception of a few boisterous and bitter souls who believed this trip represented their last ride. Each found his or her own spot on the floor of the transport vessel. Each knew that the person next to them might be their worst enemy in just a few hours. They took a suspicious look around at the others and made assessments about which competitors they thought they could beat in battle, which they might try and make an alliance with, and which they should avoid altogether. They conjured up scenarios in their minds about how they thought the event would play out. Some were confident in their own abilities; others were terrified.

Some undesirables recognized Jett and initially scoffed that he was closely associated with the Venom Society. Although they weren't fond of him, they did respect his influence.

Once in transport, Jett gained the confidence of the undesirables by offering them coveted food and nutritional supplements that they had never before seen. With that, Jett captured their undivided attention and began a difficult conversation with them.

He explained that in this upcoming "special" Expulsion, everyone involved could be a winner if they listened to him and pulled together as one. A bunch of low-hanging heads raised with enthusiasm and interest in whatever Jett was going to say next. Jett, in his own deliberate way, got right to the point.

He divulged to the undesirables what the Venom Society had done with the previous Expulsion winners, to include details of human body experimentation and biological modification. He explained how undesirables who were tough enough to survive the Expulsion were physically modified and enhanced against their will and transported to a planet that only the Venom Society knew about.

The rest of the low-hanging heads perked up this time, and the entire group started to become agitated at the idea.

Jett explained how there were valuable, medicinal chemicals located on the planet, and the Venom Society kept the undesirables alive but under the threat of starvation—solely for the benefit of their labor. Then, they hoarded their gains. He told the undesirables that the plan for them today was that all but three of them would die in the fury of the Expulsion while the Venom Society furthered their ruthless experimentation. The three individuals who survived the Expulsion would become human freaks and servants to the elites.

That news did not sit well with the undesirables, and almost in unison, several of them called out to Jett, "*Why* should we believe you? Why are you telling us this? What do you want from us?"

Those were all good questions. After all, it might have appeared to the undesirables that Jett was trying to psychologically manipulate them for some purpose of his own.

Jett insisted that what he was telling them was true. To keep from losing their confidence in him, he added that the Venom Society was so determined to serve themselves over anyone else that they willfully sacrificed the deep exploration ship, Curiosity, along with four astronauts, to protect the secrecy of their core operations.

The undesirables' faces turned inquisitive. "Could he be for real?" they thought to themselves. They had nothing to lose by placing their trust in him. Jett went silent and allowed the prisoners to converse among themselves for a minute. Then, one at a time, some feeding off the energy of the others, the undesirables indicated to Jett that they were ready to hear him out.

The undesirables had already grown physically imposing, given the difficult living conditions in which they were immersed. Their hearts were hardened. They had honed their fighting skills as part of their onerous lifestyles. What they needed to learn now, most critically, was how to turn from the mindset of killing each other to survive to pulling together as one lethal fighting force, strong enough to dethrone the Venom Society.

Comfortable with the notion that they now took him seriously, Jett set the plan into motion.

"Today, I implore you *all*; join your brothers in a show of solidarity," Jett urged them. "Once the Expulsion begins, make yourselves appear to be genuine in your actions. We must not let the Venom Society suspect anything," he explained to them.

"I will stall the onlookers so they do not vote and influence the killing devices," he continued. "This will allow all of you to be presented to the audience and loaded into the death cage, all very much alive. When the time is right, we will mount an attack against the Venom Society. I'll signal you with cannon fire. At the sound of the cannons, everyone is to converge at center stage," Jett told the undesirables.

"That is where the Venom Society will be seated. The walls adjacent to their seating area have been sabotaged so that the fasteners will weaken, failing easily. Then, my friends, the evil regime will be directly accessible to you. *This* is your chance to avenge them, save yourselves, and save *us all.* Unite and dismantle the ruling body that has deceived us."

Jett pumped his fist in the air and, in unison, so did the undesirables. Then, Jett motivated them with a snide battle cry: "*Do* what you MUST!"

CHAPTER 39

Final Expulsion

The undesirables arrived at the Expulsion site in the large containment vessel. They were systematically offloaded and herded into the staging area of the colosseum. Although the undesirables did not let on that anything was awry, most of them were approaching this competition with a different frame of mind, to form a massive fighting alliance.

They had to act as authentic as possible so the Venom Society would remain unsuspecting. They were ruthless and deadly individuals, and the target of their fury was the Venom Society. The collective group of undesirables didn't have time to rehearse a battle scenario, but most formed an incredible bond that would govern their actions of survival over the next couple of hours.

All high-ranking Venom Society officers from the tristate area were in attendance. Ivy had requested their presence to observe the event, touting it as a celebration of the discovery of a new source of acitaneum. That was a lie, but the elite fellowship didn't know that. They trusted her. As always, they were provided with their own VIP viewing enclosure, inside of the gargantuan fighting cage.

Venom Society officers were seen greeting one another with their signature *V* hand symbols across their chests as they made their way into the exclusive seating cage. They entered in a single file line, led by Grandmaster Webb.

Kamalei made her way to the death cage where a conductor's podium sat high atop the main entrance. But before she could enter, Zinnia stepped away from the crowd of onlookers and called her name. The two made eye contact and each lapsed into a moment of reflection of just how much respect they harbored for each other. Zinnia approached Kamalei and addressed her.

"I just wanted to thank you, again, for what you did for my little brother." Zinnia said. Then she looked up at the rafters of the colosseum and added, "He's somewhere up there watching over us now."

"It was truly my pleasure, Zinnia," Kamalei responded. "I'll never forget Xion. He provided me with incredible inspiration, the likes of which you may never know." She appeared slightly emotional, which was out of character for any Venom Society officer, and worked to maintain her composure just prior to going on camera.

Kamalei turned to make her way to the podium, but Zinnia grabbed her arm as if she didn't want her to go just yet. Kamalei froze and looked back at Zinnia. By the look on her face, it was clear Zinnia needed Kamalei's help. As much as Zinnia wanted to, however, she didn't quite know how to ask the Venom Society elite. She was fumbling for words when she heard a familiar voice call out from behind her. It was Jett.

"Thank goodness, he's here," Zinnia thought to herself. Although she didn't feel comfortable asking Kamalei for any favors, she knew Jett was fast approaching to do just that. He knew Kamalei had a soft spot in her heart for Zinnia, and he wanted to exploit that.

"Councilor, Councilor!" Jett shouted as he brushed by Zinnia and stood face to face with Kamalei.

"We *need* you," he pleaded to her. "We need you to help us. What the Grandmaster and his officers are doing to our people is horrific. You know that. It's time the commoners fight back, Councilor. And that's what we're going to do today. Please have mercy on us."

Jett continued, "Will you cut the lights for me for sixty seconds when you hear the sound of cannon fire? That's all I ask of you. That's all Zinnia asks of you. Please, Councilor. You know this is the right thing to do."

Jett, looking directly into Kamalei's bright green eyes, could see that she was terrified at the thought of turning on her bosses. But humanity and compassion were tugging at her soul. With one simple nod, she agreed to assist.

Kamalei placed her hand on Zinnia's shoulder to reassure her that she understood the gravity of what they were asking her to do and that she had their back. Then she took her place on the emcee podium.

But she had to fight to appear unemotional. She had an introduction to get through and didn't want to alarm the grandmaster or his comrades. She turned and faced the arena, and the camera once again captured her beauty up close for all onlookers to admire.

This time her eyes were glassy as she peered around the grandstand, realizing the extent of anguish and hurt the commoners had suffered at the hands of the Venom Society. This was a defining moment for her. After an extended pause, she greeted the crowd.

"Welcome, *good* citizens of the Chesapeake Municipality!" Kamalei poured out her familiar words while suppressing the emotion that was gripping her.

"I am Kamalei Ricinulei, master of Expulsions. Our population is in the red. We are starving. We are sick. We are *dying*." Her voice cracked slightly, as it never had before. The Venom Society elites could be seen conferring with one another as if they questioned whether or not Kamalei was on point.

"We must join together as one and respect the needs of all of the *good* people on Earth. And yet, there are *those* who decide to cross their neighbors."

As she had done a hundred times prior, Kamalei looked directly at the holding area deliberately and menacingly, waving an arm high in the air in the direction of the miscreants. The camera panned right and took in a full view of the competitors' staging area, and the crowd responded with their applause of appreciation.

Kamalei continued, "*Today*, ladies and gentlemen, we sacrifice individuals whose behavior we can no longer tolerate. Their violation counts demonstrate they do not respect the laws of our land. Their fate lies in *your* hands. DO WHAT YOU MUST!"

Kamalei signaled to the stage crew that the event was about to begin. Lights, lasers, and fireworks ceremoniously commenced the Expulsion.

The violation counts of all the undesirables were displayed on the big screens, pictures of their faces were shone, and one by one, the mechanical arm and claws loaded them into the death cage. The frantic scramble of desperate competitors began.

The Venom Society exchanged accolades of approval as they watched the event from their perceived safe haven. This was a momentous occasion for them. They shared first-rate appetizers and drinks, but only amongst themselves, and they enjoyed the best seats in the house. To them, the celebration meant that additional Expulsion winners would be sent to harvest newly discovered sources of acitaneum.

The Expulsion began just as Jett had planned, but the competitors had to work hard to make it appear real.

Gunnar, easily the smallest undesirable of the bunch, and Bundy, the largest and most intimidating, already had a plan for how they would begin the battle. They opened the festivities with a shocking scene that had Bundy attacking the smaller, more vulnerable, Gunnar. Naturally, the Venom Society elites expected Gunnar to be taken out very quickly, but they were shocked when he grabbed Bundy's head with both hands, wrenched it sideways, and snapped his neck. Bundy dropped to the floor, 285 pounds of dead weight.

He wasn't really dead, though; he just pretended to be. He wasn't a great actor, but the chaos of the event masked any lack of stage presence. Cheers rang out from the crowd in a morbid show of appreciation for the kill, and the Venom Society raised their glasses in a toast to the surprising success of the underdog.

Bundy tried not to move after that. He needed to wait until the lights went out. Then he would rise again and head toward center cage with the rest of the group. The undesirables needed his physical presence to help breach the safety cage surrounding the VIP seating area.

In another section of the death cage, the crowd watched as three Marsupan females ganged up on a female Astronian, Shyanne, who couldn't seem to form any alliances and found herself alone and vulnerable. As two of the Marsupans held her against a tree, the third charged at her and sunk a spear through her mid-section, pinning her body tightly to the trunk. This time it was real.

Shyanne slumped over and bled out. She'd been asking for it. She had threatened the Marsupans during the trip to the Expulsion, and they never reconciled as part of the planned uprising. An unfortunate ending for her, but it definitely fueled the party in VIP section. The Venom Society showed very little emotion but appeared, by their mannerisms, to take pleasure in the festivities.

Just across a small, shallow pond, a melee broke out between rival gangs. Each side armed with beat sticks and knives. They had been wanting to get at each other for months, and today they got their chance.

In a fury of flying punches and swinging weapons, multiple gang members fell to the ground. They were either unconscious or dead, but either way, no longer in contention for securing an escape capsule. But this fight was also fake. The gangs were able to make peace prior to the Expulsion. Their actions looked very real to the Venom Society . . . and to the onlookers.

Taking advantage of that distraction, one of the overall favorites to win the Expulsion, Adley, raced to an unoccupied escape capsule hidden atop a bunker. Without even being challenged, he secured his place inside and would wait out the rest of the Expulsion in safety. At least until the lights dimmed.

Adley was startled by the thump of a competitor's fist against the aluminum walls of his escape capsule, though, and a terrified face appeared. It was Quinn, one of the street preachers in the Chesapeake Municipality, staring at him through the small circular window. She was charged with fraud for deceiving the local vagrants and taking from them what little they had.

Quinn had horror written on her face, and she begged Adley to let her in. Adley couldn't open the door though, there was only room for one body inside.

She banged on the capsule trying to convince him to help, but in the next instant, she lost her head to a machete. Blood spattered onto the small window, and her torso fell backward away from the capsule. There was no faking that kill.

The first ten minutes of the Expulsion seemed like an hour, and some of the undesirables began to wonder if Jett would keep his word. Some had reverted to a self-preservation mentality. As a result, Jett lost a couple undesirables to acts of revenge. That diminished his fighting force a bit, which was not a good thing.

But because the undesirables were putting on a good show thus far, most of the onlookers were not compelled to make any attempts to leverage their joysticks to influence killing devices. And that *was* a good thing.

Twenty minutes into the competition, with two escape capsules off the board and several casualties having taken place, Jett decided it was time to make the move. He couldn't risk the hysteria getting the better of any more of the undesirables, giving them more reason to turn on each other for real.

The cannons rang out; the lights flickered, and the colosseum went dark.

CHAPTER 40

One-Way Ticket

In a different kind of battle far from Earth, Captain Pennington worked to triage the recovery of the former Expulsion winners. The last message he received from Jett confirmed that a revolt against the Venom Society was about to take place. He wanted to be there to assist Jett with the execution, but he couldn't just turn a cold shoulder to the lost undesirables.

Dead or alive, Pennington and his crew were committed to bringing the humans back to Earth—not that things were much better there with its own impeding collapse. The very people the crew aimed to rescue were individuals with the highest violation counts. That fact brought with it mixed emotions. But in the spirit of humanity, it was instinctive to attempt a rescue.

Captain Pennington ordered the crew to identify all expendable payload that could be jettisoned, to make room on the ship for passengers.

The humans waited on the ground. At first, they appeared like tiny ants, scurrying around, growing a bit bigger with every few seconds of descent of the spacecraft. Their hands were waving vigorously in the air to get the attention of the astronauts. They appeared happy to see an approaching ship.

There were dozens of men and women on the surface of the planet. Some appeared weak and malnourished. Some could be sick. But many others seemed physically fit and healthy and could potentially provide support to Jett's new fighting force.

"What to do, what to do," the captain thought to himself.

As Pennington pondered how he'd handle his interaction with the Expulsion winners, DAISIE alerted the crew that the air pressure in the cabin would rise a bit as the spacecraft approached the surface of the planet. The crew could hear the hiss of the oxygen production units as they worked to maintain constant pressure.

The ship landed at a point slightly offset from the crowd of undesirables, but they wasted no time in making their way over to investigate. They gathered around the base of the ship just as DAISIE shut down the engines. The undesirables leaned against the spaceship and peered into the windows trying to see who was inside. This made Skip feel a bit uneasy. Visibility through the glass was primarily one-way, though. Skip could see them perfectly, but they couldn't seem to discern much of anything inside the ship.

Skip expressed his concern to Pennington, "Captain, they've surrounded Proximity. I don't believe they mean us any harm, but they are rather intimidating—standing there peering through the windows."

"They can't really see inside here, can they?" the captain asked.

Skip responded, "No. The windows are mirrored, and they probably only perceive us as crude silhouettes."

Captain Pennington then addressed another very important concern of his: "Are they carrying any sort of weapons or implements?"

Skip responded, "Well . . . *no*, I don't *believe* so. But remember, these people are born fighters, and they've lived through incredible strife. I wouldn't put it past them to want to take their frustrations out on a few unassuming visitors. If they think for a minute that we're well-stocked with French fries and milkshakes, I imagine they'd be more interested in getting their hands on those than making friends with us."

Pennington, appreciative of Skip's attempt at a bit of light satire, giggled and answered his deputy. "Yes. I can respect that. But . . . I'm fairly certain that a chance to get back home and avenge the regime that planted them here is probably much more appealing to them than incapacitating a small team of rescuers who are trying to help them."

Skip agreed, "You're probably right, Captain. I just don't know what kind of torment they've suffered, and I don't want them venting their frustrations on us."

Pennington knew there was merit to what Skip suggested but had faith that the undesirables were more curious than aggressive. "DAISIE, prepare the doors for opening. Everyone, please remain where you are. I'm going to have a little word with them to assess their current state of mind."

"I'm already ahead of you, Captain," DAISIE responded to his orders.

Pennington muttered under his breath, "Lord, give me the strength."

Then, with a sudden burst of energy, the captain rose out of his seat and the large doors to the cabin swung upward. When the prisoners saw this, they backed off slightly, and the raucous chatter from around the ship came to a halt.

The door jockeyed into its final open position and locked into place. No one from inside the ship came into view until the doors were almost fully deployed. Then, Captain Pennington stepped forward, ducking to ensure he didn't whack his head on the upper portion of the door jam.

Perched up on the ledge, leaning his back against the ship, Pennington peered out over the crowd and raised both arms high into the air as he prepared to speak. A light chatter resumed among the prisoners as they weren't familiar with the captain and wondered what his motivations were.

"Hello, my friends. I'm Phineus Pennington, captain of this deep space travel ship named Proximity," Pennington said to them. "Please relax and remain calm; we come in peace. We received word from Captain Banes that the Venom Society placed you here against your will. We're here to help you."

The crowd began to stir, and their yammering increased. They didn't know whether to believe Pennington or not.

The captain continued, "We've brought a modest supply of food and medical supplies. Enough to supplement your stock for one day. We're aware of the task you've been assigned by the Venom Society. You will no longer be persecuted. Our mission is to take you home."

With that, the crowd noise increased significantly, in part due to the shock of the possibility of being rescued and, in part, due to the uncertainty of exactly how that operation was going to occur.

Captain Pennington tried to maintain calm among the undesirables, "Now, I need all of you to remain patient as I ask my crew to disburse to you the supplements we've prepared. Please do not come forward for your stipend. We will ensure that all of you receive a portion very quickly—if you simply trust us."

To the captain's surprise, the prisoners did remain calm. It appeared as if they had gained some measure of confidence in the captain and his crew. For individuals who had been through such trauma in recent months, Pennington seemed to have struck the right chord with them. The captain paused, turned toward Skip, and issued instructions for an orderly transfer of food and supplies to the undesirables.

Once the prisoners were comfortable and believed they had received their share of goods, Captain Pennington called everyone together again and asked for their attention. "Everyone . . . EVERYONE . . . *please*, hear me again. I need you to listen very closely. As I stated previously, we've come to take you home. I know you are feeling many emotions at this time, but we need to come together as a team to be successful."

He explained his dilemma to them: "We will return all of you to Earth, but we cannot do it in a single trip. Our android, DAISIE, has determined that it will take us eight flights to transport everyone. I ask all of you to support one another as we determine the order in which you will evacuate this planet. Please understand that although we are light-years away from Earth, with collider transform capability, a one-way flight takes mere minutes to complete. Although we must refuel, inspect the ship's engines and navigation systems, and test the communications equipment after each landing, we should have all of you safely back home in twenty-four to thirty-six hours."

A boisterous cheer erupted from the prisoners. The captain encouraged them to maintain their poise. "Friends! *Please*. I know you are all very emotional right now and most certainly ready to make your exit from this place. If I can have your attention for another minute, please . . . there's more that I must tell you."

The captain continued. "We've uncovered the true agenda of the Venom Society. Their generosity and their management of welfare and care of all of us is a cover to allow them unlimited resources as our ruling body." The group collectively nodded their heads, confirming they had learned this over the last few months, and it wasn't news to them. Some of the undesirables spoke under their breaths, cursing the Venom Society.

"That's not all! Hear me out!" Captain Pennington shouted over the chatter. "The Venom Society elites are also using Expulsion winners as guinea pigs for human biological experimentation. We've discovered the chambers where the atrocities are taking place. It's time we all know the truth and fight back."

At that moment, DAISIE finalized the ship for a return flight to Earth, and she called out to the captain, "We're all set to accept some passengers, sir!"

CHAPTER 41

Surprise Attack

The undesirables had begun to wonder if Jett had not been straight with them after all. But now, with the colosseum dark, suddenly they shared a restored faith in Jett and the plan to unite against the Venom Society.

They turned their attention toward the VIP seating area containing the Venom Society elites. This was the moment that could change the course of their lives. Their confidence grew, and their rage stewed as they navigated through the obstacles within the death cage.

They had trouble distinguishing the silhouettes of their fellow fighters from the inanimate features of the surrounding landscape. Without regard to who was next to or in front of them, the competitors had one thing in mind as they forged closer to the cage protecting the Venom Society. The executioners, under the cover of darkness, fled from manning the killing devices in fear they might be in danger.

Grandmaster Webb was troubled by the fact that the lights failed. He questioned Kamalei and Jett about what was being done to remedy the situation. Kamalei remained quiet, hoping to remove herself from any suspicion. Jett assured the grandmaster that the engineers were on top of it and that power to the electrical circuit would be restored shortly. That was, of course, a lie and a stall tactic. Jett's true intent was to keep the lights off until the fighters were right up on the VIP safety cage.

And then it started. The clank and clatter of rattling cage walls. The closest undesirables to center cage arrived there first and gave it a tug. They brought with them chains, sticks, and other implements they hoped might help them break through the wall. Some brought nothing but raw anger and spite. And all of them brought with them the will to kill.

One at a time, the lights flicked on, illuminating center cage once again. As the inside of the colosseum became visible and everyone's eyes adjusted, the Venom Society sensed immediately that they had become the target of the aggression of the undesirables.

The competitors beat at the cage walls surrounding the VIP bleachers, trying to force a structural failure. Some reached through the gaps between the bars, trying to grab anyone within range. Some climbed onto the roof of the safety cage. But no one had gained immediate access to the Venom Society members themselves.

Although startled at first, the Venom Society began to enjoy the turn of events. They assumed there was no danger within the confines of the steel bars that were erected specifically to protect them. And that's just what Jett wanted them to think. They could have drawn their firearms and sprayed the undesirables with lead, but they refrained.

Soon, the last of the undesirables descended upon the cage. The Venom Society elites adopted arrogant grins on their faces, which propped up their dark sunglasses. They entered into a stare-down with the undesirables. They said nothing to the prisoners but rather taunted them by standing in line shoulder to shoulder, holding the *V* symbol over their chests with their thumbs and forefingers. It was a bold move.

Their confidence was short-lived, however. The undesirables appeared to have zoned in and acquired a collective predator-versus-prey state of mind, and the Venom Society officers were in their sights. To the

Venom Society, it became apparent they may be in danger. But now, it was too late to do anything about it but defend themselves.

In an instant, one of the hinges carrying the front wall of the cage snapped, and an incensed wave of undesirables rushed in. Jett had said that would happen, and he was right. He turned to Grandmaster Webb and threw a couple of punches to Webb's face before being swept aside by the rush of competitors.

The Venom Society, however, hadn't achieved such power for no reason. They were ruthless. And most had been trained killers, as well. They weren't going to go down without a fight.

Grandmaster Webb drew his weapon and started firing shots into the wave of enraged undesirables as they pressed through the gaping hole in the cage. A couple of them dropped after being hit. But there were just too many attackers, and they got their hands on the Venom Society officers rather quickly.

Chulah's weapon was knocked to the floor. But he was a large imposing figure, so he used the remaining weapons he had, throwing wild punches to keep the undesirables at bay. He then tried to escape along the side wall but ran right into the chest of Bundy, who made even the sizable deputy look small.

Bundy slammed Chulah into the side wall of the cage, knocking his glasses to the floor. Chulah's piercing green eyes were revealed, and they showed the panic he felt. After a quick stare down—just inches separating them—Bundy raked Chulah's head along the cage. Some of the flesh on his face and forehead dislodged from his skull, which caused his body to quiver. Bundy noticed a membrane beneath his skin, which was oddly textured and discolored. It didn't appear to be human and that startled the big man. But he didn't have time to process what he saw.

Chulah was still alive and fighting. Bundy finished him off by choking him out, and Chulah's world went dark.

Some of the Venom Society officers did get the upper hand on their attackers; some undesirables were killed. Venom Society elites were skilled at knowing how to inflict instant death via pinprick to the back of the neck. They were also good at hand-to-hand combat, as well as manipulation and control techniques. Most of the undesirables who fought one-on-one were no match for them. But there was strength in numbers.

Webb saw the Chulah kill take place, and he knew he and his colleagues were in big trouble. He tried to take out as many undesirables as he could. He was a master at close contact kill techniques. The cage hadn't given way completely yet, so he was still protected by the back and side walls.

Jett realized the momentum was swinging in favor of the Venom Society officers, so he rushed back into the cage and rejoined the attack. He wasn't as young as he used to be, but he could still put up a good fight. And that he did. His attack skills had been gained through extensive training as a security guard, and they kicked in instinctively. He made his first kill by grabbing the esophagus of a Venom Society elite and ripping it through their skin. It was an ugly sight but effective.

It wasn't enough, though. The Venom Society was too highly trained, and their perseverance put them at a slight advantage. The bodies of undesirables laying on the cage floor outnumbered those of the Venom Society. The crowd, although stunned at the turn of events, had exploded into cheers.

Jett was exhausted. He ran away to avoid being overtaken by some of his former colleagues. He was able to make it to the exit gate, where he tried to catch his breath. He feared his plan was failing. In disdain and exhaustion, he collapsed to his knees just in front of the exit. Going against his innate desire to succeed at all costs, he was about to give up hope.

But then, as he hung his head low, a pair of snakeskin boots caught his eye through the smoke and debris. He recognized them immediately.

"It's Ivy! Ivy Breez!" he thought to himself. She had come to assist in the overthrow. And she hadn't come alone.

Jett looked up at the big screens to see if he had any fighters left. To his delight, an android came into view from high above the arena. It was REX! "What is he doing here?" Jett asked himself.

The answer became quite apparent when REX extinguished his hover power and all 800 pounds of his titanium frame descended rapidly upon the VIP seating cage. It was a calculated fall though. Right smack dab on top of a cluster of four Venom Society officers. All four officers were killed instantly. Grandmaster Webb among them.

REX's devotion to winning DAISIE over, along with a little coaxing from Ivy Breez, led him to turn against the Venom Society. His heroic gesture shifted the advantage back in favor of the undesirables.

The skin of the injured and dying Venom Society officers began to crack. From underneath, an altogether different body covering appeared, one alien in nature. In fact, after just a couple of minutes, entirely new bodies emerged from their fake human husks.

"They're not human," Jett said to himself. "Not in their minds nor their bodies."

Most of the onlookers had scurried out of the colosseum by this time, but those who were left were mortified and followed closely behind. So did Ivy, who feared she would be targeted if she hung around inside the colosseum.

As a result of REX's fall, the cage had fully collapsed. The undesirables then outnumbered what was left of the alien carcasses. They pounced on them and made sure they were dead.

That left just one member of the Venom Society, who remained unharmed—Kamalei. She was in a vulnerable spot over in the control booth, and a group of crazed competitors noticed her standing there. They took off after her. They knew that Kamalei had a soft heart at times, but they also knew that she had been loyal to the ruling body all along. "And, after all," they thought, "she was likely an alien underneath her stunning, flawless human covering." They wasted no time in scaling the base of the control booth.

As the gang made their way upward toward the horrified alien, Zinnia realized Kamalei was in danger. Even though it was likely that Kamalei was also alien, Zinnia didn't want to see her die. This was one Venom Society elite that had actually showed compassion to her and secretly tried to save her dying brother.

Kamalei knew that there was an open escape capsule situated just off to her left, atop a small cliff. If she could make her way to the capsule, she could at least barricade herself there and hope that the humans would give up on their pursuit. She climbed onto the ledge of the booth and began working her way across the scaffold. The undesirables saw that she was getting away, but they didn't give up chasing her so easily.

Kamalei made it to the unoccupied escape capsule, jumped inside, and slammed the door shut. She reached in her pocket for a remote controller, which would initiate the extraction of the escape capsule so that it would whisk her out of danger. But her pocket was empty. She was stuck there. This was the end of the line for her.

Zinnia saw everything that was going on, and she was upset that the undesirables were still intent on killing Kamalei. She tried waving them off, but the competitors were oblivious to her.

Then, it occurred to Zinnia just how she might be able to return the favor to the benevolent alien. She began climbing up the chain-link fence that led to the conductor's podium where Kamalei had dropped the capsule extraction remote control. The undesirables were steadily approaching the escape capsule with Kamalei secured inside.

As Zinnia clung to the fence just inches below the podium, she stretched and peered across the floor of the podium. There it was! The remote control appeared, intact. She reached her arm across the podium floor as far as she could and was barely able to grab it. Fumbling to press the buttons, she gave them all a push, not knowing which one might trigger the capsule to exit. One of the buttons worked, and Kamalei glided down the rails, out of the colosseum, and into the underground tunnels. That effectively ended the attack.

The carnage was gruesome.

In a daze, Zinnia backed her way down the fence and trudged wearily to the exit. A recollection of life events played in her mind. Her difficult childhood, her personal losses, her inner conflict between right and wrong, her spiritual strength, and her destiny to save her fellow commoners from the bondage of alien invaders.

Zinnia saw Jett lying on his side, just outside of the exit gate. He was wounded but very much alive and conscious. Relieved that the uprising was successful, he was deep in reflection. Zinnia ran over to him and helped him to his feet. They stood together in silence, staring back at the colosseum where the profound events had just played out, wondering how to pick up the pieces now that the head of the snake had been severed.

CHAPTER 42

Earth 2.0

Jett was now in a position to become a true leader of the Chesapeake Municipality and the greater Delmarva Peninsula. Not that he, prior to the final Expulsion, had ever endeavored to seek that responsibility. But now, he was hailed a hero. He was familiar with the recent history of Venom Society atrocities. He was forward-thinking and strong-willed. He had ties to deep space exploration and experience in law enforcement and security. But most importantly, he was a champion for humanity.

Jett had spent part of his life as an enabler of the dark side of society—although he didn't realize it at the time. But he had become enlightened and turned his energy toward compassion and the defeat of the evil empire. He had gained the confidence of the commoners and possessed the mental, emotional, and social tools he needed to ensure their survival. The deep space mission showed glimpses of discovering new, habitable planets. But he would need much help if he was going to be successful.

Jett turned to Captain Pennington for assistance. Proximity had just completed its mission to return the former Expulsion winners to Earth a few days earlier and was prepping the ship and its crew for another exploratory flight. Pennington was an obvious choice for someone of high intelligence with prominent leadership skills, one who could manage the wellbeing of the people of Earth. Jett asked him if he would work with the commoners to stabilize their resource production and distribution methods.

But the captain wanted no part of that. He was a born space explorer, tried and true, and wanted nothing more but to get back out there and find a new livable territory to expand man's footprint. Pennington respectfully declined, put his hand on Jett's shoulder, wished him well, and headed back to the ship for his next mission.

Pennington rounded up his team and restocked Proximity with supplies. The crew was ready to follow his lead. Code-named *Mirror Image*, this mission sought to confirm the existence of a planet believed to have developed exactly like Earth.

Proximity had discovered the planet on a previous mission and noted it as having the exact chemical makeup as Earth's. DAISIE had also concluded that the conditions in the atmosphere, and most likely on the surface of the planet, were one hundred percent conducive to life, just like Earth. They had been unable to approach the planet at the time because they were conducting an emergency rescue of the crew of Curiosity. However, DAISIE had recorded the exact coordinates of its location, and it didn't take them long to get back there.

The crew worked meticulously prior to landing by taking air samples and confirming the planet's human-friendly atmosphere. For their own safety in this unknown world, the captain chose a remote location in a mountain range to land the ship.

The newly designed collider ship eased its way to the surface of the planet, stirring up very little dust and making hardly any noise. Skip landed the ship safely and inconspicuously in an area where no sign of life was detected. Dr. Moss and Kassie gathered soil samples and noted the same metal and mineral contents as Earth. This was exciting news.

Captain Pennington asked the crewmembers to prepare their spacesuits and calibrate their instrumentation to explore the surface of the planet. DAISIE allowed the crew to carry out their orders, but at the same time, assured them that it was completely safe to exit the ship without protective layers. She insisted there was no need to suit-up because the climate, temperature, and air quality were exactly like that of Earth. After some hesitation, the captain laid his trust in DAISIE, opened the ship's door, and lowered the ramp to the surface of the planet.

The crew quietly discussed their methods of data and sample collection as they prepared emotionally to leave the perceived safety of the spaceship. That bit of small talk was a self-distracting way to diffuse their nervous anticipation. But soon, Captain Pennington made the first move. He extended his head just around the side of the door frame and took the first close look at the surroundings. He then started into a slow and steady saunter down the ramp.

One by one, the rest of the crewmembers followed, cautiously edging their way out of the belly of the ship. They found themselves safe and comfortable with the temperature, oxygen, and other comfort factors, just as DAISIE had suggested they would. Even the star at the center of this solar system seemed to be overly friendly. Not menacingly hot, nor distantly cool. Soon the crewmembers were all freely exploring the immediate area.

Skip, Cassie, and Dr. Moss began the STARS NET transmitter installation while the Captain, DAISIE, and Max moved further from the ship, combing the nearby landscape. They saw streams, rocks, and even insects—all of which were familiar sights. They recorded every little detail so that a report could be drafted and forwarded to mission headquarters.

Kassie Lomax was able to identify multiple species of trees and cacti and ants and beetle bugs —all identical species to those on Earth. Truly stunning, it was, to see these familiar things on a planet so far from home. Everyone was silenced but not at all slowed from continuing with their mission.

Exploration soon took an even more fascinating turn, however, when DAISIE wandered off on her own and encountered the unimaginable. DAISIE found people. *Real* people, just like the crew themselves. They were some sort of alien people, but they looked just the same as Earthlings. DAISIE had considered that this was possible, but she was never terribly confident they would actually make this discovery.

By now, the android had adopted some natural human emotions, and she began to panic. With a flurry of electrical impulses stimulating her central processing unit, she struggled to maintain her focus. Without making a sound, she reversed her momentum and swiftly hovered her way back to the spaceship to find the captain.

"Captain," DAISIE called out to him. "Captain . . ."

Pennington was quite busy; he heard DAISIE but unintentionally ignored her.

"CAPTAIN!" DAISIE called to him again, increasing her volume significantly.

"What *is* it, DAISIE?" Pennington replied.

"There's *life* just beyond the ridge there. *People*, sir!" She pointed the tip of her pyramid-shaped torso in the direction of the cliffs that lead to the alien humans that she'd just spotted.

"WHAT!" the captain responded, not actually wanting the android to repeat herself.

But DAISIE didn't know that. Recalibrating her audio instruction set to repeat the last sentence listed in her voice database and increasing her volume by twenty decibels, DAISIE blurted out, "THERE'S LIFE JUST BEYOND THE RIDGE THERE. PEOP—"

The captain, who was short on time and patience at the moment, cut her off before she finished repeating her sentence, "*I got that*, DAISIE, thank you. But . . . you said . . . *people*? And . . . you saw them?"

Adjusting her volume back down to normal, DAISIE explained, "I sure did, sir. And the scientists were right: they look exactly like us. Well, you know, sir . . . exactly like *you*." DAISIE seemed to elicit a bit of emotion, knowing that she did not look or act like her beloved colleagues and having grown the capability for humanistic feelings, including being viewed as *different*. Had they built her with tears embedded in her titanium face, she might have just shed a few.

The captain lapsed into a blank stare and spoke outwardly but to no one in particular, "Incredible. Simply incredible. And we . . . *we* get to be the first to make contact with them."

"Skip, secure the ship, initiate the force field around the perimeter; we need to say hello to some new friends!" the captain ordered. "And everyone, if what DAISIE says is true, we may have just discovered another Earth and a new place to call home."

The crew set out on foot, down the trail and over to the cliff, following DAISIE's lead. In less than five minutes, the crew descended upon a small group of human-like bipeds, gathered in a circular man-made colony. DAISIE was right.

The captain and crew took cover, huddling behind a series of boulders just one hundred yards away from the alien humans.

The beings did not spot the crew and knew nothing about the collider spaceship sitting just beyond the hills.

The physical characteristics of the beings made them appear entirely human from a distance. From the feathers on their headdress to the moccasins on their feet. They had long, dark hair and took on an aura of what the crew knew as indigenous Native Americans from a thousand years ago. But whatever they happened to be, or call themselves, they were, in fact, another, very different, civilization from the humans of Earth.

The captain and crew had seen it all up until now—a lava beast, alien dinosaurs, and floating jellyfish creatures. They had experienced things that most had never even imagined. But actual human-like aliens were enough to render the crew speechless on the spot.

DAISIE quietly reminded the captain that the chemical components of this planet's core and crust were exactly the same as planet Earth, and its atmospheric and surface attributes were equally indistinguishable from that of Earth. She further noted that the alien humans were breathing the air around them just like the crew, and so, they must be similar, if not identical, biologically.

She explained that in this vast universe, this must be one of the planetary bodies that formed in the exact same manner as planet Earth, even if it were thousands of years out of calibration in time from Earth. Then, she hypothesized that it was possible—in fact, probable by her calculation—that these beings also communicated with a language similar to their own.

Without hesitation the captain rose from beyond the boulders and slowly made his way toward the colony. The crew stood and instinctively followed the captain but stopped short of leaving the safety of the boulders. Captain Pennington continued on his own.

A young colony member, small in stature and obviously an adolescent female, spotted the captain first. The other alien humans were oblivious to what was going on. The young alien human stopped in her tracks and stared the captain down. Taken by surprise, she didn't quite know what to make of the captain. He looked much like the alien colony members but was somehow different. The captain's hi-tech shirt and pants looked completely unfamiliar to the little alien girl. She turned and ran to a mother figure for comfort.

As the mother figure turned and gazed at the odd-looking captain, he raised his hands slowly and deliberately in a universal gesture of peace. Soon, the entire colony set their sights on him and assembled together in a natural show of strength in numbers.

The captain understood their concern and simply dropped to his knees to indicate that he represented no threat or harm.

What appeared to be the leader of the colony took two steps forward, and what happened next caused the captain to nearly pass out.

The alien leader vocalized three bursts of sound toward the captain. Although the language seemed choppy, and somewhat primitive in nature, the captain understood the spoken words: "Who are you?"

After a rush of blood and color returned to his face, the captain stood, gathered his thoughts, and had but one way to answer the alien leader.

"I am the captain of the deep space exploration ship, Proximity," he said. "I come from a planet millions of miles from here, along with my crew." Captain Pennington turned and aimed his right arm toward his crewmembers, who, in a lesser show of courage than the captain, receded quickly back into their positions behind the boulders.

The captain giggled under his breath, turned back to the colony, and continued: "Our android, DAISIE, noted on a previous voyage that your planet was just like ours, and we've come in search of other life forms besides our own kind. Our planet is in peril and our people are suffering. We need your help."

The captain hesitated for a moment, gazed around the lay of the land, and then continued to address the leader of the colony. "I am in awe of the sight of your people as I stand before you. If you please, sir, may I ask your name? And what do you call your beautiful planet?"

After a pause and a short, quiet consultation with a warrior-like colony member holding a spear and standing to his right, the leader again spoke out, "I'm Chief Sunami . . . and this is our home, on the only planet that we know . . . we call it . . . Earth."

ABOUT THE AUTHOR

Troy Suesse is a professional employee with thirty-five years of federal service in the Intelligence Community. Raised in the nature-rich suburbs of Maryland, he developed a fond appreciation for the planet and the majestic beauty of all living things. It's humbling that the Earth is but a speck of dust in the grand scheme of celestial things.

Inspired by science, nature, and outer space, Troy hopes his audience will enjoy immersing themselves in a fascinating dystopian world as a troubling scenario plays out and at the same time, garner a greater appreciation for Earth's precious resources. He invites readers to share in his fascination that there simply must be another "planet Earth" somewhere out there, one capable of perpetuating the existence of man. Join Troy's quest to find it. In the interim be kind to the planet, and each other.